T0036594

Trondheim

Trondheim

CORMAC JAMES

Bellevue Literary Press
NEW YORK

First published in the United States in 2024
by Bellevue Literary Press, New York

For information, contact:
Bellevue Literary Press
90 Broad Street
Suite 2100
New York, NY 10004
www.blpress.org

The translation of Derrida is by Alan Bass.

Cover photograph by Jeremy Bishop on Unsplash

This is a work of fiction. Characters, organizations, events, and places (even those that are actual) are either products of the author's imagination or are used fictitiously.

Library of Congress Cataloging-in-Publication Data
Names: James, Cormac, author.
Title: Trondheim / Cormac James.
Description: First edition. | New York : Bellevue Literary Press, 2024.
Identifiers: LCCN 2023003093 | ISBN 9781954276239 (paperback) | ISBN
    9781954276246 (epub)
Subjects: LCGFT: Novels.
Classification: LCC PR6060.A4525 T76 2024 | DDC 823.914--dc23/eng/20230123
LC record available at https://lccn.loc.gov/2023003093

Bellevue Literary Press would like to thank all its generous donors—individuals and foundations—for their support.

 This project is supported in part by an award from the National Endowment for the Arts.

 This publication is made possible by the New York State Council on the Arts with the support of the Office of the Governor and the New York State Legislature.

The author acknowledges the generous support of the Centre Culturel Irlandais, Paris, where part of this book was written during a residency.

 The author thanks the Arts Council/An Chomhairle Ealaíon for its generous funding during work on this book.

Book design and composition by Mulberry Tree Press, Inc.

Bellevue Literary Press is committed to ecological stewardship in our book production practices, working to reduce our impact on the natural environment.

♾ This book is printed on acid-free paper.

Manufactured in the United States of America.

First Edition

10 9 8 7 6 5 4 3 2 1

paperback ISBN: 978-1-954276-23-9

ebook ISBN: 978-1-954276-24-6

I recognize that I love—you—by this:
you leave in me a wound I do not want to replace.

—Jacques Derrida, *La Carte Postale*

Trondheim

Montpellier. November 27. Friday Morning.

ON THE DAY THEIR SON WAS GOING TO DIE, Lil had given herself the task of carrying forty-plus sacks of rubble from their fourth-floor apartment down to the street below. The rubble came from the closets and partition walls she had knocked out between kitchen, hall, and sitting room to open up a bigger living space for the family—now a long wide tunnel with bright windows at each end.

"It's physically impossible," Alba told her. She meant the number of sacks, the total weight, and all the stairs up and down. After twenty-five years together, she ought to have known that such a statement was the opposite of discouraging to Lil.

Lil had already used the bathroom scales for dosage, knowing that too much weight per sack would soon exhaust her, but too little would mean more trips than were absolutely necessary, down the five flights of stairs to ground level, then all the way up again.

"You know I can't help you," Alba said.

"I'm not expecting you to," Lil said.

The main difficulty, at first, was loading up, because at forty-five years old Lil could no longer clean heft that kind of weight onto her shoulder, as she might have ten years earlier. Instead, gripping the sack's topknot, she used a two-hand kettlebell swing to get it onto the kitchen counter. Then squatted down, as deep as she dared, and toppled the thing toward her.

She wanted all the work for her quads and glutes, and as little as possible for her back. With the sack on her shoulder, she lifted her chin, clenched her abs, and drove herself upward, straight through the weight.

Alba followed her through the slit sheet of plastic draped over the front door to keep the dust in, and on the landing leaned over the balustrade to watch her descent.

Ten minutes later, Lil stepped through the front door slit with a box of tiles in her arms.

"It's not hard enough as it is?" Alba said. She was sitting at the kitchen table with her mug of coffee.

By bringing supplies up from the cellar, Lil had decided, she was saving not just one trip but two: an empty-handed trip (now) back upstairs, and an empty-handed trip back down (later), if she were to move rubble and renovation material on two different days.

"Are you punishing *yourself* for something, or punishing *me*?"

Lil was already hefting another sack onto the counter. To have paused and actually engaged Alba's jibe would have been a first concession. With a sick groan, she stood up. She had used their seven-year-old daughter, María, as a yardstick of how much to put in each sack. María was now nineteen kilos, a weight Lil still carried with relative ease, piggyback or fireman. A game Alba had given up a long time ago because of her back, but which Lil never wanted to end. She had carried each of their two sons even longer. It was just one of the many reasons she kept working out, and always insisted on doing any donkey work available, rivaling everything her younger self had ever done. That was why she was so surprised, today, at how hard the work with the sacks got, and how soon.

She split the forty-plus bags into sets of six. Six was a good number, small enough to be always achievable, like overloaded reps in the gym. Then, she promised herself, she would stop for water and rest.

She did not know that Alba was waiting overhead, leaning over the balustrade again, watching her come up. Twenty-five years ago, coming together had been their first, dramatic success. They would grow closer, Alba had hoped. That would be a different kind of task, and a different—less euphoric—kind of accomplishment.

"You're just going to leave your mess there?" she said when Lil set her next box of tiles against the wall.

"*My* mess?"

"The mess."

"Our mess."

Lil started down again. Even the pause to bicker with Alba did not much revive her, and within an hour she was failing, physically and mentally. She recognized the signs, from all her failures in the past. But today was worse: she felt herself not only tiring and weakening, but aging. And not only trip by trip but flight by flight, almost step by step, a lifetime's incremental changes made flesh, time-lapsed. How much older—how many years or months per flight—she could not have said, but by noon she felt and moved the way she imagined an old woman must.

On the living room wall was a sun-faded square where a calendar and a clock hung side by side. An overturned bucket stood beneath. That was where Lil sat for long minutes after every trip now, head bowed, sweat furrowing down her gray forearms, dripping from her fingertips onto the gray floor. She should have felt encouraged by all the boxes of tile and bags of cement set along the weight-bearing walls, where only that morning sacks of rubble had been. Just as she should have felt a surge of satisfaction with each sack dropped onto the footpath down below. But fatigue debunks even the useful lie: the growing heap of sacks only meant more work, to get them to the dump, and the supplies upstairs only showed how much renovation remained to be done on the apartment. She sat on the bucket staring into space. The living room walls were scored with long scars where she'd pulled out the old silk-wrapped wires in stuttering lengths like varicose veins. Like her forearms and face, the windowpanes were blurred with dust. Every waiting sack was another dead weight for muscles now melting with fatigue. Everything said age, failing powers, endless work. She was spent.

As surprising as her body's capacity for fatigue was its ability to revive: a few minutes later she was dragging a new sack toward the kitchen. Silent angel, Alba watched from the apartment's corridor, from behind a sheet of transparent plastic. The whole apartment had been divided into different zones by such sheets, taped to the ceilings and floors, with vertical slits where the doors were, to contain the dust.

"Are you trying to make me feel sorry for you? Admire you? What?" came her voice.

Lil waddled to the front door, through its slit, and started down again. On the third-floor landing, she heard a distant phone that might have been her own. Then Alba's voice, far above, calling her name. "*Lil!*" It sounded strident, almost panicked—exactly the kind of coercion Lil couldn't stand.

She didn't answer and didn't stop. Somewhere below, robot hands were playing piano scales.

She dropped her load on the footpath by the building's front door, went to the basement for another, began the long climb back up. By now it was like climbing to a higher altitude, where she had to work so much harder to milk the life she needed from its thinner air. The weight in her arms too—a sack of grout this time—increased steadily as she mounted the stairs.

As in the final reps of a final gym set, each additional effort now brought her closer to the absolute limits of her physical strength, and by the time she was halfway back up, her legs were trembling. She paused to rest and looked up. Alba would be sulking, of course, because her call a few minutes before had not been answered obediently.

With a conclusive thud, she dropped her bag of grout onto the living room floor, then straightened herself as best she could. Alba was sitting at the kitchen table with a stupid look on her face.

"What?" Lil said.

"Pierre is in the hospital," explained a sick voice. "In Trondheim. They said his heart stopped. They said he had a heart attack. They said he died."

"*Our* Pierre?" Lil said, absolutely baffled, because their Pierre was only twenty years old and in perfect health.

"They said his heart stopped, but they revived him and now he's in the hospital on life support." With ferocious anxiety, Alba was waiting for the love of her life—the woman always so sure about everything, especially her own ability to endure or overcome—to contradict all this.

"You keep saying *they*," Lil said as patiently as she could, though there was already a taint of panic in her voice too.

"The hospital," Alba said blankly. "They called your phone. I answered it. They just hung up." Her mind was grabbing at solid facts.

As gently as she could, Lil pried her phone from Alba's hand, brought up the last incoming call, hit the number. It was a 59, which meant Norway, where Pierre was currently spending his Erasmus year. Waiting for Norway to answer, she poured a glass of water and put it in Alba's hand, where her phone had been.

"I'm Pierre Casals's mother," she told the phone. "I'm calling from France. You just called us, yes? . . . No, that wasn't me, it doesn't matter, just tell me from the start, please, step by step, what the fuck is going on."

Their son Pierre had been found dead in the street, a woman's voice said. In Trondheim, yes. In Norway, yes. Lil heard the words, but her mind refused to travel so far north, because the woman was speaking French. "Your son, Pierre Patrick Martí Casals," the voice said deliberately, like someone explaining something unpleasant to a child. "Your son Pierre suffered cardiac arrest at a bus stop. The bus driver who found him performed CPR," she said, "and succeeded in restarting his heart, and now he is in a coma, on life support, in the ICU of St. Olav's Hospital, in Trondheim.

"Whether or not he will come out of that coma, they cannot say," the woman said. "Whether or not there has been any brain damage, they cannot say either."

"Who's *they*?" Lil asked, already angry in every available direction. "Why don't you say *me, I*? Isn't that what you mean?"

"I have nothing to do with your son's case," this woman said calmly. "The hospital asked me to liaise with you. They thought you might like to hear the news in French."

This too made no sense. Lil was Irish. Alba was Catalan. French was neither's mother tongue.

"I myself am not a cardiologist," the voice continued. "I work in St. Olav's Proctology Unit."

It was another outrageous fact, from perhaps an endless fund. A shit doctor, given charge of their dying son.

The news sounded like one of the masochist fantasies Lil regularly indulged in. Yet she found she had no reaction rehearsed to meet it, and had to ask the woman to repeat what she had said four or five times, as though the line were bad and she was not sure of having heard correctly.

She put the phone on speaker and set it on the table so that afterward Alba could corroborate what she'd heard. In the meantime, she kept spitting out every question she could think of. This was not confusion, nor was it curiosity, for information to analyze. It was cold calculation. Keep the woman talking was Lil's play, because if kept talking long enough, she might say something that showed this was all a misunderstanding, or something far less serious than what they were so ready to believe.

Patiently and calmly, the phone explained once more that their son had been found lying on the ground, at a bus stop, on the street. His heart had stopped. The woman who found him had somehow gotten the heart going again. Now he was in a coma in Intensive Care. This had all happened that afternoon, just after lunch.

"We're on our way," Lil said.

"Call me," the woman said, "for anything at all, day or night."

"We will," Lil said, but it sounded like a concession just to get the other end off the phone.

And then the call was over, and Lil and Alba sat staring at the handset on the table, like a freshly used weapon they were afraid to touch.

THEIR DAUGHTER, MARÍA, WAS AT a birthday party. Lil called the mother's number and asked her to send María home immediately. Hearing the courage in Lil's voice, the other mother did not ask why. Then Lil called the Odysseum climbing center, where their fifteen-year-old son, Noah, was at his Friday evening class, and asked the woman who answered to find Noah Casals wherever he was on the wall and get him to come down.

"Could you get changed and come home, please?" she said when Noah came on the line. She didn't want to give him the news over the phone, but the boy was standing in his climbing slippers and swami belt, hands all flour, body all revved up for an overhang, and he blankly told her No.

"Noah—"

"*No.* I'm sick of your bullshit. Leave me out of it for once."

"I wouldn't ask if it wasn't important," Lil said as flatly as she could.

"So tell me what it is or I'm hanging up," said the boy, who still believed in the power of defiance to ward off the unwanted. It was also a dare, and also a rare chance for Lil to show her teenage son just how unschooled he was, and how laughably intact.

"Your brother's in the hospital, in Norway, in a coma," she announced. "Now, please get changed and come home as quickly as you can."

Alba was still sitting motionless at the kitchen table, her lukewarm coffee mug in her hands.

"You need to get María off the tram," Lil told her. "Plus, you need to call your mother and get her to come over to mind them. I need to start looking at flights."

Quite dreamily, Alba lifted her head, located Lil's stare, but showed no sign of having taken anything in.

"María, the tram, the Comédie," Lil ordered. "*Now.*"

Waiting for her daughter on Montpellier's main square, Alba stood drenched in the neon lights of the Gaumont cinema—the spot they used for all their rendezvous. Every tram that came in, she scanned the crowd it spewed. There was a famous poem about faces in the metro, but she could not remember the line. Then she was waving wildly with both arms, and María was plowing straight toward her, through the Friday night shoppers' crisscrossing trajectories.

The girl stood listening, head down, refusing to meet her mother's eye.

"*Mon coeur,* you know the way I always say it's not what happens, it's how you deal with it?" Alba asked. María nodded mutely but willingly, as though that very thought had been foremost in her mind. But whatever that movement woke, the girl started to shudder, then to cry, right there by the cinema queue. Two slightly older girls twisted around to stare openly, and Alba put an arm around her daughter's shoulder and led her away into the safety of the crowd. They walked to their building without another word, there they squeezed past the huge heap of sacks by the front door, and Alba marched up the dark stairwell ahead of the girl, punching the light switch on every floor as the timer ran down.

From Noah's bedroom, Lil heard the front door open, the flap of plastic, the door close. She did not go to meet them. She had Noah in her arms. He was crying quietly. She handed him a bunch of tissues, kissed the top of his head.

"I need to go," she said as kindly as she could. "We need to pack and get on the road." There was such appeal in a crisis that was logistical and nothing else: how to get to Trondheim as quickly as possible.

Just to stand up, she needed to set her palms on her knees to brace herself. Already her legs were stiffening. With a low animal groan, she got to her feet just as a blur flitted past the doorway.

"I've booked the flights," she called after it. The blur came back. "We're flying out of Barcelona tomorrow at noon. We'll drive down tonight and he can drive us to the airport in the morning." *He* meant Alba's father, who lived just across the Spanish border, in Figueres, just under two hours from El Prat Airport.

"There's nothing easier?" Alba asked.

The question did not deserve an answer. "We need to get packed and get on the road. And where's your mother?"

"I don't know."

"Call her."

"I called her. I told her to come straight over."

"Call her again. And call your father and tell him we're on our way. And Noah's home."

Then she was packing her case. Fugitive. Flinging clothes at the bed. From her drawer she grabbed handfuls of panties, bras, socks, refusing to count. From the back of the wardrobe she dug out her walking boots, ski gloves, a parka. Clothes for trekking in the mountains. She could tell herself no better story about where she was preparing to go. It was altitude subbed for latitude. These were the equations she was making now. As though Norway were only and entirely its own climate and landscape—another physical ordeal awaiting her.

Bag packed, she fed it and herself through the slit, out into the corridor. Passing María's bedroom, a rodent sound stopped her. She barely had the courage to go in.

María was sitting alone on the edge of her bed, sniveling in spasms. Lil looked around for tissues. There was one balled on the floor which she dared not touch. The whole room—which she had spent weeks stripping and scrubbing and patching and painting until it was an impeccable modernist cube—was a nest of dirt and disorder, of too many kinds. On the far side of the wall, she could hear Alba talking to Noah. María wiped her nose on her sleeve and snorted hard.

"I know you're upset," Lil said gently, sitting down and taking the girl in her arms. "We all are."

"Is he really *dead*?" María said.

Lil quickly reached out to shut the bedroom door. "You want your mother to hear? His heart stopped and they started it again. There's a big difference." She loosened her hug to lean back and look her daughter in the face. "I know it's hard, but you need to be brave," she said. "That's the best thing you can do for this family right now. Because if the first thing Iaia sees when she arrives—"

"Iaia's coming over?"

"She's going to mind you while we're away."

"You're going away?"

"We're driving down to Avi's tonight and we fly out from Barcelona tomorrow morning."

From far away, they heard the front door buzz.

"But how long will you be gone?" the girl asked. "When are you coming *back*?"

"I don't know," Lil said. "Look at me. Look me in the face. I don't know any more about what's waiting for us up there than you do. I'm saying that because I want you to know, no matter what happens, I'm going to try to be honest with you."

Just now the girl was disarmed enough to listen, and Lil herself had the courage—perhaps it was recklessness, equally welcome—not to threaten, or order, or harass, but simply speak.

"I'm going to say this in here so I don't have to say it out there and make you sound like a little kid," she said, speaking more softly than before. "I need you to be good." It sounded like the opening line from almost any of Lil's famous speeches, the point of almost every one of which was, Don't embarrass us, and don't embarrass yourself. But this time she meant, We're desperate, we're weak, help us, please. "Don't give me that look. I know you think I'm too tough with you, and maybe I am sometimes, but right now I'm not telling you, I'm asking you, can you just do that for us? Because if we get up there and a day or a week later we get your grandmother calling us up hysterical—"

"All right," María said. "I understand."

"*I promise,*" Lil said, and made sure to stare straight into her daughter's surprise.

"I promise."

"Good. Now fix your face and go help Noah set the table. If I even look at him, I'm going to start bawling too." She pressed her face to the top of her daughter's head to kiss it, and to torment herself with the smell of her hair.

"Mam," María said as she turned to go.

"What?"

"You *stink.*"

Stepping out into the corridor, Lil turned toward the bathroom, but was blocked by Alba and a suitcase.

"My mother's on her way up," Alba said. "Are you ready?"

There were three loud bangs on the front door.

"Could you deal with her? *Please?*" Alba said. "I have to say good-bye to María."

At the front door, Lil checked the peephole, opened the door, reached through the loose flaps, and drew Alba's mother inside. "Don't say anything stupid," she ordered in greeting. The old woman couldn't answer, still breathless from the stairs. "You can sleep in our bed," Lil said, stripping her coat. "I haven't had time to change the sheets, but you know where the clean ones are."

The old woman's hands were rooting in her black vinyl handbag, deaf to Lil's instructions. Precious seconds passed. "Alba!" Lil shouted. Her mother-in-law held out a tiny plastic pillbox. "One of these before bed every night and you'll sleep like a baby," she said, pressing the gift into Lil's hand. "Pierre needs you in good shape, not a wreck."

"Why don't you just take the whole box now yourself?" Lil said, with what sounded very like professional concern.

"And we'll wake you when we get back. That's what you're going to do anyway, isn't it?" The first shock of the news was gone and now something else was kicking in, and feeding off her absolute physical fatigue. She felt like she'd been up all night drinking, and drunk herself right the way around to sober, and was now wired to some pitiless juvenile buzz.

Alba brought the two children to greet their grandmother. There were long indulgent hugs, which felt to Lil already too much like a tribute to loss. The longer they went on, the more desperate she was to get away, pull the front door shut behind her, as though the apartment itself was the scene of the crisis, not Trondheim. To break the spell, she peeled the dust sheet off the kitchen table, carefully folding it on itself and setting it on top of the fridge, as though to preserve every crumb of dirt and gravel and later resume exactly where they'd left off. She got the red tablecloth from its drawer. With one brutal shake, the thing billowed, hung suspended, then floated peacefully down. Even as it settled, Lil ushered Noah and María away from their grandmother and told them to set three places.

"Oh no," Iaia said. "I couldn't eat now."

Lil stood to her full square. Dozens of crises had taught her how futile, with this woman, suggestion and politeness were. "Listen to me good," she said quietly, so that the children could pretend not to hear. "You're not a passenger in this house, you're the example. So I don't care if you puke it all up afterward, but you put it in your mouth, you chew, and you swallow. That's how this thing works."

Behind them, Noah and María were laying out cutlery, glasses, plates. Noah setting them down and María straightening, sometimes minutely, like a supervisor tracking a silver-service trainee.

ON THE AUTOROUTE, WITH QUIET PURPOSE, Lil pushed the needle all the way to 130, then let it sit just over the line, like a clock hand on its shadow. She had rarely driven so smoothly or read the unfolding world so well. With cold precision she was scanning cars far ahead, knowing in advance exactly what they were going to do. One by one, by sheer force of will, she shifted them out of her way. She was glad of the task. It let her feel a thrill of anger, even defiance, for long moments she wished would never end.

"You're going too fast," Alba said eventually, with great pressure in her voice, and instantly Lil saw a flash—the splashed image—of a car accident, as it might be. The gross confectionery. The scatter and squash. The balled-paper crumple. The side mirror dangling like an ear in an abattoir. She almost wanted it, and did not immediately slow down, or calm her slalom. There is something in physical proficiency that borders on cruelty, even toward oneself.

The headlights fringed the autoroute with hard scrub. The distant sea was bottled black. Closer, the lagoons were sheets of tinfoil in the dark. Then came the word *KEOLIS*, red neon, suspended in the night—an oracle's warning—on a long corrugated metal shed. The land began to roll a little. Mostly vineyards now. The moonlight caught the iron supports keeping the training wires tight, all leaning inland as though bent by the wind. The exit signs came at them one after the other, FRONTIGNAN, SÈTE, AGDE, PÉZENAS, tearaway calendar days, telling them where every other road led. Lil already knew. They led through the back country of the

Faugères, the Minervois, to the ingrown towns where she'd played much of her rugby career, and seeing those signs her grip tightened on the steering wheel, as her body heard the old call to arms.

Each in her own way, both women were still anesthetized by the news, as though in preparation for the terrible shock that same news must soon bring.

They drove on. Alongside the autoroute ran a long double row of bare plane trees like inverted broomsticks. It was the old national road, escorting the autoroute for a while, now near, now far, like a shadow over uneven ground. Then a black mass like a dead ocean liner. The Stade de la Mediterranée, Lil knew. Monument to the legendary Béziers team of the seventies and eighties, past glory that would never come again. Eventually, they passed the sign for Narbonne, and she could feel herself leaning into relief as the danger zones were left behind.

Alba too seemed to have loosened a little in her seat. She got out her phone, made a call. Lil listened to her repeat the conversation they'd had earlier with Trondheim, only now it was Alba's turn to deliver the bad news.

Lil herself would call no one. Part of her believed the news less real if it was not sent out into the world.

PORT-LA-NOUVELLE, PORT LEUCATE were the next names to pop up. La Catalane, the autoroute called itself now, and the name alone made her think the air warmer here, and she turned the car heater off. She had caught a whiff of her own sweat, her fear, pushing through the pores like day-old drink.

At Perpignan, the autoroute veered over the river and into the suburbs and rose high enough in places for them to look down like nosy neighbors into hotel grounds, nightclub

terraces, and occasionally over a private wall, into the gem-
stone magic of a swimming pool. The gardens' spotlights
shouted, Look, oranges, lemons, brightly dripped notes of
the warm south. Off to the east, the city's avenues plowed
straight for the sea, rows of palm trees like some postcard of
a colonial capital's prime. But they pushed by all that and on
to the city's ragged edges, past peeling hangar roofs, moon-
scaped factory lots, paired-up Senegalese girls patrolling
dirt parking lots for trade.

Out in the countryside again, the cherry orchards still
had their leaves. Here, the first proper frost had yet to come.
Driving south, they were reversing the tape, reeling themselves back a full month or more to a season they'd already
mourned and memorized farther north. Not rushing toward
the news but away from it.

Alba was on her fifth or sixth phone call by now. Everyone
had to be told, she seemed to think, and all with the same
words and inflections, as though to confirm and calcify not
only what had happened but how she felt. "We don't know
if," she said. "We think that." Quoting the doctor verbatim,
as though they were both on the same side. "Because there's
no way of knowing how long he was lying there before being
revived," she explained again. "That's the key. Less than
three or four minutes, the damage might be limited. Any
longer is not good."

They drove on in silence. Miles ahead, the night sky was
hung with what looked like a string of cheap Christmas lights.
They were wind turbines on the mountainside, churning mer-
cilessly in the dark.

"Not three or four minutes," Lil eventually said. "The doctor said three minutes tops."

N<small>OW THE ROAD WAS CLIMBING TOWARD</small> S<small>PAIN</small> like a ramp. Lil had her foot on the floor, and still the needle was working counterclockwise down the dial, as on a waning pressure gauge. She shifted down and grounded the pedal again. They could see the border post far ahead, lit up like a stadium, some great communion gathering its tribe. But at the frontier all barriers were pointing skyward, all the customs posts empty, and they sailed straight through. Lil had a small bottle of water between her thighs, felt it shrink and cringe as their descent began.

About fifteen minutes after the border, in a graceful peeling off, like a wingman quitting a fighter formation, the car left the autoroute, while the solid stream it had been part of plowed onward, dead south.

Then they were in Figueres, in Alba's father's house, with Alba folded into his arms, his little girl come home for another cure. Lil stood behind them holding the bags, knowing it would be her turn next.

It was late but the table was set. There were chunks of bread in a basket, and a terra cotta pitcher of wine, and a cast-iron pot in the center. Lil dabbed a finger at the metal to check was it still warm. As soon as they sat down, Alba's father started to pour wine into Lil's glass, and kept pouring, pouring, almost to the brim. For his daughter he poured nothing at all. Lil lowered her head to take a first sip. There was a fresh white tablecloth underneath.

With a shaking hand, he ladled lumpy soup into a bowl.

"I couldn't," Alba said.

Instead, he set the bowl in front of Lil—some kind of fish stew—and she didn't dare refuse. He'd caught them himself, he managed to say, meaning the fish, but the conversation didn't take. They ate in silence, with no tears and no open lament. The edges of the old man's eyes looked a little red, that was all. He was as troubled as he was upset. Age had promised to take the emotion out of certain unspoken laws and replace it with a mathematical type of truth: first him, then his children, then his children's children, and so on. But here was another sadistic plot twist.

They carried their cases upstairs to Alba's childhood bedroom, and Lil had to force her legs to make every step. In the bathroom mirror their faces looked indecently aged, or maybe it was just the fluorescent light. They brushed their teeth and their tongues and undressed in silence, as though these things were all the terms of an agreement.

"You're not going to have a shower?" Alba asked as kindly as she could.

"I'll have one in the morning. Now I'm dead."

Each lay stiffly on her own side of the bed. As ever, the room seemed far too small to Alba for all the memories it contained.

"Should we set the alarm?" Lil asked.

"You really think you're going to sleep?"

"What time did you tell your father?" Lil was already twisting a knob on Alba's old windup clock.

"I can't sleep if there's an alarm," Alba said.

"Did your mother give you those pills?"

"Yes."

"He needs you in good shape," Lil said. "Not a wreck."

Alba ignored the cue. "Do you want one?" she asked eventually.

In the dark, Lil shook her head. "I'm so wiped now, the second I close my eyes I'll be gone."

But the night was long, on both sides of the bed. Lil listened to Alba settling and resettling herself in the darkness. Eventually, as though it was just another shift, she rolled up against Lil's warm body and Lil obediently rearranged herself to take Alba in her arms. She was glad to be useful in at least that one way, and liked the idea of herself as the protector, the haven, but felt inordinately afraid of the moment Alba might start to cry. She did not know if that was entirely selfish or not. She certainly feared contagion, and where she herself was liable to go.

About 6:00 A.M., Alba finally folded back the quilt and slid quietly from the bed. Lil listened to her lift her clothes from the chair and sneak away. Then she fell into a deep sleep.

In the kitchen, looking for coffee, Alba opened one cupboard door after another, and could not understand why everything was no longer where it had always been. All she could find was an old tin of loose tea. She tugged at the lid. It was stuck. *Imperial Or,* the label said. *Dammann Frères. Marchands de thé à Paris depuis 1692.* The back boasted of this particular blend's forceful personality—brightened by a hint of jasmine, it said. She had bought it for Father's Day eight or ten years ago. She drew a steak knife out of the block and slid the point under the cusp and off it popped. Underneath was a virgin foil seal. He had never wanted it, and never thrown it out, and she could favor whichever of those two facts she preferred. Inside were short stiff curls like burned bits of wick. She lifted the tin to her nose. That big personality they'd been bragging about seemed faded almost to nothing now.

She could find no strainer either, so scattered a few pinches directly into her bowl. She watched the water turn honey, rust, ale. The leaves all sat on the surface at first. Then, soaked and swollen, each in turn began a graceful descent, like divers who'd come up for air and were now heading down again. She stirred carefully, to sink the stragglers, before taking her first sip. Every now and then, as she drank, she stuck out her tongue and pinched at it, then held out her forefinger and thumb for inspection, like an oldtimer smoking a hand-rolled cigarette.

Three hours later, Lil stood at the kitchen sink, looking out the window. Alba had gone to take her place in the shower, and her father was making a fresh jug of coffee.

"There's a parrot in your tree," Lil announced.

"*Què?*"

"A green parrot."

"*Parrot.*" The old man repeated the new word diligently.

"*Uno perroquet verde,*" Lil said, improvising.

A large green bird was hopping about the crown of the garden's kaki tree. Now, at the end of November, the tree looked like Christmas dressed by someone who preferred Halloween: spindly branches bare but for dozens of perfectly round, rust red fruit, like baubles individually hung. The fruit was not yet quite ripe, and the bird could hop and pick with no danger of any dropping off.

Already Lil had her phone out, was trying to open the kitchen window for a clearer shot. Her father-in-law stepped closer to show her how the handle worked. "Ah," he said, his face brightening. "*El loro.*"

The bird was a gaudy green. An escapee, Lil presumed, from private cage or pet shop or zoo.

"This one, I call him my best friend," the father said. "He come to see me every morning of my life and I tell him, Hello, how are you? And I talk to him, I tell him my thoughts and he listen. He really do."

The old man sounded glad of the chance to talk about something so harmless, but as usual Lil struggled to understand. He seemed to be saying that the parrots were invading—invaders?—moving farther up the coast every year. But invading from where? Farther south was the Spanish desert, then North Africa, and the bird was an advertisement for everything tropical.

To get to the airport by noon for a one o'clock takeoff, they left the house at half past nine. It was almost an hour too early, but Alba's father insisted, in case anything went wrong. In the driveway, his car looked like a slightly blurred photo of itself. It was that fine dust the sirocco sucked up from the Sahara, then blew over the entire Mediterranean coast. That, too, was something Lil wanted a picture of. When Alba got in, her father began to dribble a bottle of water over the windshield, then said something that made her lean over, start the engine, and flick the wipers on. He held his pose for a few moments, plastic bottle aloft, still dribbling, waiting for his daughter's face to reappear. The mess the wipers made reminded Lil of the whitewashed windows of bankrupt shops.

AT AIRPORT SECURITY, A YOUNG WOMAN with a ponytail and a swinging badge pointed them out from afar and wheeled her arm, traffic cop, to steer them into a particular race. In the queue, the girl in front lifted her arms as in a grandiose yawn to unhook her necklace. "Don't touch me! Don't you dare!" roared a woman up ahead. Without being asked, Lil and Alba started to peel their outer layers off.

DELAYED, the Departures screen said of their flight, which gave them an extra hour to kill. They sat at a café table by the plate-glass walls, with the runways as a backdrop, exactly as the architect had imagined them. Alba poured a packet of sugar onto her cappuccino's froth, watched the grains subside and sink, then poured a second packet into the hole the first had made.

"You see what they did to that boy?" she said, because she desperately wanted company and conversation, as distraction from the sickening fear she felt.

"What boy?" Lil asked, with a pinch of expectation in her voice.

"In the security line. They swiped him with those paddle things. All over. Front and back. Then they swabbed his hands and stuck the swab in their magic light." She was nursing an image of the little boy's face, caught between duty and fear, eyes begging his parents to tell him what his rights and obligations were, even as he'd lifted his arms out from his body, celebrant.

"So?" Lil had no surplus sympathy.

"What I'm saying is, who's going to load a six-year-old boy

with a bomb?" Alba said. It was precisely the kind of opinion Lil loved to mock, for it was a point of pride with her to see all naïveté as willful, and all idealism—even optimism—as self-serving deception.

To kill the conversation, Lil stood up again. Her legs were stiff from yesterday and she had to keep moving, she said. But she went nowhere, just stood at the glass wall, looking out. Far away, an orange emergency light was flashing near the perimeter fence. In a field beyond, someone was burning leaves. Farther off again, the haze-faded mountains were a rubbed-out sketch. To live with, she was a half-hearted dictator, whom the slightest splinter infuriated with suspicious ease. But she had often fantasized that a great life crisis would bring focus and calm. How maddening, now, that Alba seemed determined to make it another version of their petty everyday game.

In the newsagent's, Lil scanned the strident headlines from around the world, and the showcase abs and glutes fronting the women's fitness magazines, and the celebrity sailboats, and the mind games. The book rack rated the week's best-sellers from 1 to 10. On the children's shelf, the spotlight series was of Greek myths redone as comic books. Odysseus, the Minotaur, Orpheus. The comparisons were facile and of no use at all.

In the restroom, pretending she was checking her messages, she took a photo of a pilot leaning into the mirror to touch up her lips. At the far end of the Departures hall, through the glass partition, she took one of a little girl sitting on a baggage carousel, waving royally at everyone as she passed. She shot a young backpacking couple slouched in their seats, leaning into each other, both fast asleep. They looked dressed for the beach, bare arms draped across bare shoulders, flip-flops toyed from painted toes at the end of long tanned legs. Unearned reward, the perfect skin said.

Without being called, they went to their gate. The lounge seats were brown leatherette, cracked and flaking at every seam. Every few minutes another announcement came over the tin-can tannoy, lifting people from seats all around the lounge like hypnotized bodies obeying a trigger word. But none was the call they were waiting for. A man beside Alba was talking too loudly on his phone in a language neither of them could even recognize.

Finally, "those requiring assistance" were called to board, and there was a rush to form a line. Lil and Alba stayed put. It looked too much like the panic they felt inside.

From the boarding queue, Lil took a photo of the Norwegian Air plane taxiing toward their slot. She took the refueling and baggage crews surrounding it, then the first passengers emerging when the door opened, arms raised in mock victory, hostages, free. She took the same plane again from the tarmac while she and Alba stood waiting to mount the steps. Then the terminal building, framed in their porthole. The stewardess sealing the airlock. The same woman pressing a dummy oxygen mask to her face. These photos would be their adventure, in retrospect. They showed the solid overground world to which they would bring back their son.

THEY WAITED AT THE END OF THE RUNWAY, pointing north, for what felt like a very long time. As the plane finally began to move, Alba blessed herself, kissed the tips of her fingers, and closed her eyes. She would not open them again, Lil knew, until they leveled off.

They were immediately over the sea, banking left, and already the world's surface looked safely distant and small. The passengers were quiet. The hum was loud. The cart brought the homesickening smell of fresh bread.

Two and a half hours in, Lil saw a first tint of orange to the far west, like unstirred cordial at the bottom of a glass. The farther north they flew, the more that orange bruised to ruby, purple, mauve. Through the port windows the low sun now shone gold on the overhead lockers, and in perfect synchronization those orbs danced up and down, left and right, telling on maneuvers being made by the plane that they could not physically feel. Then those halos descended onto the heads of certain passengers, and for just a moment set a few random faces aglow, like faces in candlelight, over there on the other side of the aisle.

The captain came on to announce their descent and almost immediately began a gradual downshift of the engines, as though the pitch of their whine was being tuned to a slightly flatter note.

"There it is," Lil announced, nodding at the porthole, the tiny amber dots threaded through the velvet black.

Those lights did not swell or brighten, merely gained in detail, like something being brought into ever finer focus under a microscope. A single orange dot became three. An orange thread now showed the stitches from which it was made. Then those lights somehow separated from the surfaces they lit, showing walls, roads, houses, an entire solid world—one wiped out in an instant by the sudden upsweep of the starboard wing.

THEY MARCHED THROUGH THE LOVESICK STENCH of Duty Free, past the stacks of cigarettes and chocolate, the locked watch displays, the whimsical underwear, the bullion bricks of single malt whiskey. Even up here, Lil thought, the prizes are all the same. They rode the conveyor belts most of the way to Domestic Transfer while Alba sifted through her phone. There had been calls and texts from Noah, and her mother, and several friends, but nothing from the hospital. It was a letdown for which she felt strangely prepared. They'd been indoors since Barcelona Airport and felt like they'd never really left: the set and props they were now coasting past—white granite floors, brushed steel fittings, franchise food halls—were exactly the same as those they'd left behind, as though they'd taken off and circled awhile, waiting for fog to clear, but been obliged to land again at Barcelona—its new terminal—or another airport made by the same mind. The real world—time and fact and effect— was no closer here than before.

At the café closest to their gate, Lil grabbed an uncleared table while Alba joined the queue. She came back with two coffees and a sandwich. Lil peeled off the lid and peered into the cup.

"That's the way she gave it to me," Alba said.

"What did you ask for?"

"If you don't like it, don't drink it," Alba said.

This was the problem they called "dairy". It was an alibi, Alba knew, for something far more personal and far less precise.

"I'm not saying it's your fault," Lil said. She had already peeled open her sandwich, and now peeled back a slice of ham, found a thick layer of butter on the bread, and closed it over again.

"You can scrape it off," Alba said.

"They didn't have any beer?"

"I don't think beer is what you need right now."

At the ping of Alba's phone, her hand jerked as by reflex and hit her coffee cup. A brown spurt shot from its nipple, and the cup wobbled, but Lil's hand closed around it before it could tip. Alba lifted the phone she had been grabbing for.

"What does it say?" Lil asked, but Alba turned away, as though this were her private crisis, which she was not yet ready to share.

It was merely a Welcome text from her new network, with a price list.

Sip by sip, Alba finished her coffee, then started on Lil's. At a black baby grand nearby, a young woman in a chapka was playing something politely sinister—Satie, perhaps. Eventually there was an announcement to say the flight to Trondheim was delayed. At that, Lil set the sandwich in front of her, pulled it open, pulled out its guts, and began to scrape the butter off with her spoon.

"You're such a child," Alba said.

"You're such a mother," Lil shot back.

"Why don't you just go over?" Alba said finally, nodding

at the young woman playing the piano. "It would be easier on your neck."

She had been in Lil's unrelenting presence for twenty-four hours, and now she was tired, and excited, and terrorized by the growing certainty—as in an escape dream—that she would never manage to get any closer to her son.

To calm herself, she called home, told the children where they were. "Like clockwork, all the way," she told the other end. She was talking to Noah, Lil could tell. She had resumed her favorite role, all selfless concern and skillful calm. She asked if they'd eaten, and how his sister and grandmother were. When María came on, she asked the girl how Noah seemed to be. Her mother was sleeping. "Good. No, leave her be," Alba said. "I love you," she said to each child in turn, flagging the end of their allotted time.

Lil gave no sign that she wanted to be included in the conversation. The performance was mostly for her sake, she thought—a convoluted corrective to Alba's earlier sharpness. Refusing to participate, even as a witness, she stood up and walked toward the beautiful pianist. Beyond her, on the far side of a wall of soundproof glass, passengers who'd just arrived from the north were trooping past, and Lil checked their faces for news. She did not need to hear what they said. All around them in the café and waiting areas, Norwegian was the only language to be heard, everyone talking loudly to their neighbors, as though they were all part of one big family and excited to be almost home.

Trondheim. Saturday Night.

THE TRONDHEIM PLANE WAS THE SAME MODEL as the one from Barcelona. Inside, too, the color scheme was the same black and red, and they were seated again by the port wing, so that to Alba it felt like they'd just stood up, got out to stretch their legs, then sat back down in their old seats. What looked like the same stewardess went through the same moves for their imaginary emergency as before, putting the same slicker yellow life vest over her head and in a preschool mime pretending to tie it on.

"Noah said the neighbors were complaining about the bags of rubble you left on the street," Alba said.

"Not much I can do about it from here" was Lil's answer.

The takeoff was straight and steep, no banking this time. They sat in the machine-room hum. The cabin was dark, but the overhead lights never came on. Most of their neighbors were dozing. After a while, Lil turned on her own individual light and flapped through the inflight magazine. It showed photos of radiant women on massage beds, tastefully draped. Norway's best restaurants and bars, all candlelit. Ads for skiing resorts, trekking, fun outings on snowmobiles. Well-groomed thrills and body luxury on every page.

In the captain's next announcement, Lil was sure she heard the word *Trondheim*. Soon after came the first flutters of descent. Inside Lil's body, as in a zero gravity environment, something had been loosed that would never again be grounded, she felt.

The touchdown was brutal, but woke only half the sleepers. They taxied toward the lights. Eventually came the grandiose hiss of the doors, like long pent-up pressure released. "*Trondheim*," the captain said again over the PA—a sound, apparently, it gave her particular pleasure to make with her mouth.

The first screen they saw inside the terminal read 23:46, and as if on cue they began to stride, then to jog as best they could, suitcases yapping at their heels, because the last bus into the city left at midnight on the dot. They arrived panting at Passport Control to find a queue already formed, but Lil grabbed Alba's arm and tugged her past them all to the head of the line. What she wanted, she now wanted without quibble or confusion. The policewoman inside the cubicle barely glanced at their faces. The clock behind her head read 23:56.

At the far end of the hall, a big red arrow pointed down into the mouth of the exit tunnel. Alba's fears were sloppy and contagious. It was not Pierre's crisis that tunnel led to, but her own, and Lil was dragging her toward it with something bordering on brutality.

A single-decker coach was waiting directly outside. *Sentrum*, it said. *Direkte.* The driver was standing by the open hold doors, and waved grandly to gather them in. He didn't speak much English but it didn't matter, there was only one bus, going in only one direction, with only one price.

The bus windows were fogged up, and for the first few minutes they could see nothing but the slurred lights of the oncoming cars. They entered a long tunnel. The wall-mounted lamps flashed by in a slow strobe. Eventually the driver made an announcement and a lone hand rose to press the STOP button above its seat. Just as quickly, Alba took a piece of paper from her purse. She stared at it helplessly, trying to match the imagined phonetics with what she'd heard. Lil had always found her strangely eager to ask others the way, yet now she did not dare. Lil herself generally preferred to stumble on blindly, as though determined to accumulate evidence that she was indeed lost, but now plucked the paper from Alba's hands and offered it to the woman across the aisle. The thing was as limp as a bit of rag and the woman held it at arm's length, as though in distaste at how it looked or felt, or at what it said. When the driver announced the next stop, Lil turned again but the woman shook her head. Half a mile on, the bus pulled over and three women got off. Across the street, a billboard showed a knight in chain mail wielding a double-handed sword. WELCOME TO TRONDHEIM, it said, MEDIEVAL CAPITAL OF NORWAY'S CHRISTIAN KINGS.

Soon they were passing run-down apartment buildings, snowed-over playgrounds, dark supermarkets. At the deserted train station, no one got on or off. Then they were driving through the night city proper, its garish shop windows, Christmas decorations, rowdy students queueing outside clubs. At the next announcement, Lil again looked across the aisle, and this time the woman pointed at the floor and gave the thumbs-up.

An arrow marked NEVROSENTERET sent Lil striding down a narrow side street. The path was covered with slush, in which her wheelie case left two thin tracks. She had not even turned to check that Alba was following, but paused at the next junction, where a sign pointed to BLODBANKEN, straight ahead. She waited for Alba to come close enough to spot her, then pushed on.

They passed block after block of squat buildings lining the wide empty streets. Soon came the vintage sound of a helicopter overhead. The paths here were harder, less trampled, and the gritted ice sounded like broken glass underfoot. By now Alba's wheels were clogged, and the hauling harder. She stopped to switch the hand dragging her case, and as she did so, both feet shot off the ground, just like in a cartoon when the rug is whipped away. Somehow she did not fall. But afterward she shuffled along even slower than before, suspecting treachery everywhere.

Still Lil didn't wait. There was bullying—and relish—in her rush, as though she could feel Alba's aversion, and the terrible fear behind it, but knew there would be no protest. Beyond the next junction, a sign said EMERGENCY, with an arrow pointing straight ahead. In between, path and road dipped into a slush-filled gutter. Without pausing, Lil jumped clean over the puddle, in a stiff leap very like one of María's *grands jetés*. By the time Alba caught her up, she was trying the door of a building whose ground floor lights were on. Behind her, in the cold air, Alba was panting audibly. Lil began rattling the door hard. She could see a gray-haired woman behind a reception desk at the back of the foyer. Then she began to bang brutally—Let me in, let me in—but still the receptionist refused to look up. So Lil ungloved her hand and started to tap with her wedding band, louder and louder, as though actually trying to crack the glass, until the woman got wearily to her feet and began the long walk across the hall. She looked through the locked door at the two figures and suitcases outside, faintly lit by the aquarium glow in which she stood.

"*Heart, Emergency,*" Lil said, pronouncing the words deliberately, and pointing at her own chest.

The blue woman shook her head, apparently disinclined to help in any way, but for once in her life Lil knew instinctively what to do: she slipped her hand into Alba's and—barely moving her lips—whispered, "Don't move." Like a couple posing for a formal portrait, the two women stood stiffly hand in hand and stared calmly ahead, making no gesture, no facial expression, no excuse whatsoever for the receptionist to turn away. Finally the woman raised a finger, telling them to wait. She returned with a sheet of paper, which she pressed against her own side of the glass. It was a map, with a big red *X* markered on one of the buildings across the street.

"Floor four," the woman mouthed. Her right hand lifted and stiffened like a salute. Her left held up four fingers, the whole hand minus the thumb.

At the building opposite plus one, a long line of foot-high letters was bolted to a wall: AKUTTEN, the first word said. Directly underneath, stuck to the wall, was a bronze mold of what looked like a bear rug, head and all. Some kind of sculpture, they supposed.

"Acute?" Lil offered. "Do you think this is it?"

Alba's look was hesitant, fearful. Since the plane, Lil had been driving her toward the danger with an oddly obsessive energy. She backed away from the word and the wall and Lil, and the nearby doors slid open, inviting them in.

On 4, they walked the corridors. At every turn, Lil looked back and hissed, "*Come on!*" The minutes passed. Precious minutes wasted is how it felt to Lil, as though their number were limited, and Alba deliberately running down the clock. They turned another corner and found a woman in a lab coat at a nurse's desk, scanning some kind of list with a pink highlighter. She listened politely to Lil's explanation, and in impeccable English sent them back the way they'd come. "*Hjertemedisin*," she called after them, once they'd gone far enough not to turn back.

At the end of another corridor, on the dead wall, arrows pointed left and right. They tried to pronounce the words written underneath, hoping the long strings of letters might sound more familiar than they looked. Eventually they found themselves back where they'd started from. The elevator doors were just closing, and Lil jumped between them. An empty gurney was parked inside. HJERTEMEDISIN: 5, the panel said. Over and again the doors squeezed and shied, trying to close on Lil, while she waited for Alba to arrive.

Directly opposite the elevator on the fifth floor was a set of wired glass doors, with another interphone and a badge swipe. Beyond, a long wide corridor led to glass doors at the far end. Who was it, Lil wondered, they needed so badly to keep out? She picked up the interphone and pressed the bell.

"Did that ring?" she asked.

"Yes."

"You're sure?"

Alba did not reply.

Lil rattled the door handles hard. "Well," she said, "next time you play deaf, I'll know what to think."

Still Alba gave no answer. All her mortal attention was on the corridor beyond the wired glass, and on the mint green doors leading off it. Behind one of those doors was their son. Within minutes—perhaps seconds—they would be at his bedside. The thought made her sick.

With her wedding band, Lil began to peck at the glass.

"Lil," Alba said. It was a plea.

The taps were loud, and painfully regular, as though made by a machine. No one came and the tapping hardened.

"Stop!" Alba ordered.

The tapping was now so sharp that she expected the glass to crack or explode any second. It felt like the point of a pickax tapping at her own head.

"*Please*," she begged, all her authority gone.

A minute later, a young nurse came strolling toward them. At the door, she merely raised her hand to her ear in the gesture of a phone. So Lil picked up the interphone and explained in English that they were here for their son, their French son, that they had come from France, and their son was here, somewhere in this building, in a coma, because of a heart attack. As though to introduce themselves, Lil pointed at herself and Alba. "Pierre Casals," she said, and watched the nurse's face change.

They followed her down the hall, and roaring within them now was a great hunger simply to see their son, no matter what state he was in. Without the tapping, the entire building seemed terribly quiet, no sound but the whizz of their suitcase wheels and the suck of their soles on the rubber floor. There were mint green doors left and right, each bearing three numbers made of molded brass. Odd to the left, even to the right. 501. 503. 505. Everything depended now on which door this woman chose.

LIL WOULD HAVE EXPECTED THE LONG THIN BODY in the bed to be the room's only point of attention, but it was not. The rumpled bedcover felt far less important than the stacks of machines left and right of his head, where bedside nightstands ought to have been. Those were the big personalities in the room. Her eyes followed the tubes and cables and pipes they sprouted to the forearms, laid outside the bedcovers as if for deliberate display. Other wires and cables snaked up the short sleeves or down the collar of his gown. The biggest pipe by far took root in the mouth, with two lengths of thick white tape—a clumsy X across his face—holding it firmly in place.

Alba had already knelt by the bedside and taken hold of her son's hand. It felt cold, and she sandwiched it tight between her palms as though to warm it up. "Pierre, *cheri*," she said, pronouncing the words with difficulty. "It's Maman. I'm here now. Everything's going to be all right." She was trying to hide how frightened she was, much as she used to when he was sick as a child.

Lil approached the bed more cautiously. She was wary of touching him, for the great surge of emotion it might bring. Misunderstanding her reserve, with formal grace the nurse raised a calming hand. The hospital had found from experience that describing what the family saw helped reduce their shock. "As you can see," she explained, "he is connected by quite a number of tubes and wires to quite a number of machines. The one you may find most disturbing is the tube we have inserted into his trachea to help him to breathe. The other wires and cables are to regulate his temperature and to monitor his vital signs. And of course there are a number of drips, for his medication. One for glucose, antibiotics, anti-inflammatories, anticoagulant. And another one for—I don't know what the English name is, something to keep the blood flowing, fluid, *fluidifier*—is that a word?"

Waiting for the list to end, Lil remained standing as though out of respect, but wanted very badly to sit. She was tired and sore and was shifting her weight discreetly from left leg to right, by holding one foot and then the other slightly off the ground. Physically, the arrival had brought a terrible feeling of deflation, and she felt close to collapse.

"He won't respond to you in any way," the nurse was saying now, "but that's absolutely normal. It's because of the sedative we're giving him, to maintain the coma, and to palliate any physical distress."

Palliate. The word stung.

She talked them through every drip and drug, and seemed strangely conscientious about not missing a single one. It was like a legal disclaimer of some sort, and as near an admission of helplessness as the hospital would ever give.

Alba barely heard, but Lil welcomed this flood of facts. She stood stone-faced, arms clasped across her chest. For the past twenty-four hours, this room had been the prize and the punishment, and now that she was here she didn't dare relax the grip she'd been keeping on herself. It would have loosed something too strong—some deeper, purely personal grief.

Pierre's progress would be monitored over the next few days, the nurse went on, and when the signs were right, they would lift the artificial coma they had induced. But whether or not he would then—or ever—come out of his coma, and, if he did, whether or not he would be brain-damaged—as matters stood there was no way to know, she told them, because in order to know how long Pierre had been lying at the bus stop before being found and revived—in order to know, in other words, if the brain had been without oxygen for less than three minutes, or more, and if more, how much—

The walkie-talkie on her belt began to beep loudly, much like a reversing truck. She pressed a button to acknowledge the alarm, raised a finger in apology, and left the room.

Lil had spotted a wooden X-chair against the wall. She pulled it close to the bed, where she would be within reach of him, and tried to sit down, but found it a strangely difficult thing to do. Leaning forward, her gaze lit on his ears, lips, fingernails. He was a lover's body after the split. Intimacy, access, care—all banned. It was the logical conclusion, perhaps, of a process begun years back, when he had started to withdraw. Noah, too, was doing that now.

When Alba went to the bathroom, Lil shifted her chair even closer and reached out to touch his arm. She rubbed her thumb back and forth across a patch of skin near the wrist not occupied by any kind of tube or cable or tape. It was as good a contact as she was going to get in this room. "Pierre," she said quietly. Saying anything else would have felt like a performance of some kind. "*Pierre,*" she said again, winding the clock back twenty years, to the delivery room, when they'd finally learned it was a boy, and it was only then, postpartum, that she'd dared to test the name aloud, its music with his face, to convince herself of the fit.

When the nurse came back, she gave them each a bright red swipe card on a red lanyard. "For your apartment," she said, pointing at the ceiling. This was their first real piece of news. Their fret had been to book flights, get to the airport, catch the bus on time, find the hospital, find Pierre, and neither had plotted anything at all beyond that.

"It's a long time since I've seen twin beds," Alba said, when they were in the apartment upstairs. "Not since the boys shared a room."

"If you don't count every hotel we've ever stayed at in Spain."

"Not hotels. *Pensións* maybe."

"I always wonder what they expect couples to do," Lil said. "Screw in a single, then someone goes overboard? I guess we could push them together. Most hotels now, that's all the double really is."

"Leave them," Alba said. She hefted her case onto the bed closest to the door and watched it bounce. "I'll take care of you if you want. If that's what you mean. But that's as good as you get tonight."

Lil stood at the big window while Alba unpacked. Below were the whiskey-dark hospital grounds. The building opposite looked a mirror image of their own but was entirely clad with netted scaffolding. She did not want to be taken care of, like some child getting its ass wiped. She wanted a mouth and hands hungry for her flesh.

"You remember *A Short Film About Love*?" she asked the glass.

"Kieślowski?"

"Yes."

"Which one was that?"

"Poland. Eighties. Grim."

"That narrows it down."

"Young guy in an apartment block, obsessed with an older woman in the block opposite."

"I must have seen it because I've seen them all. How does it end?"

"What really stayed with me are those scenes of him turning out the light so she won't see him, and standing in his flat in the dark, waiting for her to come home and turn her light on. You always think of yourself as the one in the dark, looking out. Never as the one in the window with the lights on. He slits his wrists, I think."

"He looks so thin and frail and helpless," Alba said. It was her first confession. As though she'd had to wait to be out of Pierre's room, to be sure he couldn't hear.

Lil turned to find her sitting on the edge of her bed, pressing her hands very hard against her face, as though to keep it in place. "He was always thin," she offered, knowing well that Alba meant something else.

"I didn't expect so many machines," Alba said, releasing her head. "I don't know what I was expecting. Not this."

Each in her own way felt deeply afraid and exposed. The greatest danger to their son, Lil felt, would be to acknowledge this. So she sat on the bed beside Alba and took her hand, to keep her calm.

"It all looks so complicated," Alba said. She meant all the tubes and cables and machines. She meant so many things to go wrong.

"It's not," Lil said. For her, the apparatus was a distraction from the essential: either Pierre would come back or he would not.

Alba cried for a while and Lil held her patiently. Finally she wiped her eyes, sighed loudly, then leaned forward as though Lil was nowhere near, and began to lace up her boots.

"Where are you going?" Lil said.

"Where do you think?"

"We need to pace ourselves," Lil said. "In the morning we have to get up and do this all over again."

Alba finished each double knot with a hard jerk. What looked like resolution was a clear new thought. As a child, Pierre used to nod off almost as soon as the car got moving, sleep through everything, only wake at the trip's end. Tonight too he had looked so comfortable that it seemed his eyelids might lift at any moment and she'd hear him ask, "We're here? Already?" It was a moment she didn't want to miss.

When Alba was gone, Lil toured the apartment alone. On a side table, beside a stainless steel kettle, was a white porcelain bowl holding two packets of instant coffee, two packets of cane sugar, two minuscule tubs of long-life milk. There were two cups, two saucers, and two spoons to stir it all in. Beside that was a pile of tourist brochures and a bilingual city map. The bathroom had a stack of towels, a basket of toiletries, a hair dryer. There was even a special cupboard with a fold-down ironing board. It should have been a relief that so many practical considerations had been anticipated, but it was not. It left her with nothing incidental to negotiate.

The permanent lesson of her childhood had been how to mask her great fear, which was that her mother was going to die, and in doing so confirm how absolutely unimportant she—Lil—was. Pierre was now making precisely the same threat, her whole body was primed for danger, and when her phone gave a loud beep she felt it as a punch. She forced herself to breathe deeply, then forced herself to look. It was a text from IKEA. *BLACK FRIDAY STARTS TODAY!* Sweden and Norway were still on speaking terms, apparently.

Unpacking her case, she found that Alba had already set her clothes all to one side of each shelf, leaving the other half bare. The wardrobe had those hookless hangers, to foil the hospital hanger thieves. She got into the shower and stayed there a long time, turning the temperature down by increments, until it was as cold as she could stand. Afterward, she left the bathroom light on and the bathroom door ajar, to help Alba navigate the strange room whenever she came back. Then she turned off the main light and the bedside lamps and lay on the bedcovers in her underwear with her phone, deleting all the messages of sympathy and support without reading a single one.

In the dark, the thoughts came in an orderly stampede. One was bigger than all the rest: money. Maybe only now that she'd seen the level of care could she let that thought speak. The private room for Pierre. The apartment for them. The round-the-clock nurses. The Space Age machines. She was already so worn down from worry that for a few minutes she could not defend herself, and her thoughts rushed toward catastrophe, skipping every intermediate step. She saw herself ruined, bankrupt. Bankrupt was how she already felt. As a fact, she knew that the money was not important yet. If Pierre was saved, it was a price they'd be willing to pay. If he was not, it would be just another detail in their new life.

At Pierre's bedside, Alba got out her rosary beads and prayed for a long time. There was such violence in his absolute calm. He had been so restless in the womb.

When she put the beads away again, the nurse asked, "Does it help?"

"It does something to your mind," Alba said. She did not mean her faith, but the mechanics of prayer. How Lil was managing her own head, she could not even conceive.

The hours added themselves up. Overhead, the tide of shadows washed back and forth. She had been awake for almost a full day, and every now and then her eyes began to close, but those were precisely the moments—as though tuned to her body rather than to his—that one of the machines chose to blink or beep.

"I forgot to tell you," the nurse said, hearing the cue. "His phone has been beeping. Messages, I presume. I managed to turn down the volume, but I didn't want to turn it off." She held out a transparent plastic box, into which the staff had emptied everything from his pockets—wallet, keys, phone, random wrack—when he arrived.

The leather wallet was worn smooth and molded to the slight curve of his hip. Alba emptied it onto the bedcover and rooted through the contents. His French *carte d'identité*, his library card, credit card, some kind of travel pass, ticket stubs, a foil-wrapped condom, folded receipts. Then she used his dead thumb to unlock his phone and sat scanning through his latest messages and missed calls. She could have answered, and brought all those strangers back into his life—their lives—but just now she wanted to keep him all to herself.

Tidying up, she put all his money into her purse because they had no kroner of their own yet, not even coins for the vending machines. It felt like the poverty of their early days again, when any need beyond the absolute basics carried a threat. And now the ICU's state-of-the-art facilities, the dedicated staff, the apartment, even (the nurse said) a subsidized canteen in the basement, and a sauna, and a gym—everything was being laid on without their asking, and all of it covered by Pierre's student insurance, apparently. What was no doubt designed for relief only provoked suspicion in her: that these things were compensation for disaster. One way or another, they were going to have to pay.

FOUR HOURS LATER LIL WAS AWAKE AGAIN. The facts were no older. She managed to sit up and set her feet on the floor. Her legs and back were stiff to the point of pain, and she was grateful. It was something concrete—physical—to push back against.

Downstairs, she found Alba lying by Pierre's bed in what looked like a dentist's chair, fully reclined, with her eyes shut. Outside, it was still as dark as when Lil had gone to bed, as though she'd simply gone upstairs and showered and changed and come straight back down. Under the orange streetlamps, the whole world looked varnished and set.

"She actually slept like that?" Lil asked the nurse.

"At one point she wanted to lie beside him on the bed and sleep there," the nurse said.

"But Kristen brought me the chair and a blanket and tucked me in," Alba said, opening her eyes, smiling weakly.

Apparently Kristen was their nurse's name, and Alba's new best friend.

On the overbed table were two cups of coffee and two plastic-wrapped plates of food. Under the transparent layers were rolls of smoked salmon, scrambled eggs, some kind of thick crêpes, but the thought of eating in Pierre's presence was sickening to Lil. How far down the big black tube went, she didn't want to know but couldn't help imagining. She tried to keep her eyes fixed on the monitors and machines instead. Advertise the unseen, seemed to be their endless drill. The life of the heart, the lungs, the brain. Any hitch in flagging that work—no more beeps, no more blinks—meant the work itself would stop. To occupy her mind, she counted the tubes. She caught herself counting the seconds between each drip. Soon she knew the names on all the bags by heart.

While Lil drank her coffee, Alba called her father and described the hospital, the special room, their son in his special bed. The version she gave him was about the best it could be, and she made no mention of all the machines or cables or drips or the huge plastic tube shoved down Pierre's throat, or the double mouthguard keeping his teeth apart, preventing them from clamping down by reflex and cutting the tube off. Talking to her father, she wandered out into the corridor, as she often did at home when she had things to say she didn't want Lil or the children to hear.

When Alba came back, twenty minutes later, she stood at the threshold but did not come in.

"Pierre's doctor is coming," she said.

They waited by the open stairwell beside the elevators. From overhead came the sound of hard running up the steps. Lil looked into the waiting room. On the wall, a big flat-screen TV was showing rolling news from around the world, on mute. Under it was a dark leather couch, four yellow plastic chairs, a vending machine in the corner, and a coffee table scattered with white grains. Who had spilled the sugar? Lil wondered, and wondered what their crisis was, and wondered would it be a comfort to compare. Between her and Alba, so far, there had been little but code about what they actually felt.

"Apparently she's not scheduled to work today but is coming in specially to meet us," Alba announced.

Lil knew she ought to be grateful for this, but resented it as she would have a derisory bribe. A few minutes later they heard heavy steps below them on the stairs. Someone was coming up at pace. Lil leaned over the balustrade to look down. The steps grew louder.

"I can feel my heart beating," Alba said.

"Me too."

"I don't want her to come."

"I know."

"I want to go home," Alba said weakly. "I want to just wrap him up and take him home with us, right now." She didn't expect to be taken seriously. It was just childish bleating, a relief to admit and to hear, after so much brave good sense.

Soon a red-faced young woman in black lycra and orange running shoes sprinted past them, two steps at a time, going up. They listened to the dying pitter-patter overhead. The corridor was quiet as before. The minutes passed, and they heard more heavy steps coming up the stairs. Alba kept her right hand in her pocket, working her rosary beads.

The same runner as before passed them, going up again.

"Please do not adjust your screen," Lil said.

"You think this whole thing is a joke?" Alba sniped. "That's our son in there, breathing through a plastic tube. What's your quip about that?"

Five minutes later, with a polite ping, the elevator door opened and a young woman stepped out. Her face was shame red and damp with sweat. It was the runner who'd passed them twice on the stairs. The only difference was that she was now carrying a long rectangular vinyl case, as for a musical instrument.

"Dr. Mya," she said. Her right arm was in a plaster cast to the elbow, so she set down her case and offered her left instead, and shook each of their hands with a strangely nonchalant grip.

"Let's go take a look at him, shall we?" she said, gesturing down the hallway with her casted arm.

Standing at the foot of the bed, she went through Pierre's story from the start, repeating more or less what they'd been told on the phone on Friday, and by Kristen the night before. At present, she said, there was no reliable indicator of how long Pierre's heart had been stopped. That being the case, it was better not to try to resolve but to maintain and indeed artificially reinforce his comatose state, for a time. That was the best way to help his heart—and perhaps his brain—recover from any trauma and stress they might have suffered. Explaining all this, the doctor held her hand patriot over her own heart, as though she herself were the vulnerable one, or had once been in Pierre's situation and was living cause for hope.

"For the moment we're keeping his core temperature several degrees below normal," she explained.

"Who's *we*?" Lil asked, because the implication seemed to be that there was someone else they should be talking to—someone more senior, perhaps—and Lil liked such conversations face to face, confrontational, the way she liked her sex.

"I mean the hospital," the doctor said. She had a blond comb-over fade, neat in the extreme.

"The hospital is a building. Buildings don't make decisions," Lil said.

"Well then, I mean me."

"Then say *me, I, my*," Lil told her. *We* sounded to her like decision by committee. She had always preferred one person, alone, to take all the responsibility and all the risk.

"Well then, *I* am keeping his core temperature several degrees below normal," the doctor said. "To slow down his whole metabolism, let his heart recover from the trauma it suffered on Friday afternoon. And when *I* feel the signs are right, *I* intend to raise that, and simultaneously lower the level of sedative *I* am giving him."

"How long might that be?" Alba asked.

"It might be a day, a week, a month," Dr. Mya said. "Who knows?" Like some canny garage mechanic, she managed to make the uncertainty sound predictable, and the delay a point of pride. "He'll have some new tests first thing tomorrow morning, to get a better indication of cerebral activity, the level of infection, and so on. Once the results of those are in, *I* will be in a much better position to decide."

She had unhooked the clipboard from the bed frame, was flapping the pages over one by one, until she came to a chart that looked like the plot of an economy in decline.

She did not explain it, but was talking about brain function now. The hospital had gone to considerable lengths, she said, to find out how long Pierre had been lying by the bus stop. They had talked to the bus driver who'd found him, and the driver of the previous bus. They had studied the transport network's GPS logbook to calculate the interval between the two. Five minutes maximum, the police said. But five minutes is an eternity for the brain. At even half that, damage is likely, if less severe.

"But all this is academic," she said to end. "We won't really know anything until we try to wake him up." She flapped the clipboard shut and hung it back in place.

"And now," she said, "let's talk about you two." The days to come would be a strain, she told them. To face it, they had to stay in good condition, mentally and physically. They had to sleep and eat well, and get out of the hospital a few times every day, if only for a short walk. Even if—especially if—they didn't feel like it. "I'm telling you from personal experience," she said. "Just being brave won't work. It certainly doesn't work for me. And I leave it all behind me at the end of every shift. You need to find some way to let out the steam."

"So what do you do?" Lil asked.

"Personally, I exercise every day, and twice a week I shoot, but everyone is different. We have a gym downstairs available to all residents and family members. Have you got your ID badges yet?"

"When you say *shoot*," Alba said.

"Is that your gun?" Lil nodded at the tall case by the door.

The doctor knelt by the case and pulled at a zipper.

"I don't want to see any gun," Alba said.

"Don't worry," Dr. Mya smiled, "no one's taking out any

guns in my ICU." From the case's outer pocket, she took a wad of paper. The small sheets were the size of a Polaroid, printed with concentric black and white circles. Each had several holes in it, as though punched through with a pencil. Most in the medium or high orbits, but one in the bull's-eye.

"I thought you used life-size silhouettes," Lil said, unimpressed.

"These are biathlon targets. I finished my medical training in the army, where the biathlon is a big thing, and I got hooked. But as I said, you need to find what works for you."

"What kind of gun is it?"

"*Lil,*" Alba said, a lesson to the whole room on how to pronounce the name.

"This one is a laser rifle, for training," Dr. Mya said in her most genial voice. "And even the competition rifles just shoot these tiny lead-tipped twenty-twos. They wouldn't even knock you down."

"I don't want to be impolite—" Alba started to say, and immediately Dr. Mya made a formal bow of concession, picked up the case, and carried it out into the corridor.

"I'm sorry," Alba said when Dr. Mya came back, "but it just feels like bad luck."

"You don't have to apologize. In situations of stress, we become hypersensitive to threat. I understand."

She offered to show them the gym. It was in the basement, but a little tricky to find. "I'm going down there now to take a shower," she said. "Come on, I'll give you the tour."

"We don't have our IDs yet," Alba said, because she did not want to leave Pierre.

"I'll sign you in."

"You go," Alba told Lil.

"I have no gear."

"We have mountains of gear people have left behind," Dr. Mya said. "Practically brand new, most of it."

"Go," Alba said again, because she'd be happy to be rid of Lil for a while, and because the gym felt too much like a strategy for a long campaign.

The place was big, modern, and well equipped, with treadmills, steppers, ellipticals, a dozen weight machines, and even a barbell rack. It smelled of old diapers, deodorant, and steam. Dr. Mya set her vinyl case on a slatted bench and caught Lil looking.

"You want to hold it, don't you?" she said, smiling.

"The last time anyone said that to me, I was fifteen years old," Lil joked.

"I'm afraid I can't even show it to you. Not in here." She nodded at the other people in the gym. "I know it's safe and you know it's safe, but most people feel about it the way your wife does."

"I apologize on her behalf."

"Lil," Dr. Mya said in a new, adult voice. "She's allowed to be afraid, and stressed, and even superstitious. So are you." Saying this, she had come around to set her foot right against Lil's, standing shoulder to shoulder, as though they were running side by side. "Forty-one?" she said.

"Forty-two."

While the doctor went to the storage room, Lil imagined snapping open the clasps of her case, lifting the lid. Each part would have its own nest sculpted from the foam. She imagined assembling it too—the neat lock and click—and looking coolly down the sights at every available target, holding each head in the crosshairs a moment before moving on. Nearest was a frail old man in leg braces, inching along between parallel bars toward a physical therapist, who was turned to face him, arms outstretched, but backing away. Beyond him, a heavy old woman sat on a plastic chair facing the mirrored wall, with a man in blue scrubs standing behind her, gently lifting and lowering her arms, exactly as a ballet partner would. Beyond them was a pair of younger women—staff?—shunting back and forth on rowing machines, moving in and out of sync like the flattened orbits of two planets.

Dr. Mya returned with a red plastic washbasket just like the one they had at home. It was full of sports clothes, with a pair of silver sneakers on top. Before Lil could object, the doctor was on her knees, unlacing Lil's boots, then pulling them off. She cupped her hand under Lil's heel and smoothly slipped the running shoe on.

"Made to measure," she said, smiling up at her, and apparently expecting Lil to smile back.

Over her shoulder, Lil sighted a woman about her own age and size on a Power Plate, very like the one she'd used ten years ago to rehab her torn ACL. The platform lights were leading the woman's feet left and right, forward and back, in an apparently arbitrary but complicated dance.

The doctor stood up, blocking Lil's view, picked a blue breathable T-shirt from the basket, held it against Lil's torso, then dropped it on the bench. "If you don't mind wearing men's," she said, then held up a pair of green shorts.

When next Lil looked up, a cleaning woman was working the vacant Power Plate over with a wad of tissue and a spray gun, bang bang, wipe wipe, effacing every trace on every surface, even the touch screen.

They talked about the doctor's training routine. She said the cardio itself was simple enough. Practicing shooting with her heart rate over 180 was not. On her workdays, the solution she'd come up with was to sprint up the nine flights of hospital stairs, then take the elevator down to cut recovery, over and over, until she got herself into the red. Then she practiced shooting at a special target up on the roof.

Lil was still listening, but her eyes were on the woman who'd been on the Power Plate, now bouncing on a trampoline. Straight up and down at first, then from one leg to the other, side to side. She recognized the exercise from her own days in rehab. Next, still bouncing, the woman had to catch a ball the therapist threw to her, now high or low, now left or right. Then the same routine over, but hopping on one leg. The longer she watched, the more anxious Lil felt, about how much further the circus act might go, and at what point you said no, enough.

FOR HER DEAD MAN'S CLOTHES, Dr. Mya had given Lil a tourist tote bag. She hooked the handbag to her elbow and carried her boots upstairs, one on each hand, like the front end of a panto horse. Approaching Pierre's room, a blue scrubs stepped out from the nurse's station to cut her off. She held a cardboard box in her arms.

"I'm sorry," she said, smiling, "they were meant to give this to you last night."

Lil took the box in her booted hands, turned around, and

walked back to the elevator, away from Pierre's room, where Alba was. Why gift her another cue for grief?

In the apartment, she set it on the bed and tore open the flaps. On top was a checklist of the contents. Prison release, was Lil's thought. She flung the worn socks and briefs on the floor, where last night she'd flung her own. The box also contained a thermal undershirt, a wool sweater, jeans, his red puff jacket, ski gloves, a red beanie. At the bottom were those good Gore-Tex boots they'd bought him last year for that trip to the Alps with his on-again, off-again girlfriend. One by one, Lil tidied every item away in the wardrobe, mixing them in with her own as camouflage.

Sitting on the toilet, she force-fed herself the best facts. Their son was still alive. Moored to the machines now. Stable. Safe. Despite what Alba said about his weight, he looked much the way he had before. In any case, the doctors always gave the worst possible impression first, from which point any change could only be an improvement. That was how they worked. Set a low expectation, to make the family easier to manage, and afterward make a miracle of every baby step.

Washing her hands, she spotted a second door in the mirror. A linen or cleaning cupboard, she supposed. With her wet hand, she turned the handle and pulled, but met no resistance. It opened onto an apartment the reverse image of their own, with the same curtains, carpet, and furniture, as tidy and empty as theirs had been when they arrived, ten long hours ago. The bathroom was shared, apparently, between the neighboring apartments. Each had its own door, both of which had to be locked from the inside if you wanted privacy.

She sat on the bed for a minute, facing the dead TV, then picked up the remote control. On certain buttons—OK, VOL,

CH—the primary colors were all but worn to gray. She put the thing back exactly where she'd found it, then pulled open the drawer in the lowboy underneath. It was empty. So was the next drawer down, and the drawer under that. She checked the wardrobe. No trace of life there either. Then checked the bedside nightstands, right and left. Then lowered herself stiffly to her knees and put her cheek on the carpet to peer under the bed. She was a jealous wife now, determined to make her suspicions come true. It hurt her legs to get upright again, and hurt them to pull the bed frame away from the wall. In the seam between carpet and baseboard lay two plastic pegs—one red, one white—from a Battleship game, and a strip of red foil about the size of a fingernail shard. From a condom packet, was her guess.

When she'd pushed everything back into place—carpet dents perfectly tailored to the furniture feet—she sat on the bed and got out her phone and scrolled down through her contacts to *Plumber*. After a moment's hesitation, she pressed CALL, and counted the rings.

"It's me," she told the phone.

"I know who it is," said the woman at the other end. "I can read."

"How are you doing?"

"If it wasn't so early in the day I'd ask are you drunk. Are you?"

"I can't even call you now, even to talk?"

"To talk? Never thought I'd hear you say that. What do you want?"

"Not so long ago, you'd have been very happy to have me call you."

"Lil, I thought we beat all this out. I thought I was very clear."

"You were. You sounded like you were trying to convince yourself."

"I knew what you wanted, you knew what you wanted. Probably that's why it lasted as long as it did."

"It was good, you have to admit."

"You know Socrates' story about the river?"

"I know *your* story about the river."

"I don't need to repeat it then."

Lil lifted herself stiffly from the bed and shuffled to the window. The view was no different from next door: a hospital building identical to the one she was standing in, except for the scaffolding and netting in which it was clad, to protect those below from falling debris. Looking at the ensemble, she found it impossible not to imagine the building without it—perfectly repaired, all but new—because the daylight now showed her that the giant net was printed with a picture of the building itself, life-size. She wondered what happened to those nets afterward, when the finished work finally matched the image used to hide it.

"You never were much of a talker," Valerie said.

"I guess that's what I liked most. The not talking part."

"I'll pretend I didn't hear that."

"You used to tell me, If you have something to say, say it, but don't make conversation."

"Listen, I've got to go. He's gone for a run and will be back any minute."

"What time is it there?" Lil said. "I hope I didn't wake you up."

"What do mean *there*? Where are you?"

"I'm not standing drunk outside your door, if that's what you're worried about. I'm calling from Norway."

"At least you never did that. What's in Norway?"

"Pierre."

"That's right. I remember now. How's he liking it?"

"He's in a coma. He had a heart attack. They don't know if he's ever going to wake up."

First, Valerie needed a few seconds to force herself to believe this. Then she needed to think about what to say. Lil apologized for having just sprung it on her like that. Valerie asked what had happened. Lil told her. The story was a self-portrait of sorts. It made her sound stoic, refusing to go near hope or despair, or any place else that strayed too far from the facts.

"Whether or not he will ever come out of that coma," Lil heard herself say. Explaining, she found she already knew whole chunks of Dr. Mya's spiel by heart. The phrases slotted one into the next with admirable craft. "Whether or not he will be brain damaged," she said next, standing trancelike at the window, staring at the hospital block across the road. Immediately to its right stood a much older, redbrick building with tall arched windows, which looked like some kind of Victorian institution, made to house a well-meaning but paternal brand of care.

"They're really laying out the red carpet for us," Lil said. "State-of-the-art facilities, round-the-clock care. They've even given us our own apartment, on a special floor, right upstairs."

"Is that where you're calling from?"

"Yes."

"It must be costing you a fortune. So must this phone call."

"No," Lil said. "They say Pierre's Erasmus insurance covers everything. Apparently it's going to cost us nothing at all."

"Listen," Valerie said, "send me a text. When you have news. I mean it. I'd like to know."

It was another curtain call, which Lil answered with: "You seeing anybody else now?"

"You really expect me to answer that?"

"No."

"So why do you ask?"

"You know me. I like picking at those scabs."

"I know you like stirring up the shit. I know you don't like taking no for an answer."

"Any more than I like giving it," Lil said. As long as she kept the conversation going, she felt less of an understudy to the woman she wanted to be.

"You can't talk your way out of this one," Valerie said.

"I thought I was trying to talk myself into something, not out of it."

"Lillian, you couldn't screw your way out of it then and you can't talk your way out of it now."

"You know—" Lil started to say, with a new fault in her voice.

"Don't," Valerie warned. "Don't go soft on me now."

"If I'm not allowed now . . ."

"That's the last thing you need. Especially you. It's an awful situation you're in, and my heart breaks for you. It honestly does. But I'm going to give you one piece of advice, as a friend." She had switched to business mode. "You need to keep the tissues in the box. You can open the floodgates afterward, when it doesn't matter anymore. But right now you need to be that tough pigheaded bitch we all know and love."

Afterward, Lil showed herself the screen as though they'd been cut off and she was waiting to be called back. The truth was probably the exact opposite. Two thousand miles south, Valerie was probably rushing to wipe all trace of the call. And there it was, the dregs of the fantasy. She'd chosen her words well, to say one thing only. Lil wondered what she herself had been hoping for. Maybe she'd needed to kill it off, like an old dog gone beyond dignity.

She thought she heard movement on the other side of the wall, and stood up to go back. She cast a last look over the room, as a cleaner might, and gave the bedspread a little tug to smooth its wrinkles. Then stepped backward through the bathroom door and silently pulled it to. Turning the lock, she heard the mechanism click but did not trust what she heard, and pulled the handle again, hard, to be absolutely sure.

Bolted to the bathroom wall was a dispenser for antibacterial solution, exactly the same model as in Pierre's room. Lil pumped herself a dose and wrung her hands one in the other, a little too hard and a little too long.

"Who's been standing on my bed?" Alba said, immediately she came out. "Look at these footprints. Look at the size of them."

"They're Pierre's," Lil said. "I put his boots on the bed. Sorry. It never occurred to me they might still be dirty."

"Where did you get his boots?"

"The ward nurse or desk nurse or whatever she's called. She gave me all his clothes. I guess they undressed him when he came in."

"That's what's in the bag?"

"No, those are for the gym. Dr. Mya kitted me out with stuff other people left behind."

Even as she was talking, Lil was stripping down to her underwear. She got Pierre's heavy trousers from the wardrobe, pulled them on. Alba asked where she was going.

"Out," Lil said.

They'd been awake for five or six hours already, running the labyrinth of corridors and rooms, and by now Lil's brain and body needed a change of scenery, exactly as Dr. Mya had said she would.

"Out?" Alba echoed. It was one of Pierre's words. This summer his brother Noah had learned it too. And here was another ventriloquist. They had their own little gang, Alba felt.

"I thought you were all sore and stiff," Alba said. The best cheerleader, she knew, was the skeptic.

"I am." Lil pulled on Pierre's thermal undershirt. *Active recovery* was one of her pet remedies. Doing more of what made you sore in the first place.

"You won't get lost?"

"I have my phone."

"When will you be back?"

"I'm not a child. I'll be back when I'm back."

Whoever had undressed Pierre had yanked his bootlaces loose, and now Lil sat on her bed rethreading the empty eyes. Their feet were the same size, they often shared or swapped shoes, and she'd actually worn these same boots only three months ago, on his last weekend before leaving for Norway. They'd gone picking mushrooms together in the Auvergne, and she'd led him deeper and deeper into the woods, until he eventually announced, "We're lost." "Not completely," she'd answered, "we just don't know the shortest way back to where we started from." That was the joke she'd managed to make of it at the time, but knew now that he would have been condemned had his sick heart picked that moment to give out, so deep into the forest, so far from help.

In his boots and hiking trousers and thermals, Lil stood at the wardrobe, where the rest of his clothes were hidden among her own. She pulled out the long twine-colored scarf and twisted it several times around her neck. His gloves too were obviously much better than those she'd brought for herself. The tag on his beanie said ONE SIZE FITS ALL. She lobbed it and his gloves across the room, onto her bed. Next layer down was the heavy oxblood sweater Alba had knit that summer when she heard he was going north. Lil held it against her torso to check the fit. Only then did she see that it had been slit from neck to navel. Some minor bond—static?—nonetheless held the sweater in place. All in a splurge she saw the rattling gurney wheels, blue lights flashing in the scissors' steel. Her instinct was to hide the thing from Alba, but it was too late.

Lil folded up the remnants of the sweater and put it up on the highest shelf, out of sight. Then she went and sat beside Alba on the bed and let her lean in, hide her face. Lil listened to her sob and snort and felt her heave, then reached both arms around her, in a hold so firm that the throes of that other body were all mimicked in her own. It was permission of a kind, given the only way she knew how. Twelve hours after their arrival, they'd finally caught up with the facts.

Sunday Noon.

L IL HAD FOUND A FLYER IN HIS JACKET POCKET for a Student Sports and Activities Fair being held this morning, somewhere near the docks, and had decided to go in his place. It was the one concrete action she could conceive of—to do what he might have been doing himself, were he awake—that kept at least the idea of him alive. Getting his boots and his clothes moving again, in time with the rest of the world, in the place he'd planned to go, among the people he'd planned to meet.

At the bus stop where they'd gotten off the night before stood a group of students about Pierre's age. Under their winter coats, most seemed to be in costume, as for some kind of carnival. Two were carrying rifle cases very like Dr. Mya's. Two others were twirling majorette batons. It was easy to imagine them as Pierre's classmates or friends, and when they began to move en bloc in the direction she was already headed, Lil slowed down and fell in behind them.

They crossed the long bridge to the north bank, as though heading for the cathedral spire. When a bus cruised close to the curb, spraying slush, the volley of shrieks it raised made her smile, and somehow endorsed her decision to track them. They turned into the riverside park. On either side of the path was a smooth white spread of fresh snow it would have been a pleasure to spoil.

The students pushed on at a good pace and Lil had to drive

herself hard to keep up, because her legs still felt old. They led her all the way to what looked like an old grain store, its entrance guarded by two bearded men in peasant costumes— thick cloth, autumnal colors, roughly cut—blowing into carved wooden whistles, like hunters summoning ducks. A long queue of other students was already waiting to get in, and Lil joined the end of the line. Both sides of the river, she saw, were lined with rows of revamped wooden warehouses just like this one—their long vertical planks stained mustard, terra cotta, laurel green. Seeing those ahead of her reaching inside their jackets and drawing out lanyards with their student cards, she searched Pierre's jacket pockets, found his, and hung it around her neck. The guard didn't even look at the photo, just pointed his scanner at her chest, got her barcode in the crosshairs, pulled the trigger, and waved her inside.

The hall was huge, perhaps half the size of a rugby pitch, and filled with row after row of stands and stalls, each presenting some kind of sport or pastime. Immediately inside the door, as though to block entry, stood a man with a wild white beard and a shaved head and what looked like a genuine, razor-ad samurai sword. A crowd had gathered to watch, but the sense of threat kept them at a distance as the blade whipped back and forth. His invisible opponent was trying every conceivable thrust, jab, and sweep, every angle of attack, but as by telepathy the man anticipated them all.

Lil backed up and let the crowd hustle her into the next row over, past Greco-Roman Wrestling, Jiu-jitsu, Tai Chi Chuan. Nearly everyone around her was in their early twenties. Some were undoubtedly Pierre's friends—had probably even arranged to meet him here, and were expecting at any moment to get a text from him saying they were waiting at the Krav Maga stand and where was he? It was that Mossad thing Pierre had done for a year as a teenager with a Jewish friend, and Lil stopped to check it out, because that's what he would have done. The staff stared right back at her, as if sizing up not a potential client but a potential threat. He had once used her as a stooge to demonstrate a move that had nearly broken her wrist. Dancing in fancy dress, is what he called everything else.

She checked the flyer she'd found in his pocket, saw that Boxing, Biathlon, and American Football were underlined, and pushed on to find them.

Some of the stands were just two tables set end to end, and some were open cages hung with elaborate displays, but she paused only at those with English signs. First was The American Library, which had a lion-clawed bathtub filled with secondhand books. Next was Shiatsu, then Corporo-Spiritual Healing, then some cultish Christian thing. That stand had a tree contrived from scraps of driftwood, hung with brightly colored tickets like autumn leaves, guarded by a middle-aged woman who looked strangely healthy and strangely thin. Whatever knowledge that woman had, it seemed to have calmed her. She caught Lil's eye and held it, smiled pleasantly but made no effort to sell. The solution was right there between them, she knew, on the tickets of her tree. They said *Faith. Patience. Humility. Devotion.* Lil wanted to rip off every one and scatter them for the winter boots to trample and soil. She wanted to make her own tree. *Nothing*, its tickets would say. *Costs. More. Than. Care.*

At the end of that row, against the warehouse wall, was the Biathlon stand. They had opened the fire doors and set up their targets in the yard outside. One of the young women Lil had followed from the bus stop was showing members of the public how to aim and fire, and from a distance it looked like rogue snipers picking off random passersby in the street.

In the queue, Lil listened to the advice being given to an international student ahead of her. What relief, she imagined, in lining up the target, feeling the kickback, seeing the target fall.

"Take a nice deep breath and hold it in while you line up the sights," the woman was coaching. "Now, gently exhale and . . . *squeeze*."

In the distance, a dull clink, and almost simultaneously against her thigh Lil felt Pierre's phone ping. She took it out, checked the caller, and for a second was tempted to reply— maybe even to take a few photos to post later on his FB or Instagram, letting them believe he'd been here just as planned, moving among them, unseen.

"No force," the woman was now telling the next in line. "Don't pull the trigger, just imagine you're stroking it gently with your fingertip."

When Lil's turn came, the woman sidled close to help tuck the stock and to place her head and hands. The thing felt solid but light, and the fit to Lil's shoulder and hands remarkably snug, as though the designers had been imagining her body when building it, which in a way they had. She closed her left eye, lined up the sights, and touched the trigger as lightly as she could. The target stayed up.

"That's it?" she said when the woman took back the gun. "Just one shot?"

The woman smiled kindly in compensation, handed Lil the club's application form, and turned her unspoiled attention to the next in line.

She walked the aisles in a daze of failure until she came to the warehouse's central square, which had been laid with padded mats. AMERICAN FOOTBALL said a hand-painted sign leaning against a clutter of helmets, body armor, cleats. A squat man with an overthick neck was rigging up a lanky boy about Pierre's age and shape. He led the boy onto the mat, then stood behind a bright orange tackle bag. His partner stood at the mat's far end, holding another. The boy shuffled forward, bumped into the first tackle bag, and bounced off. There was a clatter of laughter from the crowd. In the other direction, the boy tried again. This time, the man propping the bag stepped away at the last moment with a dainty matador step, and as soon as he hit the bag the boy dropped to the ground. The man helped him up, then showed those watching how to clap, but few took his cue. There were no more volunteers after that, no matter how hard the bull-necked man worked the crowd. In the end he even tried to call Lil in.

She shed her coat, let them scan her code, then tucked in her lanyard and let them strap the gear on. The tight helmet set the blood pumping in her ears. From behind his tackle pad, one of the men gave a nod. Lil shuffled across the mat and pushed her shoulder into the shield, and it ceded with a quiet sigh. Her body felt stiff and tight and old, but she turned and jogged a little faster toward the shield at the far end, and hit that, and thought she heard a punctured laugh from the crowd. "Come on, Pierre!" shouted the man behind her. So she turned back and tried again, and again, and again, until she was well loosened up. Each time, the man opposite gave a nod of assent, as though his was the permission she was waiting for. Now she sprinted forward and shot her shoulder much lower into the shield, producing a nice neat punch. Landing, she used the bounce to get herself back onto her feet, whirled around, and charged at the opposite end. She hit this one even harder, bounced up, and was off again before the crowd had a chance to cheer. Warmer, looser, younger—shedding years at every impact. This time, keeping her angle higher and pumping her legs, she drove shield and man backward, knocking him right onto his ass. Up and off again, her body cruising, crouching lower, hitting harder, making the harried young men stand full square behind their shields and lean into them to give some proper pushback. To and fro she went, pinball, not noticing the souring faces in the crowd. Her body steeled yet slack—in a groove now, righteous with adrenaline. Drive through it, is what rugby training had taught a much younger Lil. Imagine another shield, identical, right behind the first. That's the one you're trying to reach. Imagine a body behind the body. The one you see is just a front, a buffer, between you and the woman you really want to smash.

When she drove one of the men all the way into the hoarding—cracking it—half the crowd winced as though in pain, and when she turned to go again she found that his partner had dropped his bag and was holding his arms in an X across his face. The foam inside the helmet, when Lil removed it, was warm and damp.

At Boxing, a ponytailed, teak-skinned man—late fifties, Lil thought—in shorts and a tank top was on the mat with a young woman wearing a flouncy red flamenco dress and two outsized black boxing gloves. As though this too were a form of dance, the man simply tilted back and forth, left and right, letting the girl try to hit him, without otherwise defending himself. When they were done, the trainer immediately caught Lil's eye and lifted his chin, to say it was her turn now, as though the thing had been long ago agreed.

Once they touched gloves, Lil came pushing forward, elbows tucked over her midriff, thumbs to her cheekbones to guard her face. She was still full of what American Football had put into her, and determined to be that version of herself, not any Flamenco Girl. The trainer seemed not to notice: as before, he just dodged to and fro like a self-righting toy. Her first proper punch came in a wild arc. With a gentle bend of the knees, he ducked under it, popped up inside her guard, touched her chin with his glove, then backed off. Maybe it was only the mouthguard, but his broad grin made it look like he was enjoying his superiority very much. Time and again he showed her the red palms of his gloves. It looked like an appeal for clemency, and was nothing of the sort. He was merely offering her another target, as though her failure to land any real blows was due to confusion as to where to strike. That was his trick, Lil decided—offering her a target, making her moves all the easier to anticipate. She had not been trying too hard, but merely obeying. That was her problem, and not only here in this ring. So now she came at him flailing wildly—*la moulinette,* they called it on the rugby pitch— as he circled backward, just out of range, and kept circling, until Lil suddenly lunged forward and caught him nicely on the chest. Mechanically, his right arm rose up and struck her temple with force. Lil wobbled but didn't drop. Neither did she take it as a sign to stop, or to calm herself: back she came, only slightly more controlled than before. The ponytail didn't let his body take over again. From then on, he simply showed Lil how much better he was at this, by staying within range, ducking and bobbing and weaving—with greater virility now—and punching back, vicious little jabs perfectly meas-ured and perfectly placed—on the cheekbone, chin, temple, nose. He was not giving her a beating but information, about how easy a beating would be. Refusing to notice, Lil kept coming back for more, as though *more* meant success, not fail-ure, but he kept ducking down and popping up again behind her, dancer, backing off, drawing her on, and on she came, too ready, reaching too far, tilting toward him, off balance, until a gentle left to the ear knocked her to the ground.

The ponytail stood over her. She was on her hands and knees, heaving, but refused to acknowledge his offer of help. She gathered her knees under her and managed to stand up. The man insisted on helping her tug her gloves off, smiled too nicely, and ran his wet pink tongue across his upper lip. Lil turned away in disgust, but he grabbed her arm.

"You bleed," he said, and once again showed her where, with his own tongue on his own lip.

To reach the exit, she had to go by the Biathlon stand again and couldn't help checking the target as she passed. From a far-off speaker came Billie Holiday's brazen voice. From some-where else came the sinister smell of frying meat. Everywhere she turned there was benevolent indifference to her beating and to the absence of her son.

In the foyer, putting her layers back on to face the cold, she checked her phone, hoping for some sign that Alba at least had been wondering where she was or when she was coming back. There were no messages and no missed calls. Pierre's phone, by contrast, now had a dozen messages—from people all around her, no doubt—asking where he was.

Sunday Afternoon.

A LBA DID NOT KNOW WHAT EXACTLY IT WAS about the butchered sweater that had so upset her. It was not the destruction—necessary, not willful—of something she'd put so much work into. She was too used to that. Perhaps it was the fact that he'd been wearing it, and not just out of duty, like a sweater on Christmas Day. Perhaps the fact that other hands had undressed him for bed, pulled up the covers, like she herself used to not so very long ago.

In the chair by the bed, praying, she proposed no bargain, no swap. "If I could take his place, I would," she had declared earlier on the phone to her father. What she really wanted was to hear that offer made by someone else. Now she just asked for strength to face whatever was to come. If, she started to say. There were certain thoughts she needed to breathe her way through. It was yoga. It was anal. Your breath cleared the way. No, your breath *was* the way. If what has to happen is he dies, she told God. Alone, each of us is sincere, Emerson says, but immediately a second person is present, in the imagination or the flesh, the pretense begins. That was why God was so useful. Your every thought had already occurred to Him and pretense was pointless. If what has to happen is he dies, she prayed, give me the strength to accept that.

About midday, she walked down to the waiting room for a coffee, and found another woman already there, slotting coins into the machine. It was Elsa, daughter of the old man in the room neighboring Pierre's. They had met and talked for a long time during the night, and from their very first exchanges Alba had found herself willing to listen to her, because not once had she said, Don't worry, everything will be fine. She just said, You don't know anything for definite yet, wait for the tests, take it hour by hour, that's how you're going to get through this thing, in here time is your friend not your enemy.

"Do you want company?" Elsa asked now.

Alba looked at the open laptop on the waiting room's coffee table. Beside it was a bunch of pale green grapes in a transparent bag.

"It's a straight question," Elsa said flatly. "You do or you don't."

"You're working."

The work was an alibi, Elsa said, clapping the laptop shut. Her sister had come with her family for a visit and they needed to stay out of each other's way.

"Why?"

"For example, our father's being fed through a tube and this is what she brought." She held the bunch of grapes formally in her bowled hands.

"I don't know how you can do it," Alba said, nodding at the laptop.

"You pray, I work," Elsa said. It was a holiday for her brain.

They took their coffee back to Pierre's room. Young and old voices came through the partition door. Alba pretended not to hear, but Elsa asked about her other two children, how they were reacting, how she herself was managing the distance.

"Lil thinks adversity brings out the best in people," Alba said.

"Not me," Elsa said. "Don't let the calm fool you."

Inside Alba's clothes, a cell phone began to ring, but she didn't take it out. Elsa thought this compensation for the closed laptop. "I can leave, if you need privacy," she said as the phone rang on.

"I know everyone is trying to show concern and support," Alba said when the ringing stopped, "but sometimes I just want to throw it out the window."

"Why don't you?"

They both looked out the window at the netted building opposite.

"All these lights on, night and day. My father would have a stroke," Elsa joked.

A purple scrubs in the window opposite was changing an empty bed. The white sheet billowed upward, hung suspended, and floated peacefully down. Seconds later, a gust of wind ballooned the building's printed veil.

"I called home earlier but there was no answer from anyone," Alba said. "Which would have panicked me before, because I'm always worried something terrible might happen to one of them. But now I feel they're immune. Like lightning can't strike twice."

From the other side of the partition door, the children's bickering swelled, then a man's voice barked, muting everything.

"I'm just glad they're not up here with us," Alba said.

"It's hard when they're so young. They don't know how to react. They don't have anything yet to compare it to."

"I mean glad for me." During the night, desperate for an

anchor, she had imagined ordinary scenes at home. María dripping her desensitization medicine onto her tongue. Noah working on his subjunctives for next week's test. Her mother staring at the iron, trying to figure out how to work the steam. "Somehow it helps to know they're back there plowing on with their lives," she said. "Like this whole thing is just an interruption and afterward we'll have to catch up." This was the most ambitious version possible—almost pure aspiration—of what she felt.

They sat in the room as an old couple might, easy with each other's silences. Occasionally, uncued, one of them spoke. Alba said it was starting to snow again. Elsa asked what were her other two children's names, their ages, what they liked. In some ways, she felt closer than ever to her father, Elsa said, now that his personality was no longer in the way. At home, Alba said, she went every Sunday morning to the Dominicans near the Esplanade. That's probably where her mother and the children were. Sometimes she wondered if the real attraction wasn't the building. The bare sandstone walls, the high windows, the remote light. They had a new brother who played the church piano like Rubenstein, all flourishes and frills, which gave a drama to Mass she was not sure she liked. She asked if there was a chapel in the hospital, and Elsa explained the official policy against it. She could find out where the nearest one in the town was, she said, but Alba said not to bother, she preferred not to leave the building, at least until Lil came back.

"Maybe then you can rest a bit," Elsa said.

Alba smiled cheaply. "This is it," she said. "This is my rest—" But she stopped there.

"Go on, say it," Elsa told her.

"Well, you get to a certain point in your life, you think you know what you're capable of. Feeling, I mean."

"But?"

"But you're wrong."

"Give it air," Elsa ordered her again. "Give it air or carry it around dead inside you. That's your choice."

"Did you ever wake up expecting a hangover but it's not there? Even though you've had a big night?" Alba said.

"I wish."

"It's like there's something strong you know you're meant to be feeling, but you can't quite connect with it. And you kind of feel *lonely* for it. Even if you know it's bad."

"I don't know if you're talking about Pierre"—Elsa nodded at the bed—"or someone else."

Alba pretended to think about this honestly. They heard the gang next door gather their things, say good-bye, go. Then Elsa remembered that on Sunday mornings there was usually a religious service on the state TV. Alba didn't dismiss the idea, because she was worried she'd been talking too long, or confessing too much, and that Elsa's tip was actually a hint she'd had enough, wanted to get back to her father or her work. So when the day nurse stood up a few minutes later to change Pierre's bag, Alba stood up also and said she might try after all to find that TV Mass.

"And try to rest," Elsa said as a good-bye. "Tomorrow's going to be a big day."

"What do you mean?" Alba asked. "Did you hear something?"

Elsa raised her hands in a calming gesture that might as easily have been surrender. "Tomorrow's Monday," she said.

"On Monday morning they do their tests, they get the results, they decide. That's the way it works in here."

"Decide what?" Alba turned to the day nurse. "Is it true?"

The nurse folded her arms across her blue scrubs and gave the tiniest possible nod of concession. At Alba's insistence, she called Dr. Mya, who answered with a cheery voice.

"It's true that tomorrow morning we'll be doing some tests," she said. "Then I'll discuss the results with the neurologist and the anesthetist, and if we decide there's an opportunity to seize, why not?"

"Why not *what*?"

"I think in French you call it a *réveil*," the doctor explained. "Like *reveille* in the army. You know, at the end of my medical training I did six months with the UN in Chad, with the British. It's funny what you think you're going to remember and what you actually do. *Soldiers arise! Scrub the bloody muck out of your eyes!*"

Alba heard none of this. She was just waiting for a break in the doctor's blather to ask her question: "Isn't it too soon?"

"For who?" the doctor said.

Upstairs, she stood opposite the TV and flipped through the channels until she found some kind of service, in what looked to her eyes like a Protestant church. But the priest (vicar? pastor?) was a woman, and her vestments provocatively plain, and her gestures mechanical, like in a student Noh play. Facing the screen, Alba's own arms rose up hypnotically, mirroring those of the woman standing in that spartan church. *Celebrate* was the verb. Guessing where they were in the ceremony, Alba tried dubbing the woman's words with her own. The contest was grating and she hit MUTE. The sound of her own voice in the empty room was worse. She could have found something better online, she supposed, from churches all over the world, archive recording or live stream, any language, any denomination, from St. Peter's if she wanted, or a Tridentine rebel's chapel, or some pagan midwinter rite. None would have been the communion she was desperate for.

She killed the screen, went into the bathroom, rummaged through Lil's toiletries bag. The first thing she brought out was the thin foil strip of the condom packet Lil had found next door. She left that on the glass shelf for Lil to deal with as she saw fit. Then took Lil's nail clippers and razor and shaving foam and rolled them into one of the flimsy hospital towels and took that back downstairs to her son.

Passing her in the corridor, the ward nurse said that Pierre's friend had arrived. Alba did not ask whom she meant, but approached his room quietly, stopped short, leaned into the doorway to spy. A blond girl with a ponytail was sitting on the far side of the bed in Alba's chair. The palm of her left hand was pressed against his unshaven face. Her other hand seemed to be under the sheet, near his groin, moving back and forth.

The second Alba strode into the room, the girl whipped both hands back onto her lap.

"Hello," Alba said.

This was more challenge than greeting, but did not register: the girl's attention was all on Alba's shabby sweatpants, shabby fleece, hangover hair. A long-term psychiatric patient, is what the woman looked like to her.

"I'm afraid of Pierre," the girl said, with a strong French

accent. "We are in the same class. I am coming from Sciences Po in Strasbourg too."

"You mean *a friend,* not *afraid,*" Alba said.

"Yes of course. I'm Julie," the girl said, hoping the name might have an effect.

"Were you and Pierre together?" Alba asked. "Are you, I mean?" She was both outraged and unnerved by the girl's provocation, but could not have said which prospect frightened her more—some reflex reaction to the hand under the sheet, or no reaction at all.

Once Alba explained that she was Pierre's mother, Julie switched to French, and Alba felt it a presumption, of common cause. Yet the girl insisted on using *vous,* and Alba felt its sting—the distance it kept her at, by contrast to the intimacy she had allowed herself with Pierre.

"*Julie,* you said your name was?" Alba said as pushback, and even pretended to sift her memory, then admitted she found it hard to keep track of all the different girls' names.

"Is there someone else we should call?" Alba asked.

"When they first called, I thought he was dead," Julie said flatly, trying to pivot to a position deserving more sympathy.

"How is he doing?" she asked when Alba didn't acknowledge this. "They wouldn't tell me anything over the phone."

"There's not much to tell," Alba said. "He's stable. But that's really just the machines and the drugs. It means nothing, good or bad."

"Do they know what happened?"

"There are some tests they want to do first thing tomorrow morning. They say they'll know more after that."

When she first arrived, Julie had stood before the bed like a dutiful tourist before a famous painting, both baffled and chastised by the deflation she felt. The cover sheet was folded to his waist, to give full access to the cables and tubes. The gown had tiny blue snowflakes on a white ground. Seeing his comatose body would bring them closer, she had supposed, perhaps even earn her rights over him that she'd never explicitly sought.

Now she asked Alba if his other friends could come to visit too. Everyone was so worried, she said.

"To be honest, I'm surprised they even let you in," Alba said. "Normally it's only immediate family in the ICU."

It was so hard just to wait, Julie explained. Everyone wanted to help, but didn't know how. Could they at least do something for Alba and Lil? Was there anything they needed? Anything from Pierre's student room? It would be such a relief, she said, to be able to help in some concrete way.

Alba thanked her for the visit and the offers of help. They were using Pierre's cell phone, she said, if Julie wanted an update. Call or text, Alba told her, feeling confident she would not.

When the girl was gone, Alba lifted and resettled his sheet a little higher and adjusted his arms and smoothed his hair as best she could. Beyond a certain point, it had pained her to see him grow. That was her own personal failing, she knew. His going off so eagerly to university had felt like a deliberate slight. Then the doubling down: exiling himself to the far end of the continent. *Norway.* An advertisement for amnesia, was what his new life had been. But now she had her son back, needing her as much as he ever had.

With great care, she peeled away the white elastic tape that kept the respiratory tube planted in his mouth and down his throat. It came away with the choke of old tape peeled off a wall—a sound Alba winced at and Pierre did not.

When Lil came in, she found what looked like a restaurant napkin gathered around Pierre's neck, and Alba leaning over him as over a quadriplegic about to be fed.

"Welcome back," Alba said without looking up.

She squelched a dollop of shaving foam onto her palm. Her forefinger took a scoop. Left swipe, right swipe, face painter pro, she gave her boy a thick white mustache, then started on his cheeks.

"That's my razor?" Lil asked.

"Yes."

"Help yourself."

"I did."

"Did you change the blade?"

"I did."

"You're not afraid if he gets cut? An infection or something?"

"Ever cut yourself shaving?"

"All the time, as well you know," Lil said. "And shaving your own body isn't a patch on shaving someone else's face." This she had learned while nursing her own father in his last months.

"But has it ever gotten infected?"

Lil thought about this. "No."

"And with all the antibiotics they're pumping into him?"

The old man's beard was now fully painted on. Alba pulled the right ear back a little to keep the skin tight, then set the blade just under Pierre's right eye and drew it downward, straight through the zone where the girl's hand had been. There was a sound very like the rasp the breathing tube made.

Once the cheeks were done, she started on the neck.

"Careful not to go against the grain," Lil said.

"You want to do it?"

"I'm not saying I'd do better," she said, but thought otherwise.

After the neck, matters got more complicated again, because Alba had left the trickiest part till last: the mouth. Here she had to work around the tube without touching it, as in a game.

"You're taking him on a date?" Lil tried to joke.

Dr. Mya's plans for tomorrow morning would have to be revealed, yet Alba could not admit to thinking in terms of a public occasion. The most she would concede was that she wanted Pierre to look his best, no matter what.

Dr. Mya had already explained that Pierre's suspended state, by definition, meant no immediate risk. She had said so as permission—for Lil and Alba to breathe easy, to sleep, to leave the hospital whenever they liked—and as a promise, that there was no threat in the room. Then an hour ago, on the phone, with perfect nonchalance, she had revealed that tomorrow, if the tests went well, a mechanical and chemical process would be engaged to wake him up. The *réveil* process, as she described it, sounded painless, natural, and timely—though it was nothing of the sort—and so simple that it allowed no chance for failure or even complication, unless Pierre refused to cooperate.

It was a kind of relief, now, to see blood suddenly beading along the line of his jaw. It was their son's heart pumping. It was his life, liquid in his veins. It would be a comfort too, Lil thought, to see his beard growing back.

After she had tamped and stopped the bleeding, Alba massaged some of her own moisturizer into the skin, as though it had been done some violence—like a day in the sun—she needed to calm. Of course she was the one calmed, by the small circular motions of her own hand, and the chance to care. But Lil found she had no welcome whatsoever for that new smell in the room. She associated it with other things.

THE BASEMENT CANTEEN HAD A HUGE BUFFET filled with cute wooden tubs of artichoke hearts, chickpeas, lentils, olives, beans. Tuna chunks. Greek yogurt. Arugula sprinkled with baby shrimp. Baby squid. Baby corn.

"Everything a woman could possibly hope for," Lil said, but felt harassed by so much choice.

She shuffled past the cold units like a judge at a county fair. Twice she stopped to read the tags of the unrecognizables aloud, as though the feeling of the words in her mouth might somehow correspond to their taste. From the last unit, solemn in her selection, she took what looked like an overcooked omelette, because that is what she thought it was.

At the cash register, a squat girl with peroxide hair and tattooed forearms asked if they would like something to drink.

"I would like three pints of cold beer," Lil told her with a TV smile.

"Just two bottles of water, please," Alba said.

"Together?"

Lil laid several different banknotes on the counter, let the girl take as much as she liked. From a drawer under the register, the girl took a roll of coins and, to weaken the wrap, banged it hard against the counter edge—once, twice, three times, in slow succession, making Alba wince visibly, as at a very real physical threat.

The canteen was empty now except for three lone men at tables that trigonometry could not have put farther apart.

"You really want a drink that bad?" Alba asked when they were seated. An old fear was awake in her, from their first years, after Pierre was born and Lil had started pushing back against the overload of the new role, going out too often, staying out too late, drinking too much, as though desperate to prolong the fun—what she called fun—of her single years. A regression Alba had managed at the time with cheap wisdom and relentless patience, and afterward rarely mentioned but did not forget.

Getting no answer to her question, she picked up a packet of sugar and began flicking at it with her fingernail, like a junkie purging bubbles from a syringe. Lil's countermove was to bite into a slice of black bread, chew, chew, and swallow. Eating, she knew, would help smother the animal craving she had. "They were careless people," wrote F. Scott Fitzgerald, of Tom and Daisy in *The Great Gatsby*. Alba and Lil were not. Their instincts had shriveled to those of children who never heard anything but cautionary tales.

"You know what that will do to your insides," Alba said, pointing a steak knife at a strange dark lump on Lil's plate.

Lil thrust the tip of her own knife into the ugly glob, then pointed it at Alba's head. "Goat, not cow," she said. Alba leaned forward, parted her lips, and Lil slid the knife inside.

Alba made a face like a face in pain. "God Almighty," she said, reaching for a napkin to cover her mouth.

"I know."

"And you let me taste it?" She spat and wiped and spat again, peering into the crumpled napkin as though looking for a lost tooth.

In Lil's sight line, behind Alba's head, an old man in a green tartan dressing gown was studying a folded newspaper, marking it up exactly the way her father used to, picking horses.

They were not being patient. They were simply stunned, by their own impotence. Every tick of the clock was a step closer to Dr. Mya's deadline. It felt like an official sentencing, D-day minus one.

"All things being equal, she said. What does that even mean?" asked Lil.

"It means that between now and the tests, there may be a definite sign of deterioration or improvement. It also means that the test results may be positive, or negative, or inconclusive. And that all those things taken together—"

"How can she just *not know*?" Lil said. She meant all those monitors, blood tests, scans.

"Whatever you say, you can't say she's not being thorough, or attentive, or communicative," Alba said. She was still taken aback at the level of care they were getting, gratis, and not to acknowledge it somehow, in some direction, felt like a form of ingratitude.

"Is the fan club open to new members, or is this an exclusive relationship?" Lil said.

"I liked her," Alba said. "I admit it. I didn't want to. I didn't think I would."

"You liked what she said?"

"What did she say?"

"Not much. Certainly nothing reassuring."

"Maybe that's what I liked about her," Alba said. "She wasn't trying to make herself sound smart, or in control. She wasn't trying to make any of this sound better than it actually is." What she meant was that there had been no encouragement or commiseration, and almost no storytelling at all, which in even banal circumstances is a feat. The effect was that Alba was not only willing but eager to trust the woman, which was not entirely a good thing, because trust is so close a cousin of hope that in an inattentive person the two are easily confused.

"She seems young," Lil said.

"She *is* young."

"To us."

"No, she really is. Your date of birth is part of your ID. Kristen was showing me this morning. They're making badges for us too, by the way, so we can come and go as we please, access the gym, the sauna, everything."

"She almost looks closer to Pierre's age than ours," Lil said.

Alba refused to acknowledge this.

"She's not, is she?"

Alba looked up and held Lil's stare.

"Christ," Lil said. "How is that even possible?"

It was now four in the afternoon. The canteen staff had started to ferry the food tubs from the salad bar into the back kitchen. Alba finally tore the head off her sugar packet and poured it onto the froth capping her café au lait. The weight of the grains made a shallow crater but did not sink. Back at the register, an *ambulanse* woman in a red uniform was chatting to a nurse. The walkie-talkie strapped to her shoulder was emitting an endless metallic garble, until the nurse reached over and turned the volume right down. Lil wished she could do the same sometimes with Alba's voice, and with the tyrant in her own head.

"The cows must all be indoors now," Alba said dreamily. "I imagine them high up in mountain pastures in summer. Then shut up in sheds all winter long."

"Like *Heidi*," Lil offered. "*Cows* or *cattle*? I never understood the difference."

"*Cow*, plural *cows*. *Cattle* comes from *chattel*, which is something completely different. Moveable possessions, alive or dead. It used to include a man's wife and children and indentured servants."

"You're going to teach me my own language now?" Lil said.

Alba poked at the sugar crater with the tip of her spoon. The grains had turned damp and brown, but the surface tension still held. "More and more these days," she said, "I think of that scene in Chekhov, in one of his early plays. Set in a country house where this mixed bag of characters has gone for a holiday but where they all feel trapped. The main character is a country doctor, who has surrounded himself with people he despises—them and everything they stand for. Yet there he is, joking with the men, flirting with the women, and despising himself for doing just that. Because he knows he's just as bad as any of them. Just as bourgeois. I'm forty years old! he starts roaring like a madman one night. At my age, Napoleon was emperor of all Europe! Pushkin was already dead for two years! Lermontov for fourteen! And what have I done with my life? Nothing. Nothing! I've wasted it! On and on he goes, ranting and raving, until eventually he rushes out of the house and throws himself in the river."

"Which play is it?"

"There's a great version in a Russian film that's a mash-up of the early plays. *Unfinished Piece for Mechanical Piano,* it's called. The film."

"Good title."

"It is."

"And that's the end?" Lil said. "He drowns?"

"His wife saves him," Alba said. "She's one of those Chekhov wives. Too good. Too forgiving. We're meant to admire them, I think. Quiet patient love turning it all around."

Rather than engage with this, Lil licked her thumb and used it to suck up the sugar grains Alba had spilled, like iron filings to a magnet. Her magic touch.

"I've spent the last hour not asking what happened to your face," Alba said then.

"A man hit me."

"I presume you deserved it."

"Maybe not for anything I did to him, but more generally, yes, I'm sure I did."

"Did you hit him?"

"I tried to, but he kept getting out of the way."

"So, a middle-aged woman goes out in a foreign city on a Sunday afternoon and comes back three hours later with a, what do you call it, *un oeil au beurre noir*?"

"They call it a *shiner* where I come from."

"That she says some strange man gave her, for no reason she wishes to share."

"I really have a shiner?" With her paper napkin, Lil polished the knife she'd used for the cheese and peered into the flat of that.

"God knows what Dr. Mya is going to think," Alba said.

"She's going to think, Poor woman, it's always the quiet ones you need to be wary of."

"Which reminds me, they need our photos for our IDs," Alba said. "I'll take yours and you take mine." She picked up Lil's phone and held it a foot from Lil's nose. "This isn't your phone," she said, when she tried to open it.

"It's Pierre's. It was in that box with his wallet and his keys."

"You knew the code?"

Lil just gave a sly smile—a boast about all the secrets a mother knows. Then reached over and swiped the phone open, without giving Alba time to see.

"You don't have to make a face," Alba said, taking the photos.

"This isn't *a* face. It's *my* face."

In every single picture, they both looked drained, of something more than sleep and more than health. They looked like people who'd lost a great deal of weight in a short amount of time, but with none of the hale triumph of those before-and-after ads.

Five missed calls, the phone said now. All Norwegian numbers, and another wound for Alba, to think that for so many people out there—professors, friends, all the walk-on parts—their son's old life was plowing on the same as ever, even now. Like that private plane she'd read about in the paper a few months back, which had eventually crashed after cruising for hours on autopilot, flying over an emptying landscape, over Wyoming, Montana, Alberta, dead north, pursuing its preset course straight and true, as long as the fuel lasted, after decompression had killed everyone aboard.

They sat in Pierre's room the rest of the evening, with the day nurse at her desk, mutely monitoring the drips and screens. About seven o'clock, she stood up and pushed back the huge sliding door that separated them from the neighboring room and said something through the gap. She'd be back in a few minutes, she told them. The open door—almost half the width of the wall—was to allow and oblige Elsa's father's nurse to watch Pierre while she was gone.

"You imagine what all this would cost if we had to pay for it?" Alba said.

Lil knew as well as Alba that they ought to be thankful, but felt threatened by the level of care being afforded their son, suspecting that every little extra—almost every gesture of the staff—was further bloating a bill that somehow, at some point—despite repeated guarantees from Pierre's health insurance—they would have to pay.

To cement her unspoken thought, she picked up Pierre's phone. All evening, the messages from his friends had kept coming in, either asking where he'd disappeared to or wishing him well. She began deleting them with a series of vicious flicks.

"Anyone can see you're as scared as I am," Alba told her.

"I never said I'm not. I just don't need to shout it from the rooftops."

"I know what hospitals do to you," Alba went on. "It almost makes me cry sometimes, to think of that frightened little girl you used to be." She could bear almost anything, she thought, except Lil's version of courage, which was the kind children are asked to show in order to shut them up.

"Is this consultation part of the package," Lil asked, "or is it going on the bill as well?"

"You really think you can plow through this thing the way you plow through everything else?" Alba said quietly. Her anger had been building for a long time.

"As opposed to what? Hourly meltdowns? How's that helping him?"

"Ah! So *that's* it," Alba said, glancing at the open door. "Bottling it all up for our sakes. Sparing us the horror of your emotions. How very big of you."

"And they're off," Lil said with pointed calm. She could be seen from next door, but not Alba. She had been set up.

"Just tell me one thing," Alba went on, her voice now hot with hate. "Why did you marry me? Why did we have children? If you never need anyone, for anything? If you can always fix everything all by yourself?"

Toying with the phone, Lil somehow flipped to the latest photo, of her own discolored face. When Pierre was a little boy, he used to call her Panda whenever she came home from rugby with another black eye. She flicked again to see if the previous photo was any better, and to the one before that, then stopped. Pierre's private life was all right there, freely available for once, if she wanted it.

"So fix this!" Alba hissed, pointing at the bed.

With measured patience, Lil let out a long breath. She knew why Alba had waited for the open door to let loose. She needed a witness to her complaint who would not understand a word of it. She wanted to produce, on Lil's face, some proof of her own grievances for the nurse watching them.

"You really think I need you, to get through this?" Lil said.

"I've wasted twenty years of my life on you!" Alba shouted.

"Twenty-five," Lil said.

That was the evening's best and last back answer. Alba leaned her face into her hands. She'd had her fair and honest tantrum and felt spent. All she wanted now was for their nurse to come back and slide that partition shut again. She knew all about the old man lying unconscious in there—what he looked like, what his disease was, his age, his weight, his prognosis—and through the open door she heard the bragging of mortality.

When the day nurse came back, she had to lean into the partition door with all her weight to get it moving. Like the door of a walk-in safe, the thing slid home with a profound thud.

COMING OUT OF THE SHOWER, Alba found Lil standing in the middle of their bedroom, her head strangely cocked.

"What?" Alba said.

Lil held up her hand for quiet. "*Listen,*" she hissed.

"To what?"

"Not what, who."

"People?"

"Voices."

"You're hearing voices now. Great."

Lil walked into the bathroom and there, in the fog, put her ear against the door that led to the adjacent apartment. All she could hear was the rumor of a helicopter nearby.

"I don't like leaving him down there all alone," Alba announced when Lil came out.

"You heard the doctor. We have a big day ahead of us tomorrow. And anyway, he's not alone."

"A nurse is not his mother."

"So what?"

Outside, the rotor blades were not so much louder as sharper.

"*So what?*"

"A nurse is not his mother and his mother is not a nurse."

"That's not what I mean."

"What *do* you mean?"

"I don't know," Alba conceded. "Maybe I mean me. Being alone."

By now the helicopter's battle whup was pushing hard at the window, cheering on Alba's fears. She knew the hospital legend, of course, of old people waiting for the family to leave the room before dying. One last assertion of autonomy, in one last private act.

"I'll admit that Kristen is nice," Alba said. "At least when she's with him, I don't feel quite so . . ."

"They're all nice," Lil said.

Speaking, Alba had opened her towel and wrapped it around herself again, tighter. The taunt was reckless rather than cruel, and almost painless.

"I remember when I was a kid, being afraid to go to sleep," Lil said. "I think I was starting to realize just how sick my mother was. I must have been six or seven years old. And I was afraid, I think, that by the time I woke up, she'd be dead. As if by keeping myself awake I was somehow keeping her alive. Like she was a product of my imagination."

"Magical thinking."

"It's funny what the stress brings out—stuff you've been carrying around unawares for years."

"Like herpes," Alba said.

Maybe they could relay each other, Lil suggested later, when they were in bed. She was trying to give Alba an out, an opportunity to rest. It was another peace offering. Lil would stay with him while Alba slept, and whenever she woke, she could come down and take Lil's place in the chair and send Lil upstairs to bed. Even three or four hours' sleep, Lil said, would do her the power of good. Like the watches on a ship, was how it was meant to work. So they lay side by side in their separate beds, Lil pretending to read her book, listening to Alba's breathing and regularly checking the mirror opposite to see were her eyes still shut.

In their early days, whenever Lil woke early, she used to slip silently out of bed, lift her clothes from the chair, and sneak down the hall without even turning on a light. In the dark kitchen, she'd put on the kettle, put some bread in the toaster, get dressed. "I'm not going anywhere," she had to tell Alba the first time she was caught. But tonight, Alba didn't stir.

Downstairs, Kristen was standing at the window, her back to the door. In welcome, she touched Lil lightly on the elbow once she came within range. Shoulder to shoulder, they watched ashlike flecks wafting through the air. Like the Spanish, the Norwegians seemed not only easy but expert with physical contact, using it—even with strangers—to score almost every exchange. But to Lil, such touches burned, because of the closer contact she worshipped but was too often denied.

She lifted her chin to indicate the netted building opposite. "Don't they realize that everyone can see them?" she asked.

Every window in the hospital complex had curtains, but she had yet to see any drawn. In dark or dusk—which was most of the day—any light in any window made it a television screen.

"We can see them, they can see us," Kristen said.

"Yes, but *everything.*"

"Did you see something you wish you had not?"

"That's not what I mean."

"If you don't want to see other people's lives, just don't look at the windows," Kristen said.

The advice was literal, said her flat, friendly tone. Lil had no answer. These past two days—the fear, the fatigue, the unfamiliarity—had infused everything with the buffed-up quality of a dream.

"Are they really going to try to wake him up tomorrow?" she asked.

"It depends what the tests say."

In their own window's black mirror, if she focused on the

reflections, the snow seemed to be falling behind them, inside the actual room, down onto the bed.

"You sound worried," Kristen said.

"I am. I'm terrified."

"Dr. Mya is one of Norway's top heart specialists. She performs this procedure all the time."

"And does it work out perfectly, all the time?" Lil asked, nodding at the partition wall.

"If she's willing to try, it means she thinks Pierre is ready for it."

"But if he's not? If he doesn't wake up?"

"Thinking that way doesn't help him, and it doesn't help you," Kristen said. This was not reproach or advice, but fact.

Each sat on her own side of the bed. It was very late. Lil was reading the book she'd bought at the Student Fair, an eyewitness account of the Allied occupation of Naples. Kristen was reading from a slim paperback, so intently that Lil could watch her undisguised. At regular intervals she closed her eyes and moved her lips. When she finally looked up, Lil raised her eyebrows to oblige her to explain.

"Actually, maybe you can help me," Kristen said.

She was in a play and trying to learn her part, and it would help if Lil could prompt her, she explained. She lobbed her book across the bed, and Lil's hand snapped it expertly out of the air.

"Sometimes Henrik does it," Kristen said, as though there were only one Henrik and Lil should know who he was. Apparently, the woman had a whole life of her own.

The part not highlighted was the one she wanted Lil to read. "Just the last few words of each speech. As best you can. It doesn't matter how it sounds. All I need is the cue."

"All the other parts?"

"It is a double-headed play."

"A two-hander. That's what we call it."

Kristen thought about that. "Shouldn't it be four hands?"

"What's it about?" Lil asked, without conceding the point.

"It's a bit adult."

"*Adult* isn't what you mean. Or actually it is, but in English that generally means something else. You mean it's violent, or sexually explicit?"

"In the words, yes. Not in the actions."

"Should I cover his ears?" Lil said with a nod at the bed, and produced a smile.

So Lil started to make the sounds, with no guidance at all, and Kristen smiled again, but more naturally. Lil was making her happy, was how it looked, and it seemed such an easy thing to do.

"I know I'm pronouncing it wrong," Lil said.

"It's actually quite moving," Kristen said. "To hear someone saying emotional or even quite profound things that they don't understand. It would be an interesting experiment, you know. Foreign actors who just learn their lines phonetically. A whole play like that."

"Like that Herzog movie where the actors were all hypnotized."

"Which one is that?"

"*Heart of Glass*. At least that's the legend. That they were hypnotized. They definitely all seem strangely disconnected from one another and from everything they say and do."

They read on.

"Then there's something in square brackets," Lil told her, "and the rest of the page is blank."

"They've gone to sleep."

Lil turned the page. "Act Two?"

"Act Two," Kristen confirmed. "They wake up."

Lil went on giving her cues—loosely knotted strings of sound, just the last three or four or five words of the lead-in line—and, as best she could, checked the sound of Kristen's answer against the strange words on the page, sometimes lifting a halting hand when she could see no relation between the two. After about twenty minutes of that, something in the room suddenly came alive. It was her phone, bug-crawling for the edge of the overbed table. Lil leaped up and grabbed it and marched out into the corridor, as though to avoid waking him.

"It's almost midnight," she hissed into the phone.

"It's Noah."

"This better be a real crisis, for you to be calling this time of the night."

"María says she doesn't want to go to school tomorrow. Says she's *sick*."

"Sick how?"

"It's bullshit. She's just jealous because all Iaia talks about is Pierre, Pierre, Pierre. She even got his baby book out."

"You're sure she's not sick?"

"Iaia?"

"*María.*"

"Her friend Anne came up and they were playing house all evening. They were climbing on the rubble sacks and everything, even if I told her not to. It was only when she had to get her bag ready for the morning."

"Did she eat her dinner?"

"And two Death By Chocolates afterward."

"Tell her she's going to school and I said so."

"Iaia told her she can stay home."

"Because Iaia needs drama to look like drama. You tell them both I said she's going to school. End of discussion."

"When are you coming back?"

"*Noah,*" Lil pleaded. "You know I can't answer that."

"Is he going to be all right?" Noah said then, and sounded embarrassed to ask.

"The doctors are going to do some tests tomorrow morning to try and see if any part of his brain has been affected. By being deprived of oxygen for too long. Then they might try to wake him up."

"So even if he wakes up—"

"Thinking that way doesn't help him, and it doesn't help you," Lil cut in. "Now you really need to go to bed. You have school tomorrow too."

"Don't you want them to wake him up?"

"Right now what I really want is for you to go to sleep. We'll message you the minute we have any news."

"And she cooks funny food," Noah said, refusing to hear his exit cue.

"Bed," Lil said. "Please. *Now.*"

Immediately Lil came back, Kristen stood up to go to the bathroom, as though they were spelling each other, tag team. She left a cherry red cardigan on the back of her chair. The thing felt like cashmere, outrageously soft. Lil lifted the mass of it to her face and took a deep breath. It had in it the whole of Kristen's smell—not just the righteous lies of her shampoo and her soap but brutal promises too, buried deep down in the weave. Lil stood at the foot of the bed with the bunched cardigan covering her mouth like a villain's chloroformed handkerchief. Had her son's eyes been open, they would have been staring straight at her, but fortunately they were not.

Later, Lil asked how she'd ended up working in the ICU. Kristen spoke of the time she'd worked in Emergency. After a while it felt like a field hospital, she said. "You patched them up and sent them back out, but you knew you'd see them again soon enough. Or someone very like them. It was that never-ending stream that got to me. So I retrained."

"Isn't there an endless stream over here too?"

"The rhythm is slower. You have time to get to know people. Like this, here," she said, moving her arm back and forth through the space separating them.

Lil told her about her first summer working as a waitress in Paris, talked about the revelation for a young Irish woman of living in France, wrote out an old girlfriend's recipe for *tarte tatin*. Kristen told her about Dr. Mya's target setup on the helipad, for shooting practice. She marked various *X*s on a tourist map, including the cheapest place to buy beer. To pass the time, Lil taught her how to play Hangman, which Kristen had never heard of. Lil's description made it sound more like a race than a game, like those thrillers with time bombs, here comes death, tick tock. With courage, wit, and blind faith, the hero must intervene. There are choices to be made. Which wire to cut—red, white, or blue? Still, what a minor disappointment it always was to lose, you cared so little about the condemned man, and hoped so meekly for the last minute reprieve.

Alba woke at four o'clock, but there was no question of falling back to sleep, already her mind was crowded with a single thought: to get downstairs again.

His arms were lying in a slightly different position from the way she'd left them, bringing a burst of hope—but of course the culprit was Kristen. It was the machine breathing, not his lungs. A plastic tube attached the two. He was the appendage, not vice versa. There was one On/Off button for them both.

She frowned too at the body slumped in the chair on the far side of the bed. A good description for what she saw is in the *Iliad*, Book 8, where Teucer's arrow flies past its intended target—Hector—and instead kills the unimportant Gorgyth-ion, whose head then tilts heavily to one side, "like a poppy in a garden weighed down by its seeds and rain."

Alba shook her awake and sent her up to bed and took her place in the warm chair. She thought of laying a blanket over Pierre, then tried to pretend this stupid thought had never even occurred to her. What she really wanted was to snuggle up together as in the glory days. That shop-fresh boy. Those showboat hugs. The memories' relentless parade. If she lay down beside him, maybe she'd doze off and together they'd sleep the rest of the night through and in the morning she'd be awakened by an indignant shaking, Pierre telling her to get out of his bed, where she didn't belong. It had happened more than once, and not only when he was a boy.

The messages of support were relentless, from family and friends, from all around the globe. It was a reminder of those outside her inner circle who did not yet know but had to be told. Monday morning was as good a time as any, Alba supposed. She'd already put it off too long. So now she opened up her laptop and started to compose a short email to the three clients expecting her to deliver translations in the coming week. She was tempted just to refer vaguely to a family or personal crisis, but in the end told them straight out that their son was in hospital in Trondheim in a coma and there was no way she could keep her promises, but when she had a clearer picture she would let them know. Less apologetic, she also wrote to the gym where Lil worked as a personal trainer, using Lil's mailbox and signing her name, telling them to get someone to cover her classes and to contact her individual clients too.

Shutting her laptop, Alba was also tempted to kill her phone, but instead texted her father. *People are so good,* she told him. *Especially all the offers of support and prayers and even money, but for the moment it looks like Pierre's student health insurance is going to cover almost everything.* She was grateful for all the support, she said, but just now couldn't field more sympathy and concern. With certain messages, her gratitude bloomed into something unbearably sweet. With others, it soured, as against premature condolence. So to stay all that, she wrote him a summary of the day's news and asked him to forward it to all their family and friends, telling them to forward it in turn. She gave the best possible version of the day's events, reassured everyone that they were trying to stay positive, and asked them to do the same.

Killing time, she counted the hollow tubes, then caught herself counting the seconds between each drip. Occasionally she glanced at the window to check for any hint of dawn. Still the night tide washed tediously overhead. It was not so very different, in some ways, from the first weeks after he was born. You stared at the stranger in the bed. You searched the empty face for clues. Do infants dream? Does your comatose son? You put your ear close to his mouth, trying to catch the merest rasp of breath. Faith healer, you slid your hand under the blanket and held it to his chest. The sheer power of your presence would keep him alive.

Lil came back down at about half past seven and found Alba praying on her knees by the bed. The sight of the supplicant made Lil angry for reasons she did not fully understand. Was she was offering to take his place? What would Lil herself have offered? Everything, of course, in whatever direction such a proposition might be made. Neither knew any other way to bargain now except completely. It was a measure of how helpless they felt.

Despite her anger, Lil kept silent to let Alba finish, and when she opened her eyes and stood up, Lil asked had she slept, and Alba said a few hours, yes, and out of kindness and strategy Lil did not call the lie. "I brought coffee," she said, raising two paper cups as for a toast. She offered one to Kristen, who shook her head, said her shift was almost over, she needed to start winding down. Alba took a sip from her cup and winced.

"Take a look outside," she told Lil.

Down in the street, the new snow was implausibly perfect. By contrast, the building opposite now looked dated and drab. In between, weightless white dots hung loosely in the air. Impossible for the eye not to track them, unless by consciously focusing on something solid in the background.

When the cleaning cart arrived, they both backed away from the bed, too far, as though a defibrillation was about to be performed. Kristen too stood up and began tidying his pipes and wires and tubes—actually gathering them together with cable ties. The harsh zip of each tie made Alba flinch, as though it were her own body being grabbed.

Immediately the cleaners were gone, two big porters in grubby white scrubs came to take Pierre away. Kristen said something to them in Norwegian and they swung up the bed's guard rails with a clang and tucked the gathered tubes behind those. They kicked the wheel brakes so hard that Alba's body jerked at the shock, then shunted the bed forward and herded the machine racks behind it and locked them in place. Lil and Alba followed the bed and its entourage out into the hall. From a distance, the elevator doors looked far too narrow, but of course everything here was a tailored fit.

"What do you call those painted boards you see at fairgrounds, with holes to put your head in?" Alba said, because the corridor was a gallery of framed photos, patients with celebrities, each with identical smiles, in identical hospital rooms, by identical beds.

Pillories, Lil thought, but didn't want to pronounce the word. "Kristen said Dr. Mya just won some big prize," she said instead.

"Markswoman of the Month?"

"I'm serious. Apparently she's the best in Norway at what she does. We're actually quite lucky it happened in Trondheim."

"Lucky?"

In Pierre's room there was now a hungry space where the bed had been. On the floor, Alba expected to see dust balls, coins, marbles, Lego bits—the kind of treasure they'd found behind so much furniture during last's year's move.

They went upstairs. There was no point hanging around, Kristen had told them, that would just make the waiting worse. "Get out," she said, pointing at the window. *While you can,* Lil heard.

From the building's main door, the footprints all turned left. Alba and Lil turned right. In that direction, the unspoiled snow made the hospital complex seem a brighter, cleaner, and less complicated place. They passed the netted building opposite their own, then the building that looked like a Victorian psychiatric home—obviously a survivor from another age, around which the modern grid had grown. Pockmarks in the brick reminded Lil of the bullet holes she'd seen in buildings in Warsaw and Berlin, but was that possible? Had the war—actual combat, street fighting— reached this far north?

Farther on, they found themselves walking along a row of black iron railings outside a stand of fir trees, some kind of park. They were almost at the gate when a stream of people came rushing past them, as though toward the catastrophe Lil and Alba had just fled. They were lycra-clad runners, all with hi-vis bibs and gloves and bobbled hats, and gaudy running shoes like those Dr. Mya had gifted Lil. Some even had third-eye lamps in the center of their foreheads, and every single one had a biathlon rifle slung across their back.

As the two women reached the next junction, they heard the rumble of a snowplow. The instant the man turned green, the signal started to beep, just like a heart monitor, but they did not cross. On the snowplow came, sowing salt and hosing its racket in all directions. The beep was speeding up, from fast to frantic, and just as it blurred into one fatal note, they both stepped backward, as though to give a wheelchair or dignitary more space, and the plow cruised past, cutting a clean swath in the snow, much as Alba's razor had cut through the shaving foam the previous night.

Afterward, they made their way across the shaved tarmac with baby steps.

"Would it be too much to ask where we're headed?" Alba said.

The salt crunched underfoot like broken shells.

"We're going on a beer hunt," answered Lil, touting the tourist map she'd gotten from Kristen during the night.

They passed a hearing aid center and a morgue-bright laundrette and the door of a Salvation Army shop wide open to the cold. The urge Alba felt to go inside was corrupt in some way. Perhaps she simply wanted to close that door behind her upon entering, to keep the heat in. The temptation let her stop to admire the strange window display, composed of two headless wicker mannequins. One wore a tailcoat tuxedo and held a conductor's baton aloft, its ivory yellowed and cracked like an old piano key. His partner wore an unironed linen nightdress creased from crotch to thrapple like a cuts poster in a butcher's shop.

Lil found her X by the revamped grain stores on the riverfront, close to where the Student Fair had been the day before. Alba let her go into the shop alone and waited outside. Across the street stood a converted warehouse with three weathered bedsheets—blue, white, and red—hanging from a balcony. Probably hung out after the Paris attacks. The neighboring balcony had been glazed in, and behind the glass a man was unpegging clothes from a line. Alba watched him drape a T-shirt against his chest as if to check the fit, then fold in the sleeves and double it down and float it into the basket at his feet. When his shirts and T-shirts and jeans were done, he began to unpeg the socks two by two, tucking each into its mate to make a pair, then shot them balled into the basket with an economy it was a quiet pleasure to watch.

Lil came out of the shop carrying a blue plastic bag with a weight of cans inside. To take the long way home, they followed the river toward the sea. Fat flakes of snow were now floating down, sticking to whatever they touched for a few seconds, then vanishing. Under the newsprint sky the morning walkers all came toward them at a plod, huddled deep into their jackets, hoods up, bandit faces behind their scarves. The paths were all slush and grit here and Alba kept falling behind and Lil kept slowing and looking over her shoulder, waiting for her to catch up. Visitor's day at the asylum was how it felt.

Eventually Lil stopped to wait at a shop window with a display of antique radios. There were a few portables, Bakelite cases from the fifties, but most were massive tabletop models from before the war.

"Just what we need," Alba said when she arrived. "Another old radio."

"Tell me they're not beautiful. As objects. Forget about the technology."

"What are you going to do, put one in your case and take it home as a souvenir?"

"One of those small ones, you could. They probably all still work. Open them up, you'd be amazed at how solidly they're made."

"You see any price tags? That's your first warning, right there."

"When I was a girl, for a while we had a set just like that one there," Lil said, pointing. "Some nights we'd manage to get Radio Moscow. This was in the seventies, when we still had only one channel on the TV. It was like stumbling on a broadcast by Martians. Longwave. I hear they're getting ready to pull the plug on that now too."

She paused to listen to a distant sound like a Sunday afternoon lawn mower. It was another chopper coming in.

"In the early days of radio in Ireland," she went on, "only the two biggest cities were covered. Dublin and Cork. Then they built a transmitter in the middle of the country, in 1932. You see it?" And there it was, at the bottom of a diagonal column of names. NÜRNBERG, LUXEMBURG, BREMEN, ATHLONE. Like a young couple at a real estate agent's window, they stood and stared. In the shop's deep doorway lay a rag of old snow. Lil remembered the night-sea static, the snug hum of the tubes, the station panel's blood orange backlight. She remembered the tuner like the combination dial of an old safe, remembered turning it through the shavings of symphonies, speeches, love songs, feeling she was turning her own mind on a slow spit. "The real reason they built the Athlone transmitter was so that those living out in the countryside could tune in to the International Eucharistic Congress, which was held in Dublin that year. A huge international event. So many people traveled to it from all around the world that they had seven ocean liners moored along the city quays, serving as hotels. Anyway, they first turned on the Athlone transmitter just for the ceremonies. And you had people all over Ireland—the more well-off, I suppose—who'd bought a radio just to listen in, and crowds gathered at those houses, you can imagine the scene. For many people it was the first time they'd heard a voice coming out of the ether, and there was a kind of magic to it no logical explanation could completely dispel. So the country people gathered around the tabletop sets just like that one"—she pointed to the most archaic model, with solid wood side panels, tubes visible under a glass dome—"and listened to the voices of the various bishops and archbishops and cardinals, and prayed along, though this would all have been in Latin, which next to none of them understood. When the ceremonies were over and the final blessing given, the voices went dead and the transmitter was turned off again, returning almost the entire country to silence."

"You know everything, don't you?" Alba said when Lil had finished her speech.

"I know a few obscure historical details. Calling that everything is a bit of a stretch."

"You make it sound like everything."

"Well, when you know any bit more than whoever you're talking to, how are they to know where your knowledge stops? That's just optics, not arrogance."

Alba's resentment was resistance, to a memory cued by the archaic radio with a dome of thick glass: a physics experiment from her own schooldays, the vacuumed bell jar, the silent hammering of the bell within. That memory opened a valve, letting her physically feel within herself the hammer's mute useless clamor, which seemed somehow to echo the time elapsed since Lil's historical radio moment, and their own distance here from Pierre's empty room. But then she heard it: the bell began to clang.

It was the vintage ringtone of her phone, and she instantly knew who was calling and why.

Monday Noon.

In Pierre's room, three doctors and three new nurses were gathered around the bed. When Dr. Mya spotted Lil and Alba in the doorway, she waved her uninjured arm—holding a huge white envelope—in a grand gathering gesture, as though to say there was nothing to be afraid of, everyone was welcome, come on in.

The tests had shown nothing alarming, she said, so she and her colleagues—she flapped the envelope at the other two white coats—had decided to attempt a *réveil*.

"There's just one thing," she added, almost as an afterthought. "When Pierre wakes up, if he wakes up, it's not for you to explain why he is here. That is my role." There was to be no echo of reckoning, she meant. Pierre's crisis needed to sound like a cold life fact, announced by a stranger. His own parents would be too complicated a source.

"You said *if* he wakes up," Lil said. "I don't understand."

Pierre had been in a coma when he was brought in, Dr. Mya explained with obvious patience. They had induced an artificial coma on top of that, by administering high levels of sedative and by mechanically lowering his body temperature. What they were doing now, today, was simply removing what they had imposed. There was no guarantee that Pierre's "own" coma would lift as well. Surely they had understood that from the start?

Lil and Alba watched the maneuvers in silence, official observers, backs against the wall. They exchanged no words, no looks. The only faces that mattered now were those hovering above the bed or at the machines. Even more than the numbers on the blue LCD, they were the real news. When the neurologist discreetly picked her nose, it was equanimity. When Dr. Mya yawned, it made the world a safer place.

From 33.2, it took almost an hour, and dozens of infinitesimal adjustments, to get to 34. 35 and 36 and everything beyond felt impossibly far away. Yet that was where everyone in the room wanted him to go.

"He's a stubborn bastard," Lil said out loud. Part warning, part worry, part pride.

By the time they finally hit 35, Pierre looked somehow less relaxed, Alba thought. The doctors seemed not to notice, fascinated as they all were by their dials and buttons and taps. But Alba was unsurprised. As the numbers on the little blue LCD rose, she herself felt increasingly tense, as though whatever was being done to him was also being done to her.

The monitor beside the numbers had been unfurling a red line in a rolling horizon all afternoon. Now that line began to climb. The graphic for a Tour de France mountain stage was what it looked like to Lil. Perhaps to calm it, the hands were tinkering more than before with the machines, the mouse, the drips. Still the red line sawed its way upward. Lil glanced at Dr. Mya, the nurses, the neurologist. They all had their poker faces on, their minds meeting abstract information, nothing more.

For the past two days, at random intervals, this or that machine had occasionally given off a polite beep. Occasionally some other machine had answered it, morning chorus, call and response. Now one of them started to cheep and would not stop, and Alba would never have thought that something so neat and well schooled could have such a terrible effect. *Cheep cheep cheep cheep cheep.* It felt like pressure rising measure by measure within her own chest, and like a repeated stab meant to make that pressure burst. And all the while the monitor's red line kept rising, and rising, as though to plow right out the top of the screen.

This was the moment Lil chose to go upstairs, to get rid of her bag of beer. She too had felt the stabbing in her chest, and as soon as she got into the apartment she cracked open a can. The sound alone produced a rush of relief. Warm foam pushed sporelike up out of the hole, and she sucked at it in long passionate gulps. Halfway through, she set the can down, strode to the bathroom, knelt at the toilet bowl, and thrust her right index and middle fingers deep into her mouth, beyond her tongue, reaching for the flesh right at the back. In three or four heaves, she hosed it all—still fizzing—into the bowl. Afterward, she poured the rest of the can in on top of the mess and flushed, and flushed again, until all trace of her lapse was gone. Straight from the tap, she flushed out her mouth in much the same way. She waited a few minutes until her heart calmed, then checked her game face in the mirror, and headed down again.

By three o'clock, they had arrived at some kind of threshold, beyond which Pierre apparently did not want to go. Resisting, the arms and legs on the bed had slowly straightened and set. The hands tried to force him by doing more—drips, dials, valves—of what they'd been doing since midmorning, and Pierre answered by starting to shake. Still they did not desist—not until, with strange pelvic thrusts and heaves, he began to buck.

In under a minute, the neurologist and the anesthetist arrived, and together the three doctors watched the shakes with what looked more like curiosity than concern. With their laboratory hearts. There was no machine not beeping or flashing now. The graphs, too, all had an exciting story to tell. Eventually they formed a private huddle near the door. When the huddle broke, the anesthetist went straight to the desk. The nail-bitten fingers of her left hand pecked hard at the keyboard while her right hand scrubbed the mouse back and forth. Then she tried the keyboard again, a one-handed, multi-key combination, pianist's fingers stretching for an extended chord. It looked like what Lil did herself—almost anything she could think of—whenever her own computer froze. Within seconds, Pierre settled down.

For the debriefing, Dr. Mya led them out into the corridor. That morning, Lil had seen the same act of discretion with Elsa, outside her father's room, and she had been jealous, as though the doctor had only a finite amount of time and care and expertise, which she was squandering on a lost cause.

"What was *that*?" Lil asked her now.

Dr. Mya raised her casted arm to tame their concern. What they had seen, as much as the body's reaction, was the body's ability to react. Which was reassuring, she insisted, even if to the untrained eye it might look like distress.

"Reaction to *what*?"

Maybe it was a withdrawal symptom, from the medication, Dr. Mya said. Or maybe, with less sedative, Pierre's body had felt how cold it actually was.

"*Maybe?*"

Or maybe there had been a neurological impact and the reaction was epileptic, Dr. Mya offered, without even the pretence of conviction, as though the process of diagnosis had not yet gone beyond brainstorm and she was just bandying random possibilities around.

Unlike Lil, Alba felt no real need to understand. What she heard above everything else was the woman's unforced calm. Her account of Pierre's reaction sounded too factual, and her tone of voice too familiar, to feel they had any right to get upset. The way she told it, it was a sound and obvious choice, first to terminate and then reverse a process that might affect their son's brain. *Affect* was the word she used, not *damage* yet. She made it sound like a perfectly reversible mechanical shift, which had nothing at all about it of failure or decline. Pierre was merely being returned to the state in which he'd been a few hours previously, Dr. Mya insisted, seeing the fear on Lil's face, and the eager trust on Alba's. They would try again later, she said, but didn't say when.

It was late. They both felt drained. Maybe they were hungry, Lil said. The thought of food was repulsive to Alba, but she followed Lil into the elevator. She needed a different set of objects to look at for a while.

Down the elevator went to -1. Its doors opened on a smart hum of pineapple and bleach. The chairs were all legs skyward on the tables, except where three nurses in white scrubs sat together near the cash register. Lil slid an empty tray along the stainless steel rails, checking all the tubs and baskets for food. Inside the display units, layers of plastic wrap blurred everything. She tried the stainless steel lock on each glass door. With no bodies to soak it up, the rattling filled the empty hall, but no one came out of the kitchen to police the noise.

Alba walked ahead to a table where they would be out of the nurses' earshot, flipped one of its chairs down onto the red rubber floor. She'd brought the unwieldy white envelope with Pierre's brain scans, and by the time Lil arrived, the table was covered with the large celluloid sheets. Lil sat opposite her with the basket of bread she'd found. Between them, upside down, the MRI and CT scans looked like film negatives, giant size. As though to check for shadows, Alba lifted one to the light.

"At least she's not telling us a story we want to hear," she offered.

"I want to hear that my son's going to be all right," Lil said. "*Happily ever after. The End.*" The bread was fresh and the butter hard, and her knife was ripping the roll's insides to shreds.

"She's not trying to reassure us, I mean. There's no spin."

"That's for sure."

"Which probably means we can trust her. That's something, isn't it?"

The next instant, they were in absolute darkness. Every single light had gone dead, even those normally visible through the serving hatch, and the backlit food displays, and the vending machines by the elevators.

One after the other in quick succession, three pale blue faces appeared in the darkness, way back near the cash register. The screens illuminating them turned outward to confront the solid black mass, but the beams were so weak that Lil and Alba still felt all but immaterial. Once those lights faded and died, the only thing visible was the register's lime green digital display.

"Do you have your phone?" Lil asked.

"No."

"Do you have Pierre's?"

"No."

"Why not?"

"Why should I? Do you have yours?"

Since being told that today's attempt had failed, they'd felt a sickening emptiness very like relief.

"Do you think we could find the exit with no light?" Alba said.

"I guess we could try to grope our way out."

"In which direction?"

"I don't know. Keep on until you hit a wall, I suppose."

"I would have thought a hospital would have emergency lights, backup generators, all that," Alba said.

"Not for down here, apparently," Lil said. Sometimes she spoke only to swap one type of silence for another, slightly more troubling.

"So we're just going to sit here?"

"Let's give it a few minutes and see what happens."

"And if nothing does?"

The table between them was covered with the scans, each a different cross section of their son's brain. Without thinking, Alba reached to check they were still there, as though this might all be a masterly maneuver for theft. Her sweaty hands patted the surface before her, not caring what prints they left on the celluloid. Then began to group and stack and tidy them safely away again.

Listening to her work, Lil's own hands patted around until they found the little wicker basket, tore off a chunk of bread and used it to find her mouth. While she ate, her eyes searched again for some flaw in the darkness, some leak from another world, but even the area over by the elevators—where she guessed the elevators were, and where there ought to have been a perpetual Exit sign—was as black as the rest. Now she could hear the women's distant voices—three of them, in three separate one-way conversations, in Norwegian, populating the dark. Every now and then, as a phone lit up, one of those faces flashed into view. The effect was familiar but grotesque, like children with a flashlight playing Scare.

"I'd sit here all night if I knew his machines were okay," Alba said.

"It's an ICU. This is exactly the type of situation they're designed for. It's probably just a test run."

"Testing what? The Off button?"

"Or a drill of some kind."

"A drill where you don't do anything?"

"Yes. Like don't panic. Isn't that the first thing they always say?"

The word *panic* was another stab, which Alba was too ready to give a home. Her body now felt that anything could strike it, from anywhere, at any time.

"Are you eating?" she said, trying to trump her fear with indignation.

"No," Lil said, mimicking a full mouth.

After twenty-five years together, they were more like

teenage sisters than lovers at times. The spiked codes and acumen. The casual vigilance.

"You remember that blind restaurant in Paris?" Lil said, hoping to calm Alba with her own model of calm.

"I remember the bill."

In fact, she remembered that Paris restaurant very well, and the envy she used to feel for Lil's inclination to try things she herself never would. Even when they turned out badly, she used not to regret it. That reckless daring—close to bullying at times—had once charmed her. Now it galled. Like her therapist said: you end up resenting in your partner the very qualities for which you chose them.

"You really don't think it's the whole hospital?" she said.

Lil refused to revive that conversation, but welcomed the image of the entire city of Trondheim cast into darkness, sharing the judgment, however briefly, until the first flickers reappeared, pinholes in a black card, as the population brought their emergency candles out, a multitude of live flames replacing the candle-effect bulbs of their Christmas kitsch. During the winter storms, there were sometimes power cuts in the old farmhouse they rented every Christmas in Auvergne, but for Lil the memory mustered no anxiety. The house had a fireplace, a petrol heater, candles aplenty, and the blackouts were never anything but an excuse to build up the fire and play cards and toast bread on the flames with the laundry fork. Nothing more fun than a good crisis, she liked to say.

"I want to go," Alba announced. "I can't stand the thought that he might be lying alone up there in the dark."

"Think about what you just said," Lil countered. "Think

what those words actually mean." She reached across the table to grab Alba's arms, but could not find them.

"*Alba,*" she said. It was their safe word, to stop the game.

Her summons was pointless. Alba was no longer available. Arching her back, she was looking straight overhead. In their new apartment, they'd found the ceiling of the boys' bedroom designate decorated with luminous moons and comets and stars, obviously in situ for years. The stars were a washed-out green, almost white, barely noticeable except in the dark. Immediately they'd moved in, Pierre had pulled them all off, but the surrounding ceiling had long since dulled, so that at dusk the outline of the absent stars could still be made out, even after two new coats of paint.

A faint blue shadow now in the service hatch. The gas burners, perhaps. Or perhaps their eyes were finally adapting to the dark. Then a lone candle flame came floating out of the kitchen, illuminating nothing but the tattooed arm carrying it. That disembodied arm set it on the nurses' table, lighting up their faces like a campfire. Hands reached in from the huddled darkness and sucked one flame after another out of the original. Not with normal candles like the first, but little night lights in pear-shaped jars of colored glass, ruby and lemon and tangerine. The women's hands gathered them up and the procession moved out, placing them one by one on the surrounding tables, in an ever-widening circle of light, like they were all back in their student days, waiting tables again in that cosy Italian restaurant and setting up for Valentine's, the biggest night of the year.

Lil discovered a washing machine in a cupboard under the bathroom counter, and took a few moments to realize its presumption of an extended stay. To shut that possibility off, she shut the porthole door, and something clicked. She immediately tried to pull it open again, but could not, so she pressed the button with the lock icon and pulled harder, then pressed POWER, and something inside started to turn.

Coming out of the bathroom, she found Alba on the phone to her father, talking about Dr. Mya. "She didn't try to sell us anything," she was saying, "which makes me trust her. I think she's always going to tell us the truth, good or bad."

This absolute deference to Dr. Mya was barely tolerable to Lil, as was the trumpeting of the doctor's honesty—a sly dig at herself, Lil supposed. They had long since reached that point in a relationship where everything seen or heard or done is just more of the same.

"The staff, the equipment," Alba went on, "we absolutely couldn't wish for more." This was her latest favorite story: the hospital's perfect anticipation of Pierre's needs. Another bad move, in Lil's mind. It meant the outcome now depended entirely on him.

On the building opposite, behind the printed net, the big red digital display had clocked down to 0°. On ground level, there was still a clot of smokers by the main door. In the dark glass, Alba was now listing off for her father all the day's encouraging signs. "And then," she told him, "when the doctors turned the respirator off to see if he could breathe on his own, for eight or ten seconds that's exactly what he did."

From a parallel world came the empty washing machine's thud thud, pause, thud, as of an unhappy, off-center load. Lil went back into the bathroom as though to investigate and shut the door behind her, to shut Alba's wanton optimism out. As her courage failed, it mattered less and less what any scan or screen or doctor said: everything was bookies' banter now until Pierre spoke or opened his eyes. But the bathroom was no refuge: in fact, the manic banging felt like an endorsement of the loose panic now rallying inside her. Here at last, it yelled, was catastrophe she'd felt shadowing her since childhood—the masochist fantasy that, all her life, had cheered on even the most minor anxiety.

Lil came out of the bathroom carrying two empty plastic cups and set them in front of the dead TV. Her loudest cue yet for Alba to get off the phone. But Alba had already hung up with her father and called a new audience: her children. Lil went to the window and opened it and instantly the room expanded, from private to public space. Hand over hand, she drew up a roped sheet with a blue plastic bag tied to the end. For three days she'd been desperate for a drink, and finally she had it, in five half-liter aluminum tins.

"It's to protect the brain," Dr. Mya had explained downstairs, and Alba now offered this explanation to the phone, as though the more people she told, the more credible it must be.

Lil cracked a can open, tilted it slightly toward her cup, then tilted more, and more, to no effect. She turned the can almost vertical. What dribbled out was the color of milk.

"We need to keep this in perspective," Alba was saying. "Everything's exactly the way it was twenty-four hours ago. No better, no worse."

To Lil, this was just one of those cheap thoughts you say out loud to see whether it is something you might be willing to believe. But it was not true: in almost everything said and done since that first phone call three days ago, back in France,

Pierre's viability had been assumed, and whatever glimpse of his brain the doctors got that morning had encouraged an attempt to test that assumption, and the test had failed.

Fed up imagining the answers to Alba's cues, Lil pulled the phone from her hands, put it on speaker, and threw it on the bed.

"Did he get my message?" asked María's voice.

"I saw it on his phone, yes," Alba said.

"But did he hear it? Did he actually hear what I said?"

"*Amor*," Alba said. "It's like he's really, really fast asleep and nothing can wake him up. You understand that."

"I want you to play it to him out loud. He has to hear it," said the small faraway voice.

"*Amor*," Alba said again, close to exasperation at having to describe her son's condition even more plainly. "I don't know how else to explain it to you. He can't hear or see or feel *anything*. That's what *coma* means."

When Alba hung up, Lil handed her a cup that was half empty and half foam. She had to lift her chin, exposing her throat, to get any liquid at all into her mouth.

"You know what my mother said?" she asked.

"That it's all part of the master plan? Mysterious ways and all that shit?"

"She said it's like the first crêpe—it always sticks, you've just got to write it off."

The top of a giant Ferris wheel could be seen beyond distant apartment blocks. Its dark empty cabins cradled in the wind, and that slight movement kept tricking Lil into thinking the whole thing was starting to turn. She wiggled the can in her hand, dribbled a little more into Alba's cup, gave herself the dregs.

"It's like living in a submarine," Alba said. She meant the dark window they were standing at, hermetically sealed against the cold. She also meant home, by comparison, two and a half thousand kilometers to the south. Just now, home meant a warm breeze on their balcony, the smell of ground coffee, the sun on her face. Minding that dream, her hand rose up and twisted the handle—then she leaped back as the entire window dropped toward her, like the toppling of a solid wall. As the cold poured in, she pushed the window back into place and worked the handle left and right, but couldn't make it open any other way.

"I guess they don't want anyone jumping out," she said.

"No one's jumping out of any hospital windows," Lil said. "Not yet."

"To stop them from falling out, then. Old people or children. Remember Eric Clapton's son?"

When they'd finished their next drink, Alba announced that she wanted a cigarette—she who'd not smoked since being pregnant with Pierre. She also wanted to get out of range of the washing machine, which was now gearing up to go into a high spin, too like the flutters of panic loosed in her by the drink.

The elevator, when it came, already had a passenger: a cleaning woman with a wheelchair carrying a tall plastic tree. They all went down together without a word. The leaves of the tree, Lil saw, were furred and gray with grime. She scraped at one with her fingernail, revealing a glossy green stripe. When the elevator doors opened, they stood back to let the tree go first, then followed it across the foyer toward the main door. Outside, the cleaning woman kept going, wheeled it almost as far as the 7-Eleven on the corner, as though taking it for a coffee or a snack.

Alba waited by the wall while Lil approached the nurses standing in a smokers' huddle. Most were staff, the grave-yard shift coming in, and one was Kristen, standing with her pelvis cocked like a pregnant woman, left hand on the small of her back, right hand dangling low as though to hide her crime. The other nurses stood with shoulders hunched, feet together, bodies clenched against the cold.

Lil nodded hello and asked if she might bum a cigarette. "For Alba," she said.

Kristen placed her hand on Lil's forearm and rested it there. "They told me about today," she said.

Lil remembered the smoke trapped in her cardigan with all the brighter smells. She remembered how her own clothes used to smell after a night on the town, back in her student days, when there was so much available that felt forbidden now. With her fingertips, she drew a single cigarette from Kristen's pack, put it between her lips, then leaned in very close, to light it from Kristen's own. Afterward she smiled weakly and turned away. Tonight Kristen had her long corn-colored hair in a French plait, and below the elastic, like a calligraphy brush, it tapered to the finest of points.

Lil had left Alba near the main doors. As she turned back, the cleaning woman passed right in front of her, leaving the building again. This time, she was holding a huge metal nozzle in her hands and hauling over her shoulder a thick white canvas strap: the fire hose. Leaning forward as into a strong wind, step by step she dragged it toward her plastic tree. On the far side of its white line, Alba had turned her face to the building, was leaning her forehead against the wall, and had the flat of her hands against it too, shoulder high, as though to support herself. She was trembling slightly, but not from the cold. This was her moment of weakness, Lil knew, and knew from experience not to interrupt. Some twenty feet beyond her, stuck to the facade, was the huge bronze mold of what they'd first taken as a bear rug. They had since realized that the animal was a wolf, with its form flattened, as though fallen from a great height, and its four legs in a star-shaped splay. But its head was not cocked back like a bear rug's. Rather, it looked to be half-embedded in the concrete— indeed, at a corresponding spot inside the building, by the elevators, a bronze snout with snarling teeth projected from the wall. From Lil's perspective, both splayed figures looked about the same size. Between her and them lay the fire hose, which the cleaning lady had pulled as far as the wheelchair at the corner, that the smokers catch no spray. Now the flat white line came alive, morphing from two to three dimensions, idea to reality. It swelled and fattened, until as tight as young skin, then the solid bar of the thing began to tremble, and lifted miraculously off the ground.

For a long time that night, Alba sat by the bed with her hands in her lap, listening to the quiet penance of his pipes. In Catalan, for privacy, she talked to him of her secret life with Lil. Her frustrations, her patience, her anger. He would understand better than any priest. Every family is its own climate. Year after year, he had breathed the same air. There was no reaction to her voice, and eventually she took his hand. Then she was petting his hair, his face, stroking his skin. He had always loved such tenderness, but now refused to respond. After a while, like someone begging for forgiveness or leniency, she found herself kissing his palms. Then she was crying openly, leaning farther over the bed, almost on top of it, with his head in her hands, like a blind-fold game where fingers must recognize a face. These things were not a provocation. They were her lure and bribe—a smuggled message about all that was good in the world, to tempt him back. The absence of all reaction still did not discourage her. His suffering tubes—amplified in the night hospital—whispered clearly of his inner life, pointing beyond the surface physical to vital function and absolute organic need, letting her feel closer to him than she had in years, almost back to the glory days, when attachment and anxiety were inextricable, in both directions.

A loud slurp lifted her head. It was a drip bag collaps-ing, as though in the grip of an invisible fist. In the slow-motion implosion, she saw threat: the shrivel and choke was her darling memory—mother and child—being strangled, crushed. Kristen, at her desk, saw a welcome excuse to stand up, go change the bag, and perhaps say something to Alba, try to calm her.

The speed with which she unplugged and replaced the bag was impressive—something she'd obviously done a thousand times before—but the expertise brought Alba no comfort, only another ruinous insight: this woman or one like her was going to be Pierre's primary caregiver for the rest of his life. He was never going to wake up. The mothering she herself could offer was redundant. He was in the hands of machines and professionals now, far smarter and more selfless than any-thing she could provide. Her job was done. The doing of it had not satisfied but confirmed her need. That was the real lesson of these past three days.

Like dreams and drink, disaster has its own quack confidence: she got out Pierre's phone, found the voicemail María had left earlier that day, put it on speaker, and set it on the pillow close to his ear, as she'd promised she would. Maybe that would get through.

The recording said: "Pierre, I love you a lot, you can't die, you just can't, stay with us, you have to stay with us, you can't die, you just can't, I can't live without you, I don't want to."

The tiny voice made Alba feel sick—merely sad sick at first, crushed and void, but then shot her out of her chair toward the white plastic wastebasket by Kristen's desk. On her knees, doing her best to hold her hair out of the spray, she puked herself empty in half a dozen ragged, sloppy hacks. Perhaps it was the beer on an empty stomach, or the cigarette. Perhaps it was the mass of disgusting emotions she'd been hoarding all afternoon, or the inexplicable shame and relief she'd felt since Dr. Mya announced that today's attempt had failed.

She felt a hand between her shoulder blades. It was Kristen, kneeling beside her, stroking her back, a kind voice saying, "That's it, that's good, let it all out." The physical comfort was welcome, but it was the wrong advice: kneeling on a rubber floor, listening to her daughter's pathetic appeal, while puking into a plastic bucket, felt like a rehearsal for defeat. So when Kristen offered her one of Pierre's baby wipes, she drew it across her mouth, dropped it on top of her mess, then began peeling the wastebasket's bag from its lip to take the evidence away. Kristen tried to object, but Alba lifted the bag free and deftly knotted the top. You make the mess, you clean the mess, was one of the few nonnegotiables on which she and Lil actually agreed.

She carried her strange little bag down the hall to the

waiting room, but found Elsa there. Elsa looked up from her knitting but her hands did not stop. Tonight she was using pencil-length needles linked by a rubber tube, with mauve wool that looked like a frayed piece of thread. Alba sat down and set her bag on the low table like it was nothing she wanted to hide, but didn't speak.

"It's hard," Elsa said after a few moments. She had seen and heard the activity in her neighbor's room all through the day.

Alba was glad to hear this from someone for whom it wasn't just another reheated phrase, but a bald fact.

"They tell you they're going to try and wake him up and you can't help it, you start to hope," she said. "Right away you're thinking maybe this has all been just a big silly scare, in half an hour you'll be smiling and hugging and laughing, the three of you. Then they say they're sending him under again and you tell yourself it's for his own good, and that's all you really care about, isn't it? You keep telling yourself the toughest part is behind you then bang, you're back at square one, like none of it mattered, how hard the waiting was or how brave you were trying to be."

On the coffee table, Alba's bag had flattened out a little, the way a ripe fig will flatten if left on the ground for a few days. For a while, the only sound in the room was the nice click of Elsa's needles, slowly sucking the whisper-thin line of wool up out of her lap.

"My mother just said, Well, he's no worse than he was twenty-four hours ago," Alba said then. It was the most useless kind of comfort, that of comparison.

"Or better," Elsa said.

"That's what I mean. The hardest twenty-four hours of my

life, and all for nothing. This place isn't an ICU"—she let her head wander—"it's a fucking time machine."

She nodded at a paper cup on the table, asking if it was Elsa's. Elsa shook her head, but Alba drank anyway, swilled the water around her sweet-and-sour mouth, gargled, spat it back. High up in the corner, the TV was rolling 24-hour news. With the sound off, the catastrophes all seemed so far away and flimsy—far less real than the very physical threat Alba felt gestating inside her now.

"I keep asking myself what we could have done differently," she went on.

Almost everything, Elsa wanted to say, because over the past week she had spent many hours at her dying father's bedside, reviewing the twin disappointments of their lives, and asking herself the same thing. But this was the exact opposite of what Alba needed to hear, so Elsa told her, "You did what you thought best at the time. It's what we all do."

From out in the hall came the neat squelch of rubber soles—staff Crocs, Alba knew by now—on the corridor's rubber floor. One of the ICU nurses appeared in the doorway. Had they any idea where Dr. Mya might be?

"Probably up on the roof," Elsa said, "taking potshots at passersby."

The nurse tugged at her sleeves, left and right, looked from one woman to the other, hesitating, as though there was something more she wanted to say. When she was gone, Alba went to the window and looked up at the helipad, as though to check Elsa's joke. Behind her, Elsa kept working her tiny square of wool.

"I wouldn't have the patience," Alba said. Her hopes felt outdated now.

"You don't need it," Elsa said. "That's the whole point. There's no bigger picture, just always the next stitch and the one after that."

"I know I've no right to feel disappointed," Alba said, trying to coach herself back to a more familiar place. Mere helplessness was where she needed to be.

"Yes you do," Elsa said. "We all do."

Alba set her bag of vomit gently in the wastebasket. "You get to a certain age, you think if nothing else, you know your own head," she said. She meant the absolute hopelessness she'd felt today, for the first time in her life. For a forty-eight-year-old woman, it was an ominous surprise. She'd always thought herself resilient, if nothing else.

Before she could explain what she meant, tacky footsteps sounded in the corridor again, coming much quicker than before. It was the same nurse, this time with a blank face.

"Elsa," she said, then a string of Norwegian words, only one of which Alba recognized: *Papa*.

Elsa immediately jumped up, knitting clasped to her chest, and jogged straight out the door.

Alone, Alba picked through the magazines sprawled across the coffee table. Some were months old, some brand new, but all felt like reports from a bygone world, no matter how loud their headlines. She snapped the pages one by one. At the back were personals, chess moves, horoscopes, gay sex lines, anti-Alzheimer mind games. If two planes simultaneously leave A, traveling in opposite directions. If a woman fills a bath at a rate of five liters per minute, which leaks at a rate of. The unspoken creed seemed to be that, with the right ratio or unit of measurement, every problem could be solved. She had been away from Pierre too long, but for fear of contagion stayed where she was: out in the hall there was still too much coming and going of personnel, too many machines rattling past.

To prove in black and white how very far she and her boy were from such danger, she got out her phone. *Hello everyone,* she wrote. *We have no good news to share with you tonight but fortunately no definite bad news either. Today the doctors began the complicated process of trying to wake Pierre up. After they initiated what they call the* réveil *(the doctor speaks a bit of French) he breathed and coughed and even moved a little, but that may have been a reflex action, or maybe a withdrawal symptom from the reduction in sedative, they don't know yet. The doctors eventually decided it was best to sedate him again so as not to stress his body or brain too much. So the full* réveil *has been put off until tomorrow at the earliest. Lil and I are trying to rest now after what has been a tough day. We're trying to stay optimistic but we're worried naturally. Love to you all and thanks to everyone for their messages and support. Please share this with anyone I might have missed, I don't have everyone's address.*

She could still hear plenty of activity at the far end of the corridor, but felt relieved once her message was sent. The facts, as she had stated them, put Pierre and Elsa's father in two entirely different categories.

Tuesday Morning.

ALBA WAS BOUNCING UP AND DOWN, to get her jeans to her waist. "You were dreaming," Lil told her, watching the way she sucked her belly in, to something like her old silhouette.

"What are you talking about? I didn't even sleep."

"Don't you want to know what you were saying?"

Alba gave her zipper far more attention than it deserved, because she was afraid of what she might have said. How many times had she complained of the terrible loneliness she felt, how uncurious Lil was about her inner life, her hungers, her needs? Then just tell me, Lil would say, in that simpleton way she had, flipping the blame, making it a failure of confession not attention. Yet here she was now talking in her sleep, broadcasting who knows what fear or fact, in the most cowardly and naked way.

Before the mirror, she lifted both hands to her head, dragged her hair back, roughly tied it up.

"Ready?" Lil said.

"No."

Now she was rummaging in her bag. Making the world wait, was Lil's thought. She pulled out two ID badges on long red lanyards. From now on, she explained, they could come and go as they pleased from the ICU, the gym, the sauna, everything, like any member of staff. It was more freedom, she seemed to believe, but Lil felt only the new weight around her neck. She would never have dared say so, but she liked having left so much behind. It gave a certain levity to her life up here. *Levity* was probably not the right word. But home and all its props felt to her more a burden than an anchor—like some outsized inheritance she'd been appointed executor of, and for which she would have to account at some future point in time. Up here, she had her wallet and phone and key card, and everything else was surplus. The new freedom she felt told her how much she merely tolerated what everyone else regarded as her real life.

They walked silently down the hall, badges swinging from their necks, left right, tick tock. Lil had last worn one of those things twenty-eight years before, working for the summer in a computer components plant in Fermoy. One day they'd replaced all the lanyards with a new type that snapped open at the slightest pressure, after someone had been dragged into a machine on the production line.

"I come bearing gifts," announced a loud voice behind them, almost as soon as they entered Pierre's room. It was Dr. Mya, with a stack of wrapped presents in her arms. "Not for you, for her," she said, nodding at Kristen.

Kristen was inserting a syringe into the port in Pierre's arm for the day's first blood test.

"From the lab rats," Dr. Mya explained, setting the presents at Pierre's feet. "They can't come tonight."

As Kristen drew back the plunger, Alba quietly resettled her chair, to change her sight line. Lil recognized the threat but made sure not to acknowledge it: the punctured shell—skin—was one of Alba's worst triggers, and the dread it provoked would now be wide awake. So Lil walked over and stood in such a way as put her own body between Alba and the nurse.

Oblivious to these maneuvers, Dr. Mya was flicking through her phone. "Want to see a photo of yourself drunk?" she asked Kristen.

"Even if it's only for another few minutes, some of us are working here," Kristen answered with mock ire.

"Look, you've got those devil eyes."

The anesthetist arrived. "You're still here?" she said.

"Don't worry, I'll be gone soon enough," Kristen shot back.

Dr. Mya showed the new arrival the photo, making her smile. Then she held it like a mirror in front of Kristen's face.

"I'm not drunk there," Kristen protested.

"That's what's funny about it."

Lil smiled defensively, at no one in particular, relieved she was not in Kristen's place. She hated looking at photos of herself. Either they were recent and she looked too old, or it was an old photo and she looked too young.

"We're doing a slide show for her farewell party," Dr. Mya explained.

"She's leaving?" Lil said, with a note of exasperation, because she meant *leaving us*?

"It was supposed to be last Friday," Dr. Mya said in Kristen's defense. "But she very kindly stayed on, just for you."

"I'll be back this evening for the party," Kristen cut in. She was tidying her things from the desk into a plastic tray. "We'll say good-bye properly then."

There was no clear nod or order to signal the official start of today's attempt. Even as Dr. Mya chatted to them about the farewell party, the anesthetist and day nurse were tweaking various dials and valves and taps, as though merely testing them for the work to come.

Like yesterday, the blue screen's baseline reading was 33.2. It took ten or fifteen minutes of tinkering for those numbers to come alive.

By the time they got to 34, their attention was focused entirely on the buttons and screens. Lil understood their charm. She herself already knew all the makers' names by heart. She liked the German brands best. She had tried to memorize the names on the drip labels too, but they seemed deliberately complicated, as in a spelling contest knockout round.

By 35, it seemed blatantly obvious to Alba that his arms and legs had stiffened again, but none of the staff seemed to notice, and when eventually the first twitch came she was almost relieved, sure it would call their attention away from the machines and back to him. But still the hands kept toying with the buttons and dials and drips, and—as though this were their intention—the twitches were steadily amplified.

Over the next hour, step by step, the numbers climbed all the way to 36.0, yesterday's record, but did not stop there. When they hit 36.5, Pierre started to shake again. Like a body in a morgue during an earthquake, is how Lil would describe it at a much later date. But in Dr. Mya this produced no notable show of concern. Watching the jerk and buck, she merely nodded once and said, "Good," like a stern father congratulating a dull but dutiful boy. Nonetheless, she took out her phone and left the room.

Lil went to the window. Hard to say that the day was any brighter, but the building opposite was no longer quite so dark against its own lights, and the street snow was no longer quite so new.

When Dr. Mya came back, it was with the neurologist and the anesthetist; each went straight to a different machine, and she herself came over to Lil and Alba, to explain.

"If his temperature goes too high," she said, "it could materially impact the brain."

The words shot Alba back twenty years, to those terrible fever nights, when all that mattered in the world was getting the numbers down.

"So you're giving up? Already?" Lil said.

"Not at all. We're just going to have to be a little more patient than we—and you, I'm sure—would like."

The women's hands worked the taps and dials quietly but constantly, as though absolutely unsure of their effect. The numbers slowed, stalled, started to drop again, until Pierre was calmed, then completely still. Lil expected them to settle once they reached a certain baseline—35? 34?—and looked forward to that as a respite, but they bounced softly back up, and a few minutes later he started to twitch again, and eventually the twitches got more showy, and he started to shake much like before, and around the bed there was a sudden rush of activity—answering Pierre's—to reel him back in before he went too far.

Through all this, Alba and Lil stood hand in hand with their backs against the partition wall.

When next the shakes started, the anesthetist kept her arm down, as though refusing to take no for an answer this time, even when Pierre's back began arching up off the mattress. It was his body objecting, the only way it knew how. Neither Alba nor Lil had ever seen anything of the sort except

in movies, where psychiatric patients were administered elec-
troshock therapy, or the possessed exorcized.

Lil now watched the anesthetist's arm with fear, afraid of
its inertia and afraid of seeing it lift again. She wanted some
kind of stay, for herself and her son, and she wanted to push
on harder and longer than ever before. She wanted the crisis
deferred endlessly, and wanted the thing resolved once and
for all, forcibly if need be.

Beside her, Alba just wanted to shout Stop, please, leave
him be. She wanted him quiet again, the way he'd been
all night, sleeping the way he'd slept as a child—peaceful,
precious, idolized—with his wrecked mother by his side.

At about five o'clock that afternoon, the three doctors gathered again by the window. Speaking Norwegian, they leaned
their heads toward each other slightly, as in a judo bow.
Behind them, waiting for further orders, the nurses stood in
front of the stacked machines like customers in a high-end
sound store, staring at the buttons and dials with civilized
dread. Many more lights were flashing now.

When the huddle broke, Dr. Mya came over to Lil and
Alba to make an announcement. "We've decided to do an
electroencephalogram," she said. "We need to know what's
causing the spasms, and why they are so violent. My colleague
is phoning now to see how soon we can get a slot."

Their silence looked like bafflement or interrogation. So
the doctor explained again—did she think they might have
forgotten, or not been paying attention?—about the high
levels of sedation they'd been administering for several days,
the physiological reaction—possibly epileptic, but probably
not—its reduction might have provoked.

"Our son is not epileptic," Alba said.

"Epilepsy can be acquired," Dr. Mya said—as diplomatic a formulation as she could contrive. "In any case," she added, seeing the effect of her statement on Alba's face, "that's just one of a number of things we want to check."

Beyond a certain point in the doctor's discourse, Lil's own brain had begun to disengage. All she really heard was the retreat from *I* to *we*, and the one essential fact: today's attempt too had failed.

Today again, two burly men in grubby white scrubs came to wheel him downstairs. *Portalliteres*, Alba thought, but strictly speaking that meant *stretcher bearers*, which was not quite what they were. Somewhere in her brain was a kinder name, but that too was beyond her now. And today again they rigged up most of the machines to accompany him. Another reminder of how utterly dependent he was. And again the stately procession made its way down the hall, royalty and its full retinue. Again Alba expected to see fur balls, runaway coins, and sunfade in the place where the bed had been, but the empty space looked no different from the rest of the rubber floor, except for the shallow dimples left by the wheels.

She and Lil sat in silence in the empty room for a time, each with her own burrowing thoughts. For Alba there was a kind of comfort knowing he was out of it for a while. Might it not be better, after all, to let his body rest for as long as it needed, to repair the torn tissues or blasted synapses or whatever the damage was, giving him the best possible chance of revival at some later—maybe much later—date? She didn't care how long it took. Weeks or months or more, it didn't matter, if it produced the right result. If nothing else, she knew she was always willing to wait a bad situation out.

A few minutes later, Pierre's phone started to ring. It was Dr. Mya. It would be longer than expected, she said, because one of the machines wasn't yet free. Someone else was being given priority, was all Alba heard.

"She said it might be a good time for us to get out," Lil said. Not considered too closely, Pierre's absence felt like a threat removed.

"I'm staying right here," Alba said coldly. "You can do what you want."

Alba sat alone with the machines the orderlies had left behind. Their cables and tubes had been coiled to keep them from touching the ground. For her too, this was a chance to rest, but as she closed her eyes the doorway gave a bright lemon blink. It was a nurse in a Hawaiian shirt, on roller skates, headed for the waiting room. Alba let the afterimage fade and tried again to relax, until the pop of a champagne cork jerked her awake. It was no good: every time she started to drift off, there came another gust of laughter or applause or another loud flash from the hall, of Fanta orange, parakeet green, poppy red.

By six o'clock Lil had still not reappeared. Alba went to look for her upstairs, and deliberately didn't look into the waiting room as she passed, despite the noise. Their apartment was empty. From the bathroom, she peeked into the mirror apartment. It was empty too. She searched the other wards floor by floor, trying not to look too deeply into the open doorways left and right. In the alcove by the elevators on the sixth floor, an old man in wheelchair sat at an upright piano. His left arm was in a sling, but the fingers of his right hand were walking painfully down the white keys. An old woman in a pink flannel nightdress and furry slippers sat on the piano stool beside him, either waiting to wheel him away or waiting for her turn. The slings were all bypasses or pacemakers, apparently. They eased the tightness of the stitches, Elsa had explained, and how quick the hope had grabbed Alba of one day seeing her son shuffling the corridors with his arm trussed up like that. But the old man sat slouched and slack-lipped and unshaven, with what looked like a dirty dishcloth spread over his knees. If nothing else, Alba promised herself, she would never let Pierre end up looking like that. Such was the poverty of her new ambitions, both for him and for herself.

She ended up on the ground floor, at the main entrance, hoping to find Lil with the smokers. In the airlock between the inner and outer doors, the plastic tree was in its wheelchair again, with a cleaning woman scanning a hairdryer back and forth across its dripping leaves. Outside, the smokers were huddled together as about a brazier—scrubs and patients, but no Lil. *"Fire! Fire!"* one of them had screamed the night before, seeing the fire hose being unrolled, and they'd all laughed. On the building across the road, the big red digital display now said -2°. Back in the foyer, she saw that one of the elevators was on its way down. It wasn't the first time she and Lil had lost track of each other in this maze. Wrong corridor, wrong turn, wrong floor. Several times a day, they had to text each other to say, *I thought you were coming up, stay where you are, I'm coming down.* Even that option was now gone. Alba still had Pierre's phone, from Dr. Mya's call, and Lil had stormed off—on purpose?—without her own. The elevator didn't stop, and she rushed after it, down the stairs to -1. By the time she arrived it was empty, but there were no customers in the canteen—no one at all except the bottle blonde with the black skullcap over by the cash register, emptying the bread baskets into a black bag. When the baskets were empty, she began to lay big white cloths like sheets over the drink machines, the stacked mugs, the condiment rack. Then she unpinned her skullcap and held it humble in her hands, as if out of respect, while she looked one last time over the empty display units and bains marie. A red dot was pulsing through the sheet on the coffee machine, so she reached underneath and blindly felt around the base until her finger found the right button and turned it off.

Alba used her new ID card to swipe herself into the gym. Near the door, an old man in leg braces stood between a set of hip-high parallel bars, tracked by a very young therapist. Beyond him, a mirrored wall stretched the full length of the big room. The machines facing it were unoccupied except for a lone woman on the StairMaster at the far end, marching smartly up its endless steps. She was wearing gray cotton leggings a size too small and a tight gray tank top, damp between her shoulder blades. Seen from behind, everything looked stout but well set, quite like Lil in her prime. Now she switched to giant loping steps, three at a time. To firm up her thighs, Alba supposed, as though there was any need of that. Without breaking her stride, she tilted her head and wiped her forehead across her bicep, exactly as Lil liked to do, and Alba was split with the thought—almost entirely self-reproach—that she hadn't been paying enough attention, that after months working on the apartment, hard physical labor day after day, on top of her time in the gym,

Lil had tightened up even more, and really did look this good again.

At the parallel bars, the therapist was no longer at the old man's side but facing him, arms outstretched but backing away, promising to catch him if he fell. Alba watched his progress, to put off the moment when she would look at the StairMistress again. By the time she did, the woman had switched to a new routine: four quick steps up, three slower steps down, like some Latin dance. Alba was glad she couldn't see the woman's face. It let her get angry at Lil—at the idea of her working out, getting her high, while Alba waited alone upstairs in Pierre's empty room for the news that would spare or condemn. Finally, in an ever-complicating choreography, the woman turned ninety degrees to climb the stairs sideways, showing Alba someone who was only a very poor version of what Lil had once been. Her resentment did not fade. It no longer depended on the facts of the moment. She had accumulated too much proof over the years, making her ability to imagine it perfectly admissible evidence that this was exactly the kind of thing Lil would do. Every second step, the outside leg stretched high into the air, right over her head, in a balletic gesture at once graceful and boastful and obscene.

She walked up the stairs to the foyer one heavy step at a time, then walked slowly to the main door, past the posters of emergency crews at accident scenes, past the plastic tree, the huddled smokers, the beast with its face plugged into the wall, then walked the gray slush all the way to the 7-Eleven on the corner. It was the last place she could think of where Lil might be.

There was no one in the shop except a clerk behind the food counter and the old man from upstairs with the sling, still in his wheelchair, at a one-armed bandit near the back. The woman at the food counter was a tall elegant fifty-year-old with strawberry highlights and horn-rimmed glasses. She said something in Norwegian, but Alba smiled apologetically, so in perfect English the woman asked if Alba would like something to eat. The food under the heat lamps—burgers, pizza, hot dogs—all looked well past its prime, but the question sounded so like genuine motherly concern that Alba could not bear to refuse, she felt so deserving just then.

Alba took the thing she'd ordered—some kind of rubbery, wrinkled sausage set in a dry hot dog bun—to the ragged-edged counter by the window. To avoid looking at it, she looked instead at the old man working the one-armed bandit. Again and again, she willed his robot hand to hit SPIN, watched the rollers blur and tire and set until her face was as blank as his, both offering the same dumb reverence to whatever result—dollar, lemon, crown—the skewed algorithm threw up.

A trembling in her jeans snapped her back to the now. It was a message on Lil's phone. *Been thinking of you,* it said. *Any news/progress? Sorry about Sunday. I was a bit of a cunt, I know. Maybe not the first time either. The news didn't really sink in until after, so I think I might have sounded really harsh. Or maybe I was really harsh. Anyway I'm sorry. You don't deserve that. I still think of you fondly, you know, and don't regret a minute of it. Call me when you get back or whenever you want. love, Valerie.*

A blast of cold air swung her around, hoping and dreading that it might be Lil who'd triggered the doors. It was the old woman in the pink nightdress and slippers, swaying slightly and blinking hard against the shop's neon blare, and holding a huge paper cup in both hands. She stepped closer, to set the cup onto Alba's counter, but somehow misjudged the distance and let go too soon. The thing wobbled and tipped over. The lid bulged outward, did not pop, but from its nipple shot a series of thick brown spurts.

At the service area on the far side of the door, a spiral of paper towel hung from a barrel dispenser. The old woman shuffled over to it—triggering the doors again—and grasped that paper tail in her fist. Instead of jerking a length free, she pulled at it hand over hand, like someone climbing a rope.

Back at the counter, she set a huge wad of towel on the puddle—it was not coffee but soup—and with a polishing motion began to move it around. Any second now, Alba was sure, the cup's lid would explode, so she backed up her stool as far as she could, right to the wall, leaving Lil's phone and her hot dog behind. Beyond the old woman, like a fallen garland, the loose cord of towel—still connected to the dispenser— stretched all the way across the shop.

Eventually, just as she'd feared, in sloshing to and fro the woman banged the overturned cup, the lid peeled—then popped—open, and a splurge of sick-like soup spewed out. In disgust, Alba turned away, only to be confronted by her own nightmare face in the dark glass. That face was both proof and accusation. Her whole life—body, brain, ambition—was melting. I am history, she thought, and held that thought in her mind like a comfort, until a group of masked runners slid across her reflection, all with rifles on their backs.

After its first surge, the soup slowed, but some invisible tilt kept it crawling in her direction, cautious but unstoppable, like an invasion graphic on one of Lil's History Channel maps. Brown for Germans, was the obvious equation, moving across the green Formica countertop. One by one, in little gulps, its advancing edge sucked up the counter's stray poppy seeds, sugar grains, crumbs, even as it left its own bigger lumps behind. Then it touched the flat edge of Lil's phone, paused, and began gathering its bulk, getting ready to swallow it.

Back at the service area, over the wastebasket, the old woman was working the huge sodden wad with both hands like a batch of dough. She swaddled the thing in fresh layers of towel, cradled it against her paunch, and waddled back. It hit the counter with a splat. With careless strokes, she began to slosh the shit-brown liquid to and fro again. The white cardboard of Alba's plate darkened, then began to melt. The bun on it began to sag. Beside it, the phone was by now just a long soft lump. Alba had long since renounced a rescue. The soup was Lil's vomit from her drinking days, and the children's diarrhea, and her own sick from the night before—so much of what she thought she'd put behind her, returning like the tide.

"Manure can accomplish miracles saints cannot," Alba's grandfather used to say. He was being literal, not wise or poetic, as so many want their peasant ancestors to be. But how smartly she had repurposed him—forgotten that he'd been a narrow-minded bigot who dealt daily with manure as almost his only reliable resource. Likewise, until tonight she had continued to believe that this trial might bring her and Lil closer, heal or dumb their differences, which for years she had tried to treat as petty irritations and nothing more.

Pierre's room was still empty when Lil got back to the ICU. The nurse's station, too, was unmanned. She stood in the corridor listening for some sign of life in the ward. Next door, Elsa's father was lying in exactly the same position as always. In the waiting room, amid the wreckage of Kristen's party, she found Elsa sitting alone. Beside her, a stainless steel cart bore the remains of a huge, penis-shaped pink cake. Half-eaten slabs of it lay in stainless steel kidney trays on the table and chairs. The windowsill was lined with champagne bottles and paper cups, the floor scattered with balled-up wrapping paper. Lil brushed the confetti from a chair and sat down.

"I saw them taking Pierre away," Elsa said.

"For tests," Lil said.

"I thought they did that yesterday."

"That was an MRI, to check for bleeding. This is an electroencephalogram."

Elsa nodded. The long word stirred an old, redundant hope.

"It's hard to keep track," Lil said, "but right now brain activity seems to be their big concern." The technical terms were a language she did not really want to learn. She could only pretend interest in the minutiae. As far as she was concerned, this whole thing was a test with only two possible grades, fail or pass. "How is it?" She nodded at the kidney tray on Elsa's lap, and at that cue Elsa's phone began to ring. Elsa checked the screen, then handed it to Lil, because the caller was Alba. Lil set it face down amid the debris, then drew the cart closer, took one of the scalpels, and cut herself a big slice. The phone rang on.

"I saw forks somewhere," Elsa said, vaguely scanning the mess. "You're not going to answer it?"

On the coffee table, Lil noticed, there was also a half-empty bottle of Japanese whiskey, a pack of tarot cards, a book of temporary Māori face tattoos. *No Pain! No Regrets!* the cover said.

"I don't need any more Alba in my life right now," Lil said when the ringing stopped. "I don't need any more blame, any more explanations, any more plans. All she ever does is tell me what I'm doing wrong. It's my accent. It's the way I sleep. It's the paint I put on the walls. I'm sure even all this"—she stirred the air—"is my fault, too, somehow, in her mind."

"She's terrified," Elsa said generously, "and you're the person closest to her, so of course you bear the brunt." She picked up a champagne bottle, lifted it to the light, and shared its last dribble between two paper cups. "This isn't the first ICU my father has been in. So I know what I'm talking about," she said, draining another empty on top of the first. "You need to remember that one day, one way or another, this thing is going to be over, and you're going to come out the other side."

"She's waiting for nothing to happen," Lil explained. "That's her plan. If from now on he just stays the way he is, that's good enough for her."

They raised their cups in a silent toast, and each took a sip.

"I remember his face when he was born," Lil said. "It was blue. Actually blue. I wasn't ready for that. Like a plum. I remember the look on the doctor's face almost as well. That's how I knew how close we were to disaster. Now I'm starting to wonder if his heart problem—or whatever it is—didn't grow out of that. And to wonder what *that* grew out of. Alba smoking for the first months of the pregnancy? Her overeating? Or the diabetes that came with that?"

"Even if you did know," Elsa said, "what good would that do?"

"I think back to all the last minute complications and wonder what if," Lil went on. "The fact that our own midwife at the very last minute had to cry off. The way they screwed the epidural up. All those little details. Maybe none of which on their own amounted to much, but all together . . . All I know is, it was a very long night, a real mess, very hard on Alba, and then when he finally came out he was blue and I thought he was dead. I really did." She wiggled the stopper out of the whiskey bottle, lifted it to her nose, took a breath. "So when he survived, I swore to myself I'd take every minute that came afterward as a gift. You make yourself those promises, in situations like that."

Elsa nodded. "And you mean them," she said, finishing Lil's thought. While Lil was speaking, Elsa had picked up the tarot pack and cleared the center of the coffee table and now started to deal out the tall cards, very loosely, as though merely checking that she had a full deck. She had no desire whatsoever to referee a couple's spat.

"You know how to use them?"

"I know what each card means. I'm not a medium or anything like that," Elsa said, even as her stubby hands kept dealing onto the low table between them.

"I thought you kind of had to be. Otherwise anyone could do it, couldn't they?"

"There's a lot of nonsense talked about tarot cards. Like they can predict the future, that kind of thing. They're just bits of printed paper with pictures on them. That's something people tend to forget."

"Then what do they do?"

"You've heard of the Rorschach test?"

"Sure."

"Well, that obviously doesn't read your thoughts; it just lets your mind go where it really wants, by a process of suggestion and association, and gives you permission to say those things out loud. The cards are a bit like that." She flipped over the latest cards more slowly, to demonstrate. They were: two dogs howling at the moon, a naked woman pouring water into a pool, a blindfolded woman holding two swords aloft, a jester, a knight on a white horse, a man crucified upside down, a dancing skeleton. "The images are archetypes," she explained. "Images of the Greek and Egyptian and even Babylonian gods. A kind of map of the human mind, cut up into seventy-eight parts."

"Says who?"

"Says the fact that we're here talking about them three or four thousand years later." She turned over another card, which showed a tall young woman scattering seeds in a field. "They've filtered down to us over centuries. Like fairy tales. The ones that survive do so because they hit the right buttons for everybody, one generation after the next."

Lil picked up a plastic fork, wiped it with a napkin, started to pick at the slab of pink cake in her tray.

"The order of the cards isn't determined by some supernatural force," Elsa said. "But it is determined, by an unpredictable and uncontrollable series of events—what we call luck. It has no more or no less meaning than all of us being here in this hospital in Trondheim at the same time. I'll show you. Shuffle the cards."

Lil took the pack but didn't immediately obey. "Why me?" she said. "What's that going to do?"

"It's going to stop you from suspecting there's some trick involved if I shuffle them, that's all. At least if you think it's random, your mind stays open. It's not like you're transferring your secret essence or pheromones or whatever to the cards."

Lil shuffled the cards sloppily, reluctantly handed them back.

"Now we lay them out," Elsa said, even as she squared up the deck like a casino pro. "I'll do that, just because it makes it easier to explain, and then I'll tell you what each card means, and you'll feel one way or another about each of them, and what you feel about the first card will influence what you feel about the next and so on, and your mind will end up telling itself the story that deep down it's most willing to believe."

She started to lay out the tall cards one by one, according to some pattern already present in her mind. Behind them, unseen, Alba stood in the doorway vetting the scene: Lil and Elsa eating cake, sipping champagne, reading the tarot. Several more cards were dealt before she walked forward to where they would notice her.

"Do you want to see this?" Lil asked, too brightly, when she did.

Alba scowled at the cards arrayed on the table. "No." Watching from the doorway, a fear had woken inside her like a sickness, and with each new card that fear had grown, the way fear grows with the number of cards dealt out in black-jack. It is mechanical. Every new card is one card closer to game's end. Of course she wanted to know the future. But if the cards announced misfortune, would misfortune be obliged to come?

"They're tarot cards," Lil explained.

"I know what they are. Where were you? I've been looking for you for hours."

"What does this one mean?" Lil asked.

"The Door," Elsa said. "It generally indicates some kind of transition."

"What's the bright light?"

"What's on the other side of the door is unknown. That may feel like opportunity or danger, which you can accept or resist. Resistance means bringing your fears with you, which is another way of saying trying to keep living your old life. To go through the door willingly, on the other hand, is to embrace change. What that change *is* will be evoked by the other cards. Maybe it means a new relationship, or seeing a current relationship differently. It could be a new lifestyle choice, a new mental perspective, a new sexual attitude . . ."

The longer Elsa spoke, the more afraid Alba felt, as though an actual door had been opened nearby, with a bright light beyond, the kind to lure horror movie victims to calamity, and as Elsa lowered the next card toward its preappointed place, Alba's right arm rose up without thought and slapped it away. Her next swing swept all the cards off the table and across the floor. She strode over them and out of the room.

Without a word, Elsa picked the cards off the floor and off the cake. She wiped them off, arranged them all face down, and slotted them back into their box. Then she gathered the box and whiskey bottle and tattoo book together on the table, for whomever would come to collect them. She drained her cup, nodded sadly at Lil, then went back down the hall to her father.

When everything was quiet, Lil stood up and moved about the waiting room, testing the heavy champagne bottles one by one. They were all empty. Sugar, she knew, would deaden her craving for drink a little, so she cut herself another piece of cake and leaned back in her chair to look up at the rolling news, holding her plate under her chin to catch the crumbs, though the room around her was already a complete mess.

PIERRE'S PHONE STARTED TO RING. It was Dr. Mya. Lil switched to speaker and pointed the thing at Alba like a flashlight.

They had not completed their tests yet, Dr. Mya said, but she wanted to let them know there were strong indications that Pierre's reaction was not of an epileptic character.

Relief coursed through both their bodies like a drug.

"However," she said, "the electroencephalogram results do appear to suggest trauma of some kind." What the extent or consequence of that trauma was, she could not say—perhaps none. "But don't worry," she added, "in light of the episode he suffered, the data is very much within the parameters of what we'd expect."

Alba's mind grabbed *episode* and little else. It was the most merciful word she'd heard in days.

"So it's normal that it's not normal?" Lil asked the object in her hand. She sounded genuinely confused. Her body was still running with its first sensation—relief—and could not switch so cleverly to dismay.

"Absolutely," the doctor said.

It was like one of her mother-in-law's nutty New Age things.

"But what does this mean, practically?" Lil said.

"It means we can attempt another revival whenever we feel the time is right. And that in some respects we do not need to be quite as cautious as before."

She could not yet say for sure when they would bring Pierre back, she told them, winding down the call. In any case, there was no point waiting up. Better to get some sleep. Tomorrow was going to be another big day.

"So what is it, if it's not epilepsy?" This was the question Lil had not dared to ask the phone, but immediately shot at Alba, as Dr. Mya's stand-in, once Dr. Mya hung up. The trembling that afternoon had been so impressive, impossible to imagine it might be anything benign.

"I'm not a doctor," was Alba's defense. Lil's fears were her religion, which no argument could dilute. "And neither are you."

"I don't have a diploma but I do have a brain," Lil countered. "I can still see it's not good, regardless of what she's saying to keep us calm. Or do I have to take every word comes out of her mouth as gospel, like you?"

The family had often gone hiking around Mont Aigoual in the Cévennes, ninety minutes' drive north of Montpellier. Near the weather station there, rain that fell on one side of a ridge flowed south to the Mediterranean, and rain falling a foot away ended up in the Atlantic. The fridge door at home bore a photo of all five of them standing astride that ridge, canteens held high, every second one dribbling it left or right. In Alba's mind, that was where they were now: Pierre's fate was balanced on a knife edge, and the slightest force—even mere suggestion—might be enough to tip it this way or that. It was this power that made Lil flinty and cuntish and shrink inside pessimism as inside a shell, Alba thought—pessimism which was as clear a threat to her son as the tarot had been. To protect him, she needed to shut Lil up. So she said:

"All those times you said you wanted to kill yourself, why didn't you?"

This was so hard a punch that Lil could not immediately counter it.

"Because it's just an escape fantasy and you're a coward," Alba told her. "That's why."

Listening, Lil's face was plaster.

"From now on," Alba ordered, "if you don't have something positive to say, keep your mouth shut."

In the shower, Lil turned the tap full throttle, twisted the head to POWER, closed her eyes, leaned in, and let it pummel her face for as long as she could stand. It was the level of violence she needed just now, to shout all the other violence down.

They were each living their own spoiled dream. Probably it was better that way. All Alba had heard was the pardon, not the new prognosis. Not epileptic was good. Damage to the brain was normal, and normal was good. She had not the courage for pessimism, or even percentages. It was another advantage of her faith: a lifetime's practice at negotiating facts.

Fifteen minutes later, Lil emerged from the bathroom in

a white terry bathrobe, with her damp hair swinging, look-ing like an exclusive spa's brochure client, smugly revived. Alba stood at the window, considering their twin building across the way. The office shelves over there were laden with ring binders, folders, file boxes, all various shades of gray: the record of every life crisis, minor and major, that had occurred in the hospital over the past few years, archived for future reference or statistical analysis.

"What are you thinking?" Lil asked. The kinder tone was amnesty, for Alba's tirade.

A blustery wind was banging on the glass, just inches from Alba's face. "I'm wondering how much I'd pay to have a bath," she said without turning around.

"Have a shower. It'll do you good. The pressure's great up here."

"A shower is for washing. That's not what I'm talking about."

"There must be at least one bath somewhere in the hos-pital," Lil offered. "In the rehab unit or somewhere. Do you want me to ask?" *Ask Kristen*, the ghost.

"I don't want to take a bath in the rehab unit. I want a long hot soak with my own soap and my own candles in my own bath in my own home."

"We don't have a bath anymore."

"I know. You took it out."

Lil refused to resuscitate that argument.

"Anyway I don't mean the apartment, I mean *home* home, in Figueres," Alba said, because she needed to show Lil that her earlier spite was still very much alive.

Lil swung open the window Alba was standing at, push-ing her aside. From below came the beachy whoosh of tires on

slush. Hand over hand, she drew up the beer bag like a bucket
out of a well, took out a can, let the bucket back down. Afterward, she brought two plastic cups and a hairdryer out of
the bathroom, plugged it in, began to work it back and forth
across the frozen can. Eventually she poured a little foam into
each cup and set them with the open can on the nightstand
between the two narrow beds. Another peace offering.

"I thought it would be warm," she said after her first sip.

Still no answer. Alba had not moved from the window.
On the ground floor opposite, in the prosthetics lab, a lone
fluorescent tube was stuttering in a slow motion strobe. Each
flash showed a trail of footprints, black on gray, from the
building's entrance to an empty parking space. Alba felt not
only wiser but better because she'd carried them. Whatever
she thought or felt was, as a consequence, more reliable. As at
a naïve child, she sometimes smiled at Lil's belief in herself as
an equal, blind to the fact that her heart had never flowered as
Alba's had, her choice was all deficit, she lived—unawares—in
the shadow of the life she might have had. Until after María
was born, Alba thought it fair incitement to put her own full
affections on display. In her kindest moments, even now, she
felt pity for Lil. That came easiest when having a cuddle with
one of the kids. Mostly María now. Bath- or bedtime or con-
solation. The wordless access, both ways. The mutual feeding.
The forgotten self.

Later, each woman lay on her own side of the valley,
drinking from her own cup. Lil was watching black and white
war footage on the muted TV. Every now and then she gave
the can another blast, then topped up each cup with more or
less equal amounts.

When the can was nearly empty, out of nowhere Alba asked, "Was Norway on our side in the war?"

"*Our side,* Generalissimo?"

"Franco wasn't Spain."

"Of course not, *camarada.*"

"Remind me again whose side Ireland was on."

"Officially, I think Norway started out neutral," Lil said, pivoting away from her own unhelpful example. "Waiting to see who attacked them first." She was already consulting her phone. "It says the French wanted the British to invade Norway to provoke the Germans and open up a second front. They didn't want to get bogged down in trench warfare like last time around. Here we go: In the end the Germans called their intervention, quote, An armed protection of Norway's sovereignty, end quote. I like that. Very nicely put."

Alba took none of Lil's cues. She was too tired, it was too late, and she had no desire to hear more of her own wild thoughts spoken aloud. She would have liked to kill Lil's chatter, but instead leaned across the divide and grabbed the remote from her hand. She no longer wanted those images in the room, no more than she wanted Lil's certainties, or Lil herself, in her own life. Tonight, like her son, she was too available to harm. So, as though obeying rote-learned instructions, she pointed the remote stiffly at the screen and pressed down hard. Perplexed at the result, she chose another button, pointed, and pressed again, and again, and again, until the screen went black.

They both lay in the dark watching far-off headlights sweep across the ceiling, like cloud shadows in rout across a snowscape. After a while Alba began flipping through her phone—all the calls and texts that had come in since that morning's attempt, and none of which she had answered.

"I think I lost my phone," Lil told the dark, to no reply.

Alba's latest message was from her mother—a photo of María holding a sheet of paper across her chest, crayoned with a big red heart. It was a whole other family once that woman got involved. Her housekeeping done, she switched to Flight Mode and closed her eyes, hoping to let tonight's resentments dilute and dissipate by the fact of not being acknowledged again.

Across the valley, Lil was still staring wide-eyed at the shadows washing back and forth eight feet above her head, making her tired brain suspect the ceiling's solidity. She turned on her side, but shadows were roaming the walls too. They came from distant headlights sieved through bare trees, and from the huge kliegs planted in the grounds to hype the hospital buildings like a landmark. Turning the other way, she saw the shadows' ghosts in the dark window beyond Alba's silhouette. There were no more solid surfaces to contain her, nothing now but warped geometric planes, some sharp, some blurred, all restless, like refracted light in a swimming pool, and Lil at the bottom, being crushed.

Hours later, Lil woke with a jerk, thinking she'd dozed off for a few minutes, no more. She could not get back to sleep. As revenge for Alba's earlier attack, her loose mind began to nurse a rival fantasy, of a new life up here, and she was thrilled at how clearly she could imagine the details—how ready to comply the future seemed to be. Her quirky little apartment. Her local shopkeeper's mute acknowledgments every morning. Her daily pilgrimage to the hospital. Her first

Norwegian words, learned by the bedside, from a children's grammar book. The day nurse correcting her pronunciation, or insisting on hearing progress, bravo. The phone calls home, to the woman still officially her wife, as they learned a new dance, of silence and information and diplomacy. Running into one of the nurses some night in town. Maybe a drink. Maybe more. The Scandinavians understood everything so well. They would have heard the real news in her stiffening phone calls to France. Afterward, Pierre would choose to stay on with her. Neither would want to return to their old life, which each in their own way had outgrown.

Tomorrow was going to be another big day, Dr. Mya had said. So, after twenty minutes tossing and turning, Lil surrendered, slid out from under the covers, crept to the bathroom, and rummaged in Alba's toiletry bag for her mother-in-law's sleeping pills. She managed to grope her way back to bed without banging into anything, then lay quietly for a while, working her jaw and tongue, trying to generate enough spit to wash down the pill, which she could still feel halfway down her throat.

"I know you're awake," she eventually told the dark, meaning, There's no use pretending, we've lived together too long, I know your sulk as well as my own. It was the silence of someone with a secret who does not trust herself. Counting the cost of every promise she's ever made. She was lying over there, Lil knew, like someone holding a brimful glass.

Through the window, she could just see the skeletal frame of the helipad, trimmed with lime green guard lights, jutting over the edge of the roof. A giant mothership promising escape.

As a counterweight to Alba's faith, she had always believed

in her own instinct for unpalatable truths. Such truths she considered almost the definition of wisdom, and thought such wisdom would protect her from dismay, self-disgust, resignation, resentment—the very things that fueled and skewed almost every thought she'd produced these past few days.

"I always used to wake up in the middle of the night," she continued. She spoke as if of a distant epoch, but recently she'd been sleeping poorly again, as panicked and rudderless as in the worst of her youth. "I used to wake up and I wouldn't know where I was, wouldn't understand what I was doing there, or where I was supposed to be. But these past few days, when I doze off and then wake up, I instantly know where I am and why I'm here, and it's worse."

Wanting to counterbalance or compensate for her earlier escapist fantasy, and suspecting the chemical sleep to come would scrub whatever she said, she began to talk to Alba as she'd not talked in years. She spoke of her sleepless nights, and then began to talk about how helpless she felt—how powerless, she meant—and how properly, physically frightened she was. Hoping to soothe the growing note of alarm in her head, she eventually reached across the valley and gently shook Alba's bed. No response. So she reached farther, patting left and right, then crawled her hand under the quilt. The bed was empty but still warm. Feeling both bereft and safe, she swapped over and slid inside and fit herself onto Alba's warmth as best she could, then lay there as the two bodies' distinct shapes melted into one. As a young girl, she had liked to sneak into her father's bed in the early morning, as soon as her father was gone and sure not to return. She enjoyed the warmth, and the perverse satisfaction that it was somehow stolen. With drink in him, he always slept on his back—arms and legs spread, star-shaped—so she would spread herself similarly, shifting a foot here, a hand there, trying to map herself to the heat that other body had left behind. The real warmth, of course, would be afterward. The memory of the shared bed, a bolster for days to come. Now as then, she was afraid of that other person—Alba, her father—unexpectedly returning, to discover her quiet but formidable need.

ALBA WAITED ALONE IN PIERRE'S EMPTY ROOM, listening to the squeals of the gurney wheels near and far. Having cleaned out her own phone, she began to go through his. It too was filled with promises. *There are thousands of interesting people waiting to meet you. Build a house that looks like the life you want to lead. Your satisfaction is our priority. Do you want an erection that is immediate and long-lasting? Don't let yourself down. Health Insurance means Peace of Mind. This is Your Last Chance. Pay Later. Let Us Take You Higher: Lapland. Climb Your Stairs Without Effort. Quick to Install, Easy to Use, and Totally Safe.*

When finally they brought him back, they plugged all his lines in again and settled his covers and arms and head almost exactly as before. When the orderlies were gone, the new nurse made several efforts to chat, but Alba refused every bait, and eventually she dimmed the room to near darkness, as on a night flight.

"You've had a long day," she told Alba. "Maybe it's time for bed."

Such ambitions she'd had—still had—for him, no matter

how rebellious he got, or lazy, or contrarian, or disheveled, or seedy, or thin. But now he looked mortal, as though all those tubes and pumps were draining him of something vital that could never be replaced.

"You need to pace yourself," the nurse said. "In the morning you have to get up and do this all over again."

Still Alba gave no acknowledgment. Perhaps the young woman saw comfort in the promise of routine. But that was the great threat of Pierre waking up: that they would all go home together, finish the renovations, and resume their lives much like before. Only him not waking up might provoke the crisis she otherwise hadn't the courage to precipitate.

"What a mistake," she told him. "And I don't know how to fix it. Maybe I can't."

"What mistake?" asked the over-vigilant nurse.

"Her," Alba said. "The day I met her. The day I answered her first call. The day I said yes. You want me to keep going? I have a long list." Strangers were the best confessors, she'd always found.

"You don't mean that. You're tired and you're upset."

"People say that in situations like this you don't think clearly," Alba said flatly. "But that's exactly what you do. All the usual distractions melt away. And I can tell you, I know with absolute certainty now that I would be better off without that woman in my life."

"The file says you have three children. I'm sure you don't regret that."

"Not for a heartbeat," Alba said.

Of course: you were always willing to take their place, when they were hurt or sick. But what she cleanly, callously wanted now was to trade Pierre for Lil, and have her never wake up. The swap would have fixed everything.

In the distance, a church bell struck three. Certain behavior could be considered a kind of communication, Dr. Mya had said. Meaning the vomiting, the shakes. At the time, Alba had heard that as permission to hope. Now she was not so sure.

"As my mother likes to say, life is short, but the nights are long," she told her son.

Hours of close study by his bedside had revealed something more than nose hairs, cuticles, pimples, pores. What he exuded, she now saw, was indifference to every offering. He was the least concerned of anyone about his state. He had never enjoyed attention, always preferred being uninvolved, withdrawn, safe. That too was Lil's fault—her childish need always to be center stage.

Earlier, Alba had texted a friend: *I wish they'd put me under too, and wake me up when it's all done.*

She was jealous of his machines, wanted to unplug them one by one. They knew exactly what he needed and how to provide it. It was not a fair fight.

Grief remembers what happiness forgets, she had texted someone else. Either she had grown wise or was quoting a love song unawares.

Kristen's farewell party had bothered her in some indirect way. It had also been a reminder that if this went on for just three more weeks, Pierre's twenty-first birthday would have to be celebrated or ignored. Would they buy a cake? Candles? Her first and only boyfriend had died in a car accident when she was fourteen. Sooner or later she and her friends had all sneaked into the graveyard to see the name and date carved on his headstone. Impossible even now to give him another age. Equally impossible to think of Pierre getting older, day by day, as he lay there in the bed. Yet his fingernails were still growing, and his hair, and his beard. Today's youth, tomorrow's molt. So how many candles did you light? Did you buy his favorite cake or one you yourself preferred? Did you take photographs to show him later, the way you showed them photos of when they were little, before their memories overlapped their own lives? Did you cut the cake for the staff? Did you blow the candles out? Did you clap?

Wednesday Morning.

ALBA CAME OUT OF THE BATHROOM with a scowl. In her hand was a *New Scientist* she'd taken from the waiting room, tempted by the main cover line: "Parallel Universes." But only the cover was in English, nothing else. She flung the magazine across the room at the wastebasket, watched it bloom and drop like a shot bird.

"I don't even miss them," she said. "I know I should, but I don't." She sat on the end of the bed, elbows on her knees, head down, like a boxer between rounds. Everything she'd thought so precious—her two other children, her parents, friends, all she'd accumulated over the years—now existed in an entirely separate life.

"If only I'd stayed at home, it would be perfect," Lil said.

"I just mean this all feels like some kind of dream."

They were both talking, in part, to put off the moment when they would have to go downstairs again. Each had a fund of shrewd but anxious anticipation, like a disturbed child or a good horse.

"Ready?" Lil asked.

"No," Alba said. She had not moved from the end of the bed.

"Come on."

"I can't. I can't go through the whole thing again."

"First you stand up," Lil said.

Alba shook her head, less in rebuttal than in disbelief at the terrible foreboding she felt.

"First you stand up and put on your slippers," Lil explained. "Then we walk down the hall and press the button for the lift. You don't have to look any further than that." Her body too had its own truth, and this morning's truth was its sense of routine: three days had passed since their arrival, each much the same as the last, and Pierre was still alive. Catastrophe had missed its chance.

Today's nurse was rigging up a bigger drip bag than any they'd seen before. The stuff inside was lime green, and the sorry way it sat—not unlike Alba's own sick bag on Monday—said it was some kind of paste. Was it because he'd lost too much weight? Or because the doctor knew what was coming and wanted him fortified? They didn't dare ask.

Like medical students, the white coats gathered around to watch the nurse carefully insert the tube tip into Pierre's nostril, then feed it down into him, pinch by pinch. Alba could feel the thing burrowing wormlike down her own nose and throat, but would not let herself look away. *Breathe,* she ordered herself, as though all she really needed was more air.

Besides the feeding tube, the doctors' other concern today seemed to be the machine that regulated Pierre's temperature. That machine stood separate from the rest and was connected by a thick white ribbon cable to his right thigh. With what looked like real tenderness, the hands turned its dials by the tiniest increments. Just as gently, other hands tweaked the taps. Eventually the numbers on the blue screen began to rise, but the body itself gave no obvious answer yet.

In tandem, the level in the lime green drip bag was visibly

draining down. Hunger striker: that was Lil's only credible comparison. Yet another adamant image from her youth. To snub it, she started to shift her X-chair toward the window, but a soft cough called her back. That first cough was soon echoed by something rougher, which sounded like it came from under the bed. Today's trial was starting, the coughs said.

"I feel like a Roman emperor, sitting on this thing," Lil told the room, because of her fear.

The third cough shot a string of green gunk from Pierre's nose, all down his chin. To check her concern, the IV nurse looked to Dr. Mya, who was sifting through a pile of envelopes at the nurse's desk. Only when she'd found the one she was looking for did she lift her head. When Pierre snotted again, she said something in Norwegian to no one in particular. The nurse then leaned over the bed and began drawing the feeding tube back up out of his nose. But the thing seemed endless, like some prop in a magic trick, giving him time to start trembling again, perhaps preparing another cough or something worse, and the nurse started pulling faster—not for his sake, Lil thought, but for her own. She managed to get the whole tube out of him without inducing another spasm, and immediately coiled and dropped it into her red waste bag, then ripped her blue gloves off and dumped those in too, and each of these gestures was done with tired finality, grim job done. To contradict her, there immediately came a muffled gag, which seemed to snag deep inside him and struggle and morph into a bizarre slow-motion jerk, like some stylized mime meant to evoke a dry heave. As inexplicably as it had come, the thing stuttered and died, with no obvious consequence. No spew, no spurt, no pressure relieved. Only a thin green line from each side of his taped mouth, like the telltale tears of a stressed valve.

Lil and Alba looked from Pierre to Dr. Mya, who was watching from the desk, and their only guard against panic was the fact that she still made no move to intervene. In fact, as though demonstratively refusing his call for attention, she picked another envelope from her pile, slid her scalpel under the flap, and, in a way that seemed particularly vicious to Lil, flicked the blade. She drew out and scanned the contents, crumpled and dropped them in the wastebasket at her feet. In answer or objection, a giant ripple now wrecked right through the length of Pierre's body, first arching his back, then lifting his head off the pillow and hosing a spray of green all over the bed.

All of the scrubs leaning over him took one step backward in perfect synchronization, as in a dance routine.

The color and texture of the stuff reminded Alba of a health-kick smoothie, some blend of avocado, seaweed, kale. It reminded Lil of her grandmother's Famine stories—relayed from her own grandmother in turn—of bodies strewn along the ditches, mouths overflowing with the slime of half-digested grass.

How he could vomit with the breathing tube in was hard to conceive. Gullet versus windpipe, perhaps. But cough by cough, spurt by spurt, his body seemed determined to eject every drop of gunk they'd pumped into it.

Still they waited for Dr. Mya to intervene, as she had on the previous two days—not just to order a pause but to send him back down, let him recover, try again some other time. But no matter how hard he shook and bucked and gagged, that full reprieve never came. Not when they hit 34. Not when they hit 35. Each time, she watched the rodeo for longer and longer before lifting her casted arm and patting the air. Then the neurologist would adjust the dials and he would be calmed, but a few minutes later the conductor's arm would lift again, to drive on.

As the morning passed, more hands seemed to be fiddling with more buttons, dials, and drips than ever before, to no obvious scheme. As though hoping to stumble on a solution by pure blind luck, Lil thought. Or trying to wear him down. Something in herself was definitely being bullied into submission by each bout of heaves.

It was because of the number three, Alba believed. The fairy tale third time. The last chance, which must be seized.

As the next bout began, Dr. Mya went to the doorway, leaned out into the corridor, and called back three of the white coats from earlier, and when that bout wore itself out, she herded the strangers to the window, to huddle and whisper, as though she'd reached the limit of her own competence and was sounding the hospital's general opinion as to what else might be done.

When the conference was over, Dr. Mya turned to Pierre's parents. Pierre could not be revived unless they lowered the sedation, she said. But less sedation meant more sensation, inevitably. She meant that the more awake he was, the more he could feel, and at present what he felt most keenly was the thick plastic tube rooted right down his throat. That's what the heaves were: Pierre's body attempting to eject the foreign object, the only way it knew how. And here Dr. Mya extended her arm toward the bed, where Pierre was trembling again, prime example of his own pathology.

So, if they wanted to wake him up, they had to take the

tube out—but could only do so if he showed himself capable of breathing without it. She pointed at the two horizontal lines on the respirator screen. The red line was labeled DEPENDENT. The green, AUTONOMOUS. She touched the point at which the green sloped up off the horizontal, then touched the point where it grounded again. "From here to here is him breathing on his own," she said. Their job now was to watch those two lines, to track how long he could survive without the machine.

Lil dragged her X-chair over to the bed, took hold of Pierre's left hand, and started to count. How many breaths per minute he managed alone. How long he lasted. How long of a rest he needed before giving it another go.

The green line would wake, start to rise, but soon droop and die again, every time. It was a taunt. Now he's breathing. Now he's not. Lil timed him by the clock in the blue screen's bottom right corner. That, not his face, was the real story now. Watching it, she mouthed the numbers. One. Two. Three. Willing him to last longer each time before the machine kicked in or another bout of gagging cut him off. Soon she was getting to four and five and six. When she finally got to ten, she could not help herself, hissed, "Keep going, come on," as though he were a client at the gym, or she one of those cranked Saturday morning mothers at the edge of the judo mat.

Even as a child, he'd always been apprehensive, all inward attention, too ready to fail. Maybe that was their fault. Each in her own way had entertained his weakness: Alba always too quick to pick him up, and Lil too eager to throw him in at the deep end. But now the day Lil had often warned of had come: he was on his own. There was nothing either of them could do any more to help.

"Eight, nine, ten," Lil coached. Her voice quiet yet rich with threat, and perfectly audible to the whole room. To Alba it sounded like hide-and-seek, or some other playground contest, see who was best at holding their breath.

"*Eleven*," Lil announced. "Well done, that's your best yet. Now rest, and when you're ready, we'll try again."

Counting the seconds, she lost all sense of time and could not afterward say how long she'd spent tracking the numbers on the blue screen. But by three in the afternoon something had definitely changed. There were no more doctors' discussions by the window, no more scrubs swanning in and out. Except for Pierre and Lil, everyone was quiet, and the whole room heard each clean beep, and the glum electric hum, and the loud gasp whenever the respirator kicked in again, as though the breath held was its own. Meanwhile, Lil kept droning out the numbers like a roll call, and even fractional headway felt like big news. The first time he made it to thirty seconds. The first time he made thirty-five. But the progress wasn't linear. It wasn't brick by brick. Now he was lasting almost a minute every time, and now he could not even get to ten.

How easy it was, she thought, to just never wake up, leave them their sick lives and embellished grief. How stupid, to leave something so important to someone so soft and unwilling, rather than to a fighter like herself. How ready she was for him to fail.

"Pierre," Lil said a little louder, "if you want us to take that thing out of you, you have to breathe. You. Not the machine."

Make it happen had been her own father's mantra, against

every appeal for help, and that is what she now ordered her son to do.

She felt a hand on her shoulder. It was Dr. Mya, squatting by the bed, her face so close that Lil could smell the sour warmth of the woman's breath.

Right now, she explained, Pierre didn't need encouragement. His body naturally wanted to breathe. "Let him be," she ordered Lil.

Let him fail, Lil heard. Waste the only window of opportunity he might ever have. But she nodded to show she understood, then she let go of his hand and sat back in her chair, and when the green line woke again, she acknowledged it only with her eyes.

A few minutes later, she stood up, walked quietly out of the room, and headed down the corridor toward the waiting room, but a gaggle of voices from that direction turned her back. The door of Elsa's father's room was ajar. She went in. He was alone. To anchor herself, she braced both hands against the partition wall, took a long deep breath, blocked it, and let the pressure build. With deliberate slowness, she let all the air inside her out. When her lungs were empty, she took another huge breath. It was the drunk's trick, trying to husband her own rising tide.

The old man behind her meant nothing, but the body in the bed on the other side of the door was a new kind of close: not her son but her choking twin. Her own breaths were what lifted the green line off the horizontal and kept it aloft.

Detach, the Buddha says. Because attachment is suffering. You will grow old. You will grow weak. You will die. You will not be loved the way you want to be.

Alba had quickly taken Lil's place in the X-chair, and immediately took hold of Pierre's hand. As a child, he had always loved her touching his face, caressing his hair, stroking his arm. So that is what she started to do now, sitting by the bed, speaking in a calm, reassuring voice, telling him over and over again, "Don't worry, Maman's here. Everything's going to be all right." After a while, in something very like her normal voice, she began to tell him his own story, backward. First she told him what courses he was taking this semester. She told him about essays he'd written for Sciences Po in Strasbourg. About his year in *prépa*, his *bac*, his bikes. Year by year, she rewound the tape. His girlfriends. His holidays. His first day at school. She talked about his crèche as if it were yesterday, and the springer spaniel, Rags—*Wags*, little Pierre had pronounced it—he'd loved more selflessly than he would ever love anything all the rest of his life. Any detail at all that occurred to her from his first years, she mentioned—the fairy tales, his favorite foods, the names of his teddies, teachers, nanny, the entire cast—until she was merely throwing phrases at the boy's head, like trigger words for the brainwashed or the hypnotized. She was somehow testing the quality of his childhood or her own mothering, and his failure to react felt like the loudest possible rebuke.

At one point, she caught Dr. Mya looking at her and expected correction of the kind given to Lil, but the woman held her eye and nodded approvingly. "Sing the songs you sang when he was a baby," she said. "Those are really burned into his brain." Meaning: they might spark something, if anything can. So Alba began to sing him the old lullabies she had once used to put him to sleep, all the while stroking his hair and face. At one point, between songs, she asked him to squeeze her hand to show that he could hear her, but got no response. And when another bout came on soon afterward, she started to bargain. If You save him, she began. If You give him back to us, no matter what his state, I will accept—*no, too mean*—I will love him as he is, no matter what. He began to hack harder than ever, and she leaned back out of the way but didn't let go of his hand. I will love them *all*, she offered now, upping the stakes. With all their faults, just as You love me with mine. That was the highest price she could think of just then.

When he was calmed, she leaned back in and began to sing again more or less where she'd left off, and between songs she kept telling him, "Pierre, if you can hear me. Pierre, if you can open your eyes. Make a noise. Squeeze my hand. Give me a sign."

About four o'clock, Dr. Mya came and stood right by Alba's shoulder, breathing noisily, nasally, for a strangely long time. Then, with a beaten tone, as though conceding to a suggestion not her own, she said, "All right, let's try taking it out."

The event gathered in several more doctors and nurses, as though eyewitnesses were needed, in numbers, to corroborate afterward the official account of the procedure, and to confirm that the proper protocols had all been observed.

"Should I get out of the way?" Alba asked.

"Keep doing what you're doing," Dr. Mya told her. "We can work around you."

First, a purple scrubs began to pick at one of the bandages holding his tube in place, jabbing her fingernail at the frayed white threads again and again until a corner curled up. Then she began to pull. The slow rasp made Alba hold her breath, then wince as it ripped free of his face.

On the monitor, the red was flatlined now, and the green ragged as a seismograph. *Even if* ghosted Alba's every hope. Even if they managed to get the tube out. Even if they managed to wake him. What would she be satisfied with? Awareness? Recognition? Motor skills? Or was that too greedy? Would she have to up her bid? What would she give, for instance, for him at least to be able to talk?

When Lil reappeared, having heard their plan from the far side of the partition door, it was to force herself to watch, the way she had forced herself to watch the birth, knowing she would want the memory, no matter how it turned out. As she arrived, the nurse was drawing the big black tube up out of him, hand over hand, like a thick rope. The thing seemed preposterously long. Perhaps it needed to be, to reach right down into the lungs. It reminded Lil of a circus-act porn scene where the girl draws an obscenely long dildo up out of her throat. With a slurp and a pop, the end slid free and for a moment, dripping, swayed back and forth above his face. As though her own body had been delivered of that same giant splinter, what Lil felt—inside her horror—was sheer physical relief.

A nurse quickly strapped a transparent mask over his nose and mouth. The machine would continue to complement his own breathing when necessary, Dr. Mya said.

Watching the mask clear and fog, Alba continued to sing.

"What makes you think he can hear you?" Lil said.

So, very deliberately, as to a failing parent, Alba asked, "Pierre, Can You Hear Me?"

It was not yet half past four, but the afternoon's dusk had darkened again completely, making a black mirror of the big window and showing them another room beyond—blind, deaf, and dumb—like a home design hack to create the illusion of space where there is none.

When no answer came to her question, Alba said again, just as stiffly as before, "Pierre, if you can hear me, squeeze my hand."

Feeling a slight pressure, she did not know how to react. She was wary of her own fantasies, and far more at ease with the suspicion that this might be further sign of his body's absolute disarray, because he was still in a coma, still heavily sedated, making it all but impossible, mechanically, for him to hear and respond to what she'd said. So she turned for an expert witness. Dr. Mya was within reach. Alba grabbed her arm.

"He *moved*," she said, and instantly had the doctor's undivided attention.

"Tell me exactly. What did he do?"

Half choked with emotion, Alba managed to say, "I asked him to squeeze my hand and he did."

"Which one?"

She lifted the right hand an inch off the sheet.

"Take his other hand and tell him to squeeze that," Dr. Mya ordered, and Alba felt pinched by such skepticism— that the woman's first, ungenerous thought could be so close to her own: that this was some freak twitch, legacy of the earlier spasms, or merely wishful thinking on a hysterical mother's part.

"Come *on*," Dr. Mya said, but Alba was afraid to test her son a second time, in case he didn't respond.

In all their time in the hospital, this was the only occasion on which they saw Dr. Mya impatient in any way. Shaking her head, she stepped in front of Alba and pulled Pierre's hand into her own. Alba expected some attempt at imitation—her touch, her voice, her Catalan—but there was none. In her distilled English, the doctor loudly ordered the body in the bed: "Pierre Casals, squeeze my hand."

It wasn't fair, Alba thought. He wouldn't respond and would be judged to have failed the test, because in his current state how could he be expected to understand any voice but his mother's, and anything but his mother tongue?

Then the betrayal: the pale fingers shriveled slightly in that stranger's hand. Dr. Mya reached across his body, took his other hand, and ordered him to squeeze that. Again, Alba thought she saw the fingers tighten, but tried to read the doctor's face for definite news. Through every trial so far, her flat, professional demeanor had checked Alba's fears, yet how relieved she would have been had the woman made some show of emotion now.

"It's definitely a response" was all Dr. Mya would concede. "What type exactly is hard to say."

A few minutes later, Alba's phone started to ring. It was her father—the witness she'd been waiting for. So she walked out into the hall, toward the elevators, where the reception was best. If the doctor was too careful to acknowledge Pierre's milestone, she was not. She would give her father the best possible version of today's events, tell him they'd removed the respirator tube, that Pierre was now breathing almost entirely on his own, that he seemed to have heard her voice, and another woman's voice, in two different languages, and understood both, and not only understood but actually responded, physically, even if he had yet to open his eyes or actually speak. It felt like her own achievement—her gift, unbreakable—which her father, for once, would have no way to cheapen or refuse.

"*Papa*," she said, all but choking on the word.

Before she could calm herself enough to go on, Lil appeared at Pierre's door, looking up and down the corridor like someone set to cross a busy street. Their eyes met and Lil made that rough sweeping gesture she had always used to call the children in from play. Alba pressed the phone to her chest to screen her father from whatever awful news was about to be shouted at her.

"Quick! He's awake!" Lil barked, then retreated through the doorway.

Forgetting to hang up, Alba ran after her, deaf to her father's foil-thin voice calling from a great distance: "*Reina*, what is it, tell me, what happened, what's happening, I can still hear you, can you hear me, I'm still here!"

On the phone, Alba's father heard what sounded like footsteps. Then a static scratching—his daughter's hand?—across the mouthpiece. Then a silence he was tempted to exploit, shout into the handset in the hope of being heard, beg someone to explain, please, what was going on.

Then: *Do you know who I am?*

The voice was Alba's, at a great distance, in Catalan.

There was no audible answer.

Next, a new voice, Scandinavian, speaking in English, asking a list of questions, with long gaps for answers he never heard. *Can you hear me? What is your name? What year is it? How old are you? Do you know where you are?* Somehow he felt those questions—and their beginner's English—were directed at him, at the lonely end of the line. It was a fantasy, of course, of the attention he wanted but knew he didn't deserve.

Before he dared say anything, he heard his daughter's voice again, saying, *It's Maman, I'm here, don't worry, everything's going to be all right.*

So it went. Alba's phone lying on the covers at Pierre's feet, her father at the far end listening to—squinting at—the scraps of sound ghosting their way to him from Trondheim. So far he'd heard only women's voices, and did not dare interject his own.

Pierre, Lil cut in, much louder, *tell me, in chronological order, the presidents of the Cinquième République.*

Lil! protested Alba.

But no objection from any of the staff. Only silence, as everyone waited for an answer. In Figueres, too, her father held his breath. His grandson was a student of political science. The question was fair.

Then—tiny, troubled—a wounded animal sound. Something like the word *all*, as spoken by a hoarse old man.

Louder, Lil ordered. *As clearly as you can. We need to know that you understand.*

"De Gaulle!" he wanted to shout, to spoil the women's quiz, or as a prompt that Pierre might hear and repeat, even mechanically, and earn himself a little more time before being condemned.

De Gaulle, came the echo down the phone.

Go on, said Lil, with little warmth. *Next.*

Pomp—, the damaged voice started to say, but the name seemed to catch in his throat, and as though to clear it, there was a cough, and the cough snagged on something solid, and started to gag.

Alba's father held his breath until the gagging was done.

Give me a wipe, his daughter said.

The silence was longer this time. But eventually: *Giscard.*

And one by one, in the right order, in that old man's voice, all the French presidents' names.

DURING HER FIVE YEARS IN THE ICU, the ward nurse had seen all kinds of sorrow and never once cried, but she was crying now, at the end of Pierre's bed. Lil and Alba, however, were trailing some way behind her in time: they looked stunned, did not yet dare push past their suspicion of these strange new facts (he could hear, think, talk), which their brains recognized but their bodies were still braced against.

Dr. Mya thumbed open his eyelids and baited his pupils with her penlight. She lifted his elbows and let them fall.

She folded back the bedcover, raised his knee to a right angle, tapped at it with her little pink hammer, then lay the leg down straight again. It was only then that Alba's body began to stir, as though the doctor had been striking her.

The staff needed no such spur. Within minutes, the rumor had spread, and from all over the ward the scrubs began to gather in the doorway, soon forming a queue out into the hall, with those at the back standing on tiptoe to catch a glimpse of the miracle.

At the bed, Dr. Mya turned to Lil and Alba when she was done. "Considering everything he's been through, most of the signs are promising," she said. "But we're not out of the woods yet. For the moment, we'll continue to monitor and sedate him."

The new word widened Alba's eyes like a spell. "*Sedate?*"

"Just to send him over the edge," Dr. Mya said, as though the image was a reassuring one. Seeing their threatened faces, she explained as best she could: that the sedative would be nothing like what they'd been giving him previously, neither in quantity nor effect; that the *réveil*, as they'd seen, had been physically taxing, flooding his body with adrenaline; that they needed to bring him down again, to let him fall asleep, rest, and begin the long process of recovery.

WHEN THE CROWD WAS GONE, the two women sat quietly by the bed, studying Pierre's face for some sign that the drugs were kicking in. His half-shut eyes reminded Alba of an infant's, unable to focus at any distance, seeing only abstract patterns of changing light—the shapes of a face, perhaps, but not the face itself. Every few minutes he gave another quiet cough, as though still troubled by the residue of what had been pumped into him. But those coughs grew softer and further apart. His body was winding down. As it did, Alba felt her own stunned body coming more and more to life, beginning to catch up with the facts of the *réveil,* and she began to pick apart with increasing vigor what Dr. Mya had said. Which signs were *not* promising? Hadn't she seen the ward nurse's tears? The vitamin smiles of all the other staff? Weren't there certain things only a conscious body could do?

When, about seven o'clock, the eyelids lifted briefly, she shifted her chair to put herself in his sight line to no effect. His gaze still slid over everything. This was a comfort to Lil: it said that the drugs were working, that he could rest and recover now for the night. To Alba, it posed more threat than the coma: despite all her attentions, she did not yet exist— even as an idea—for her son. So she took his hand and began to stroke it again, and to caress his hair and face, and spoke to him with a voice that was warm, calm, devoted, not to anchor him in the world but to send him away with the best possible impression of a mother's care, wherever he was going, to sustain him until he came back.

"It would be best to disturb him as little as possible," the nurse said, seeing Alba beginning to fuss with him again. "What he really needs now is rest."

"Rest!" she wanted to shout. "He's been in a coma for five days!" But she let go of his hand and leaned back in her chair.

"Let's go out," Lil said then.

"*Out?* Where?"

"Anywhere that's not here. Somewhere in town. Get a drink. Celebrate."

"He's just woken up."

"And now he's sleeping, and they said he'll sleep all night. He's exhausted."

Alba plucked one of the baby wipes from their box, ran it along the lower edge of the mask.

"We'll go out some other night," she said. Raising three children had taught her nothing. All her moments pointed backward. Her fear had such confidence in itself.

"Tonight's the night he woke up. There's not going to be another one of those."

"Make sure you eat something," Alba said as Lil left.

For about an hour, Alba sat and watched Pierre breathing inside his mask. The rhythm was steady, and his sleep undisturbed. Eventually she opened her laptop. *Hello everyone,* she typed. She knew no way of declaring her news to the world except with the stiffness of a formal wedding or birth announcement. *It gives us great pleasure to announce that after two failed attempts to bring Pierre out of his coma, the third attempt, made today, Wednesday 1st, has succeeded. Since then, Pierre has answered questions in English, French and Catalan,* she wrote, proud parent. *He shows no obvious brain damage or debility,* she wrote, on her own authority. Her message was trying to work the same spell as Lil's celebration. *The doctors seem genuinely surprised at his recovery. Perhaps that means they were more pessimistic than they let on, but I guess it was better we didn't know that. Only a few hours ago such a recovery was beyond our wildest dreams, and the worst outcome imaginable still seemed a very real possibility. Of course we still have to wait for official confirmation as it were from new tests the doctors will perform over the next few days but it feels like we've come a long way in a very short time. We thank you all for your support and prayers over the past week and we send you all our love. Lil and Alba.*

Wednesday Evening.

DOWN IN THE STREET, as Lil passed the Kvinne-Barn hospital block, a battered white HiAce pulled up to the curb. The driver leaned over to roll the passenger window down. It was Dr. Mya, in her running gear. "Come on," she shouted, gunning the engine. "If I stop too long, I'll stall and you'll have to push."

"Slam it," she said after Lil got in.

Lil opened the passenger door again and slammed it shut.

"Harder," Dr. Mya ordered. "As hard as you can."

Once they were moving again, Lil leaned forward to inspect the floor, then twisted around to check the back. She could hardly believe that someone so precise, so diligent, and so fragrant, could tolerate such filth.

"I'm not going to apologize for the mess because it's not mine, it's my brother's," Dr. Mya said. "I hit a deer last month. The bastard just bounced off and ran away but my car was wrecked."

The wipers squeaked back and forth across the windshield, in and out of sync with the white rosary beads swinging from the rearview mirror.

"I see your brother is a . . . man of faith," Lil said, choosing her words.

"Actually, those are mine. Salvaged from the car. But it's not what it looks like, they're more of a good luck charm."

"Didn't save your car."

"No, but I walked away with barely a scratch." She showed Lil her casted arm.

"Some people would call that more than a scratch."

"The truth is, I got them from one of my patients."

"Strange present if you're not religious."

Dr. Mya gave no answer.

"I'm sorry," Lil said.

"Officially I had no right to take them," she said, "but when someone has no family I know what happens to anything left behind, so I took them and they remind me of her, that's all. Not in a bad way. You form an attachment to certain people without really knowing why."

When they paused at the next junction, she had to jerk the stick and rev hard, learner driver overdose, to get going again.

"I guess you're going out to celebrate," she said.

"If I don't celebrate this," Lil said.

The van was now home to a faint but odious smell.

"Do you know where you're going?"

"Some place that serves alcohol. Any recommendations?"

"You're going alone?"

"Alba doesn't celebrate. It's against her religion. But you're more than welcome to join me. On my tab. A few drinks and you might tell me just how close we were to disaster."

"I'm on my way to target practice," Dr. Mya said, lifting both hands from the wheel, the better to display her gear. "But I'd be happy to show you a place that doesn't charge tourist prices. And we'll have a drink together another night. I promise you that."

She parked on a dark side street, then led the way. Standing at the first corner was a young Black woman in knee-high boots, too-tight jeans, with too-perfect hair. Lil caught and held her eye from a long way off and the girl said something in a bright voice as she passed. The doctor smiled to herself, and a few yards on Lil asked why.

"The expression she used. *Would you like something sweet?*"

"She has a good radar. I'll give her that," Lil said. "But I'd have to bring you along to translate."

"I'm sure she speaks some English. Certainly enough for the basics."

"What makes you think I'd be satisfied with the basics?"

"She probably has a card. Want me to get it for you?"

"Lead me not into temptation," Lil said. Then: "Although I definitely need something."

"A drink."

"A drink, yes," Lil said, knowing it was not the full truth. The encounter on the corner had planted a new thought in her mind.

The bar Dr. Mya led her to was grubby and dress-down gay. After her first sip of beer, she noticed a smudge of fuchsia on the rim of her glass. She didn't complain and didn't wipe it off. She drank sip by sip until the rim was clean, scanning the clientele and glancing several times at a table at the bar's back end, at a familiar-looking face. A version of a younger Alba? Certainly the type Lil used to like.

Lil didn't go to her directly, but chatted first with an older woman at the counter. The woman's English was too lame to get beyond niceties, and afterward Lil ambled about, eavesdropping, less to hear what this or that group was saying than what language they were saying it in. A group standing near the girl was speaking a mixture of English and Norwegian, and Lil lingered on the fringes but no one offered her an opening line. A few minutes later, as those people began gathering their things, the girl stood up, took a strange roundabout route through the bar, then on her way back slickly palmed a pint glass one of the women was leaving behind, still half full. This gave Lil permission to walk over uninvited and sit down.

"Enjoying your drink?" she asked.

The girl drank, holding Lil's eye.

"Do you speak English?"

The girl nodded.

"Are you drunk?"

"If this is drunk, I want my money back," the girl said. Her accent sounded vaguely Midwestern, but flattened by aspiration or exile.

The barman came to collect the empties from the neighboring table and gave a glance in their direction that was something other than care.

"Can I buy you one of your own?" Lil said.

She caught the barman's eye and pointed at their two glasses.

"What's it going to cost me?" the girl asked.

"Nothing."

"Something that costs nothing. That's a first."

Lil didn't even acknowledge that first thrust. "What are you, twenty? Twenty-one?"

No answer.

"Hard to say with that drinker's face you have."

"You'd have to see me with my clothes off, is that it?"

It was a prebaked line, but Lil needed a moment to recalibrate. The barman arrived with their drinks and slid the bill toward her.

"I'm sorry if that sounded like an interrogation," Lil said. "Let's start over."

The girl downed the dregs of the one she'd filched.

"All right, I'll go first," Lil offered, feeling the same mixture of embarrassment, dismay, and sympathy at the girl's hostility as she did whenever she thought of her younger self. "I'm forty-six years old. Irish originally, but I've lived for twenty-odd years in the south of France. How I ended up so far from home is a story in itself, but let's skip that. You want to know what I'm doing in Trondheim?"

The girl deflated slightly. "Season One, Episode One. Here we go."

"All right," Lil said. "You don't have to listen to my story. But I'd like to hear yours."

"Why?"

"Young American woman in a dive dyke bar in Norway in winter, scrounging slops off the tables. And that's the punchline. Makes me curious about the buildup."

"I knew you'd come over," the girl said. The facts of her life, and Lil's equanimity, had procured her the right to announce her private thoughts as though the world had endorsed them.

"Maybe you've a higher opinion of yourself than you like to admit."

"There's a lot better-looking in here than me," the girl parried. "Why don't you try them?"

"Because you look like someone I used to know a long time ago, who I should have been a bit kinder to at the time." The sense of recognition Lil felt was coming into focus. It was not just the priestly clothes and the convict haircut: the longer she looked into that defiant face across the table, the more she saw a younger version of herself. "Plus you speak

English," she said. "Plus you're desperate or lonely enough to let a stranger buy you a beer."

"A beer doesn't buy you anything. Just keeps me sitting here the time it takes to down it."

"What would buy me more?"

"If you're looking for a trick you're in the wrong place."

"Who said anything about tricks?"

"What then? You want to adopt me?"

Toward the front of the bar, a bearish man in a plastic Viking helmet was moving from table to table with an old-fashioned pram full of red roses, with no success.

"Talk. Walk," Lil said. "Maybe get a drink someplace else."

"Sounds like a date."

"Call it what you want."

"For how much?"

"Name your price," Lil said, partly from curiosity, partly as a dare to herself.

"You want me to eat you out, is that it?"

"That's not what I was thinking of when I came over here."

"But you're thinking of it now?"

"You really don't have to talk like that."

"If that's what you want, go down the street to the docks."

The Viking flower seller stopped before them, obviously with no great hope, but Lil asked him how much, then counted out some coins into his hand. She offered the rose across the table and batted her eyes.

The girl scoffed but refused to take it. "What the fuck am I supposed to do with that?"

"You're meant to take it as a token of undying affection. Or a peace offering. Or a joke, to break the ice." She stood the rose in the girl's half-finished beer. She'd had a bit of good luck today, she explained, and wanted someone to share it with. All they were going to do was walk around the town, have a drink, maybe something to eat. "How does that sound?"

"Sounds like a thousand kroners' worth."

Lil took a moment to convert and consider the price. It was obviously a figure picked out of the air. "Five hundred an hour," she proposed.

"We're negotiating now?"

Lil raised her glass to seal the deal. Still the girl stalled. "First hour up front," she said.

Lil counted the notes onto the table one by one.

The girl folded and tucked the wad into some kind of secret slit sewn inside the waistband of her jeans.

"Plus drinks," she said.

"Okay."

"Christ, you must be desperate."

"What I am, actually, is happy. *Way* more dangerous."

"You win the lottery?"

"Even better," Lil said. "Until earlier this evening, my son was five days in a coma, and now he's awake and it looks like he's going to be absolutely fine."

The girl's mutinous look did not color even a shade.

"A real wake-up call, if you'll forgive the pun," Lil said, and sounded almost proud. Gratitude, relief, and joy were emotions she had not much practiced, and mostly they made her uneasy, but right now she was hard in the grip of a fantastic physical exhilaration and it needed a release. She needed to talk—even to brag—about her luck, as though it was an achievement, the way a child sometimes does.

They walked toward the river. Shuffling down the slope to the park, the girl grabbed Lil's arm to steady herself, and at the bottom Lil tightened her grip but the girl pulled free.

"Just talk and walk, you said."

So Lil searched her wallet and brought out a hundred-kroner note.

In the park they met no one, and their steps on the frozen snow sounded not just amplified but multiplied, like far greater numbers marching in time. A little farther on, Lil paused to approve the cathedral across the water. A pair of ducks cruised silently by. On the bank opposite, the wind was bouncing the snow-stacked branches of a fir tree up and down, and she thought—tried to imagine—she heard them groan.

"She know you're out here tonight with someone half your age?" the girl asked, to spoil the silence.

"She knows I'm not with her," Lil said. "That's what counts."

Farther along, set well back into the park, stood a lone wooden house with a white picket fence, a porch, dormer windows in a pitched roof, like an isolated farmhouse in some hardship tale of the American Midwest. A line of small—children's?—footsteps led to it across the snow. Frozen solid, like forensic molds. As soon as she saw them, Lil let go of the girl's hand and veered off the path. "Now I know where I am," she called back. "Come on. This is a shortcut."

Left, right, she set her boots into the dark sockets, hoping the compressed snow would hold her up. Sometimes it did—bore her entire weight—for two or three or four steps, but then her leg would pass through the crust as through paper and plunge to the knee. Following, the girl took care to place her feet exactly where Lil had, where the compacted surface was less likely to give way.

They came out onto the cobbled streets of the Old Town. Left and right, each wooden house—painted mustard, olive, rust—had its own blue enameled number plate, just like in France. With the girl on her arm again, Lil strolled past them proudly. The trek uphill through the snow had set the breath pumping in and out of her and set her whole body aglow—an exhilaration she'd been desperate for, unawares, since Pierre woke.

To welcome them, the shops and restaurants were havens of polished silver, shining skin, sparkling glass, and it felt not just like a less troubled part of town, filled with a sense of celebration, but a new, better part of her own life. Every uncurtained window she looked into confirmed the fantasy. Yet for once she did not feel excluded. The outdoors was just as magical. Skeletal trees beaded with bulbs and wired with secret speakers piping a childhood Christmas into the street. Every door hung with a fat Christmas wreath. Even the first café they came to had tea candles inside storm lanterns on the terrace tables, and a big basket of sheepskins for anyone who wanted to sit outside. The temptation of something so soft and safely animal made Lil pull her free hand from her glove and caress them as she passed. Lone snowflakes swam the air. She too was floating along. She hadn't yet called or texted anyone. Plenty of time later to share. Just tonight, she wanted to be a tourist again in her own life.

Farther on, they passed a violin maker's, a snug little basement shop aglow with wood-toned ochers and ambers and burgundies and a workbench scattered with clamps and skeletal body parts and pots of glue. Farther on again, they passed scabby club chairs and fraying Louis XV fauteuils set outside a brocante, under a vast plastic sheet heaving and sighing like the night sea. They passed an empty sushi place, low lighting on brushed steel, with a circulating conveyor belt inside the window, carrying just one lonely plate—a pair of labial-looking tuna sashimi—instead of the endless selection it was made for. Next door, a Salvation Army store with all its lights out. They crossed a footbridge, on the far side of which the snow underfoot was no longer dry and clean, but gray slush stirred with grit. They passed a tackle shop, two Asian supermarkets, two tattoo parlors, the Glory Revival Ministry. Like Lil's beer buzz, the dream had begun to stale.

"I should have said I'd pay you per word," she said to raise a spark, but got no reply.

As they passed the Little Big Horn Steak Restaurant, Lil saw the girl glance in the window, where a dozen lobsters were writhing one over the other in a grubby fish tank. Beyond them, a big group of businessmen were all laughing and leaning back in their chairs.

The waiter led them to a window table facing the dock across the street. The other tables were all middle-aged couples except for the businessmen and a family party against the back wall. Lil watched her date reading down through the menu line by line, whispering the dishes' names under her breath, as though the feel of the words in her mouth might suggest their taste.

"Do you eat meat?" Lil asked.

"Every chance I get."

Across the street, three blue plastic barrels stood just

outside the Ravnkloa Fish Shop's front door. Beyond was a loading area, and a lone trawler moored at the quay.

The waiter came back with no notebook. Lil folded the menu shut.

"The Chateaubriand, *saignant,* with Lyonnaise potatoes," she said. "*S'il vous plaît.*"

"*Très bien.* Would you like something to drink?"

With a perfect accent, Lil named a bottle of Saint-Emilion.

"*Très bien,*" the waiter said again.

"You like getting exactly what you want, don't you?" the girl said.

"Know anyone who doesn't?"

When the waiter came with the wine, he showed Lil the label and poured a splash into her glass without even looking at her companion. Lil tasted, swilled, swallowed, then nodded sternly.

"Knock yourself out," she insisted, seeing the girl look warily at her wine. "All you can eat and drink, on someone else's tab. And in exchange, you just have to make a wisecrack every now and then."

Offering herself as an example, she took another drink. Then got out her phone to immortalize the moment: a middle-aged woman and her wineglass in a world of light. Across the table, as though taking her cue, the girl got out her own phone.

"No screens," Lil said with real hurt in her voice. "Please."

But the girl wanted her phone as a tool, not a distraction: she tapped it against the bell of her wineglass, hard. Several heads turned. "Time's up," she said, and downed the rest of her drink.

"Remind me of the rate."

"Ten kroner a minute."

Lil fished out a hundred-kroner note and laid it on the table.

"No rose? The romance is going out of this relationship fast." She took the note and poured herself another full glass.

"Now the meter's back to zero," Lil said, "why don't we try to have some kind of an adult conversation?"

"You mean why don't I sit here listening to you talk about yourself and your good luck?" Instead of placating her, the latest payment had provoked another surge of resentment, that Lil could make it—and she take it—so easily.

"Is someone else's good luck really that hard to listen to?"

"You're paying me to listen. Are you also paying me to shut up?" Not to give Lil time to answer, she stood up, said she was going for a smoke.

"If you're not coming back, I sincerely hope you have somewhere better to go," Lil said as the girl lifted the jacket from her chair.

"What does that mean?"

"You're not on the street, are you?"

"What do you care?"

"You're certainly working hard to make me not care, but for some reason I do."

"Why?" It was an open challenge, to hide her curiosity.

"I've been asking myself that same question," Lil said. "Maybe I'm just trying to treat you the way I'd like to have been treated when I was your age, no matter what I said or did. Or maybe there's something about you I like, behind all the bluster. Or maybe I'm trying to pay something back." She was speaking now with flat sincerity and no power play.

"You've already paid me, we're quits," the girl said, patting her waist, then turning and walking away to clinch the point.

When the waiter arrived with the Chateaubriand, he set it in the center of the table.

"Will your companion be returning?" he asked.

"I'd be surprised."

He leaned in farther to clear the setting, but Lil shooed him away.

"The Chateaubriand is quite substantial," he warned. "Normally even two people . . ."

"I know what cut the Chateaubriand is, and what weight it should be, and what sauce it is served with, and what chef first created it," Lil said.

"*Très bien,*" the waiter said, with a deferential nod.

Before there was time for the side dishes to arrive, Lil swapped the near-full glass opposite for her own. This was not greed, but to slow the girl down, if she came back. Lil herself already felt more high than drunk, like smoking a cigarette after giving blood.

When the girl came back, she sat down as sullenly as before.

"If there's one bit of advice I'd give my younger self," Lil said, "it would be to stop smoking."

"Nothing else?"

"Believe me, the list is long, but that would be close to the top."

"And what would your younger self have said to a middle-aged stranger giving her advice?"

"Probably have told her to fuck off and sort out her own shit first before giving any lectures."

For the first time that evening the girl smiled, though

whether in appreciation of Lil's honesty or in endorsement of
the answer was not clear.

At the neighboring table, the man drew a bottle from an
ice bucket, poured the woman with him a glass, then wiped
the butt with the napkin, exactly as their waiter had minutes
earlier. The couple looked a little stiff to Lil. Perhaps playing
out an occasion decided on too long in advance. The family at
the back was having more fun. They had blindfolded the little
girl whose birthday it was and were feeding her forkfuls of
various types of food.

"I'm surprised you came back," Lil said, "but glad you did."

She cut a sliver from the bloodiest part of the sirloin,
pronged it with her fork, and offered it across the table to the
girl's mouth. "Just have a taste. It's really good."

"Should I stand up on my hind legs too, and beg?"

So Lil put the sliver into her own mouth, and when she had
swallowed, she took another drink, and as though this was
her very first sip, she pushed the wine all around her mouth,
less to savor than to wash away the taste of everything that
had come before. Around the room, near and far, neat voices
mingled nicely with the clink of cutlery. In the window tank,
the lobsters were still wrestling with their own preposterous
shapes. Across the street, the lights were still on in the empty
fish shop, casting a glow on the three blue barrels out front.

Across the table, the girl looked thin, and not in a healthy
way. Perhaps it was not possible for her to eat without showing her need.

"Why do you keep looking at me?" she said.

"I'm looking at you drinking and not eating and wondering how you do it. Personally, whenever I have a few I get
mad for food like you wouldn't believe. Have to eat a second

dinner when I come home from the pub. One of the reasons I stopped drinking so much." She patted her own waist and smiled. She was offering the girl an out.

"You ever been hungry?" the girl asked then, without looking up.

"Yes."

"I mean really hungry." She was inspecting the linen table-cloth's tight weave.

"I know what you mean," Lil said.

"People say being poor teaches you something. I'm still waiting to see what that is."

"Teaches you to do whatever the fuck it takes not to end up poor again. Gives your pride a good beating, is what it really does."

That lifted the girl's chin, made her look at Lil with a hint of recognition for the first time.

"Does it get any easier?" she said.

"No," Lil said. "I can't honestly say it does. Some things actually get harder. You wouldn't think it possible, but they do. And most of the stuff you think you're going to figure out or get on top of, you just let go. Pride and hope mostly. You stop fighting so much. Either your anger turns to bitterness or you just let yourself roll with the punches a bit more."

Then the girl was leaning forward, elbows on the table, the white linen napkin pressed against her face. At first, rather than crying or hiding, she seemed to be just feeling her head, as though to check that everything was still where it ought to be. Across the table, Lil felt the gravitational pull of the younger grief. There was no sound, just shoulders lifting up and down. After a minute the heaving stopped, but she kept the butts of her hands against her eyes. When she sat up straight again, the napkin naturally peeled away, lost its adopted shape, and dropped to her lap.

While she'd been crying, some of the men at the nearby tables had glanced in her direction, afraid of bigger drama in the offing, but there was no need. She'd had her moment of high emotion and now felt calmed. She looked across at Lil with real bravery.

"So what do I really want?" she asked.

"Right now you want to break everything, but that's just the froth. Deeper down, you want someone to fix whatever feels broken. Except you despise being the person who wants or needs that kind of help. Just as you despise anyone willing or able to give it to you. That's the tricky part."

"So?"

"So nothing. You're still too young. Still have too much dog in you. It's going to take another few years before you even start to wear yourself down."

"You really know how to charm the pants off a girl, don't you?"

"From where I'm sitting, your pants look very much still on."

"Well, get used to the view. It's not going to change. No matter how much you sweet-talk me."

"Now this is more like it," Lil smiled. "Bit of banter. Bit of fun. Why couldn't you have done this from the start, instead of wasting an hour pouting like a teenager?"

"You really think I'm a piece of shit, don't you?"

Lil thought about that. "No I don't," she said. "I think you're drowning. And your struggles to stay afloat keep beating everyone away."

"If you're so smart, how come you keep giving me all this advice you think I'm not ready for?"

"That's the wisest thing you've said all night. We're definitely making progress."

"You think I'm going to be grateful?"

"*Au contraire.*"

"Why not?"

Lil leaned in with her knife and fork and cut herself another good chunk of muscle. "Listen," she said. "I want to try and get some of this into me before it goes completely cold."

"I asked you why not."

Lil took time to chew and savor and swallow.

"A famous psychoanalyst once said that some Germans will never forgive the Jews for the Holocaust."

"That doesn't make sense."

"No it doesn't. Not until you think about it long and hard."

"Well, when I've thought about it and it makes sense, maybe I'll give you a call."

"That's a deal," Lil said, but she wasn't joking, and insisted on swapping numbers, and in doing so the girl saw the time on her phone and wielded it to tap her wineglass again. But Lil wagged her finger.

"You're telling me to leave?"

"Jesus, get down off your cross. All I'm saying is it's off the meter from now on. Stay if you want to stay. Go if you want to go."

"So I can just stand up, take my winnings and get out while I'm still ahead?" She patted her waist.

"In a while, that will be gone, and all you'll be left with

is the memory of the time we spent together and how you acted."

"Like you."

"Except," Lil said, "that when I think back on tonight, I'm not going to feel shit about myself. For once."

"Who says *I* am?"

"You never feel good about wasting someone's kindness. Not in the long run."

"Who says it was wasted?"

"Maybe you're right. Maybe you'll learn to let go of the anger a bit. I hope you do. If you don't, it's going to be a long hard lonely road."

"What made you so wise?"

"Good question." She took another drink. "The passage of time, mostly. Not getting what I wanted. That will school you good. And then getting it. That'll school you even better. Getting seriously sick will too—or someone close to you. Having kids. Losing your parents. Each of those things opens your eyes a bit wider."

"Those are your parting words of wisdom?"

"My parting words are, Good luck."

"Whatever that means. *Luck.*"

"It means I hope you don't fall off a rooftop dead drunk or OD or get raped or anything else while you're working all your shit out. It means I hope you make it out the other side more or less intact."

"Like you?"

"I hope you do better than me. That's the honest truth." Meaning she wished someone had said such things to her at the girl's age, and wished she'd been humble enough to hear them. By humble, she meant fragile, although she knew those windows—that access—never stayed open very long.

The girl didn't know how to answer. All evening she thought she'd been listening to speeches of self-promotion.

"That's it?" she said. She seemed now to be putting off her departure.

"Actually, no," Lil said. She needed a moment to muster her own courage, then said she had a favor to ask. Perhaps she thought trust was the best gift. The favor was: in a few days, she might get a phone call from Lil's son, and Lil wanted her to answer it and pretend to be the bus driver who had saved him, and to say a few specific things.

"What things?" the girl asked, not to say yes or no.

On the back of a menu, taking all the time she needed, Lil wrote down five or six phrases that she wanted the girl to work into the conversation when Pierre called. Then she held the menu out with five more hundred-kroner bills. The girl pocketed the sheet of paper but refused to touch the money.

"Thank you," Lil said, with a stern nod of acknowledgment.

At the big back table, glasses were raised for a toast. They rang like chimes. Lil took up her knife and fork and bowed her head and, with a strong sense of duty, began to work her way through the Chateaubriand, cut by cut, bite by bite. Finishing her own share, she was not quite full, but very able to imagine the point at which she could absorb no more. Perhaps that was what let her keep eating—the fantasy of absolute satiety.

By the time she finished the bottle, the restaurant sounds came as if from the next room.

"Do you know what a doggie bag is?" she asked when the waiter came to clear the table. His look told her he did not.

She explained that she wanted him to wrap up the remains of the meat so she could take it with her. His look soured to open distaste, but her celebrations and their cause had made her impervious to every qualm. "If you prefer," she said nicely, "I could just take it in my fist and drip a trail of blood across your carpet all the way to your front door. Is that really something you want all these fine people to see?"

Paying with her credit card, she refused to look at the screen—didn't want to spoil the pleasure by giving it a price. Time enough later to learn how much tonight's little indulgence had really cost.

Outside, she sat on the quay wall near the lone trawler, looking back at the restaurant. Its windows were liquid gold. It was days since she'd had anything more than a few hours' shallow sleep or an unfearful thought, but now her mind—honed by drink—had detected an utterly alien presence inside herself. It was total satisfaction, she thought, very different from what she might ever have imagined that to be. So physical, in fact, that she wondered if it was not merely the half pound of tenderloin now worming through her gut. After a few minutes, as though to test this idea, she peeled open the foil package on her lap and picked off a string of meat and ate it. Soon a black cat with white socks came and sat at her feet. She picked off another scrap about the same size as she'd given herself. The cat gulped it down without a single chew. A minute later, another disciple arrived—a tabby. He was more prudent, preferred to sniff and lick at Lil's hand before daring to take her offering into his mouth. More cats appeared, one by one, and gathered in audience around her. To draw the pleasure out, she picked off smaller bits of meat and threw them like crumbs left and right, near and far, to share the prize as fairly as she could, and keep them from crowding her. Occasionally she feinted a throw, then fed the scrap to her own mouth. She knew they were only temporary friends, incapable of real gratitude or loyalty, yet she sat with them in absolute joy as under a spell.

Thursday Morning.

LIL SLEPT SOUNDLY BUT NEXT MORNING woke tired and fogbound. It was not the hangover. It was the safety. The adrenaline was gone. For the first time in a week, her body was allowed to feel its own fatigue.

Alba was sitting on the toilet, texting, when Lil opened the bathroom door. "How was your drink?" she asked, looking up.

"Drink singular?"

"Did you eat?"

"I had a very nice meal." She patted her belly affectionately. What was inside her had solidified somewhat overnight. "How is he?"

"I left him about midnight and he was still sleeping. With no more sedative after the first dose. He must be exhausted. He's been through the mill, I guess."

"He's not the only one."

When Lil put a hand on her shoulder and kissed the top of her head, Alba's whole body tightened, and to disguise that reflex she leaned forward to wipe herself. In the course of her adult life, she had gone from being a naïve person to a disappointed one. Both were states of abdication, at one with her faith.

They walked silently down the hall, each bearing her own nervous thrill like a gift to what was waiting downstairs.

"You remember that time I went to New York for the championship?" Lil said, waiting for the elevator.

"I do."

"I went up the Twin Towers."

"I know."

"Well, one of them."

"I know."

"I know you know, will you just let me tell the story?"

"That's all gone now," Alba said.

"What impressed me most, more than actually being up at the top and how small and silly the whole city looked from that height, even the Empire State—what impressed me most was going down. In buildings that high, the elevators get up to phenomenal speed, of course. Otherwise, top to bottom would take all day. You don't really notice it, because the acceleration is constant. But when you're approaching the bottom, just as it stops, the car overshoots a few inches, then floats back up to the level of the ground floor. That's the cable stretching, because of how long it is. And these are traction steel cables as thick as your arm."

The elevator was empty when it arrived. Lil remembered that other elevator in New York, and how she had felt it sinking as the crowd piled in. They packed fifty or sixty people into those cars, four or five tons, stretching the cable like a catapult being drawn back. Here in Trondheim, this morning, the two of them alone weighed nothing at all.

He looked much as he had on the previous days. Homeless hair, doped eyes, doughy skin. For the past hour, the nurse said, he'd been drifting in and out of sleep.

Who would wake? Alba wondered. Over the past few

days, she had prayed for and promised so many marvelous and mundane things. If ever they got him breathing again by himself. If ever she felt him squeeze her hand. If ever she heard him speak. Help me, she had prayed and begged. Make me strong enough to love him, no matter what state he's in. Her prayer now was that she be strong enough to keep the promises she had made.

Before there was time for him to wake, Dr. Mya entered the room carrying a tray of food. On it was fresh orange juice, coffee, and three heaped plates. Alba smiled and said this was very kind, but she honestly didn't think she could keep anything down. With so much meat inside her, Lil too wanted to object, but Dr. Mya was having none of it.

"The Casals family are going to break bread together, whether they like it or not." She nodded at Pierre. "You need to set him an example."

One plate was a heap of scrambled eggs and shrimp, sprinkled with too much parsley. Another, smoked salmon and pickles, sprinkled with dill. The third, slices of hard-boiled eggs spliced with salami. Alba could not imagine the three of them, even in peak physical form, finishing it all.

"How did he sleep?" Dr. Mya asked the nurse.

"Almost no sedative, and all through the night," Alba said.

The doctor looked from screen to screen, adjusted one of the taps, wrote something on the chart. Alba tracked her face for hints of satisfaction or relief. Signing the daily, her hand gave what looked like an involuntary jerk.

Feeding Pierre, Alba tried a little compote first. His daft eyes stared right through her, but she paid no notice, kept bringing the spoon back to his lips, which eventually opened as if by reflex, and the instant they did, she slid it inside. She had to consciously stop herself from making darling sounds of delight.

"Take a photo for Iaia," she told Lil, because her mother was always fretting about Pierre's weight, and forever trying to trick or tempt or shame him into eating more.

In the photo, he still had the marks of the mask on his face, like a fighter pilot after landing.

At ten o'clock, a blue scrubs arrived with two hefty porters. Her pale skin looked close to transparent, and she seemed as young as Pierre himself, but introduced herself as his physical therapist. She reminded Alba of Julie, the girl—girlfriend?— who'd come to visit on Sunday and had texted for news every day since. The porters lifted him too easily out of the bed, set him in the dentist's chair, left without a word. They needed to get his muscles moving again, the therapist explained. She kicked the brakes off the chair's castors, then knelt before him, flipped the footrests vertical, and set his bare feet on the red rubber floor. Retreating a little, she lifted the left leg and moved it a few inches toward her, then lifted the right and set it slightly ahead of that. Inch by inch, the chair moved toward the wall, and as it did the cables and tubes linking him to the machines lifted slowly into the air.

Palmar reflex, was Lil's thought, seeing the feet clench and paw at the floor.

"Maybe I could do it," Alba offered, uneasy at seeing a young woman kneeling in front of her son. The therapist ceded her place, but Pierre's tubes were already at full stretch, so Alba shuffled him back to where he'd started from.

Lil lifted him back into the bed, and within seconds his eyes were closed.

"You remember sitting in the hospital with him the time he got his appendix out?" Alba said when the therapist was gone. This was not a question but a cue to herself. It was also their own special affiliation restored. "We sat by the bed the whole weekend teaching him poker and blackjack."

"Letting him win," Lil added. "Which in blackjack is no small feat."

"I remember teaching him how to bluff. He got that quick enough."

"I remember reading you the newspaper when you were in labor with him," Lil said. "Just like this, only it was you in the bed. The most painless labor in the history of the world bar none, then in walks your mother quoting Genesis, *In great pangs shalt thy progeny be spawned*, or whatever it is."

"There were pangs aplenty before the epidural, believe me. And when it wore off."

Every now and then his eyelids would lift slightly and their voices would quiet, as though to encourage him to speak. So far there had been one word answers to some of their questions, but as yet no full, coherent phrase. That morning, Dr. Mya had told them that for the brain, the only real medicine is time.

For lunch, Alba trimmed the crusts from a slice of toast and held it against his teeth. With a mechanical chewing motion, he ground it to a mush his swollen throat could accept. Lil took another photo. *from fluids to purée to solids in 24 hours #soproud*, her caption read.

He slept soundly all the rest of the afternoon, and what a smug pleasure it was to sit in their X-chairs watching and not watching him, manning their phones, sending updates to the waiting world. The news sounded so positive that Noah called the minute he got out of school. Alba talked to him for a while out in the corridor, then came and handed Pierre the phone.

"It's your brother. *Noah*," she said.

"Hey," Noah said.

"Hey," Pierre echoed, as the phone slid from his hand, down his neck.

"Noah, if you can hear me, we're still here, just hang on," Alba told Pierre's chest, reaching up inside his gown and feeling around to fish the phone out. From then on, she held it to his ear.

The brothers' conversation was one-sided and awkward, like a grandparent trying to engage a very young child on the phone. Most of Noah's questions got merely a mumble, or no answer at all, and when Pierre did try to speak he sounded blind drunk, and nothing at all like the miracle revival their mother had described.

"COME ON," LIL SAID THAT EVENING. She meant *out*, and out meant the riverside park, lights boiling on the water, glistening cobbles, the rhinestone magic of the Old Town and the quays. The danger was past. A celebration—the two of them together—would cement the fact.

An hour later they were walking onto the pontoon terrace of a dockside bar. The terrace was deserted, sprayed with frost, and looked closed but for the lit candle on every table.

Alba followed Lil slowly down the icy gangway, scraping her feet along the solid planks, then gave a grotesque spasm and shot out her arm and grabbed Lil—the nearest solid object— to steady herself.

Lil led her to the terrace's farthest edge, which looked out onto the magic river and the marina. Every building in sight was drenched with Christmas decorations.

"You know what this whole town reminds me of?" Alba said.

"Don't say Vegas."

It was high tide and the pontoon was almost flush with the quay, letting them look through the bar's big plate-glass window. At the solid oak counter, a bartender in a lumberjack shirt was working a mortar and pestle with strange intensity, leaning all her weight onto whatever it was she was trying to crush.

"Remember Caesars Palace?" Lil offered.

On the waterfront opposite, the Radisson hotel was a cruise ship in the night.

"I remember you losing our fare home," Alba said.

"I won it back. And more. We should have celebrated."

"That's not how it felt."

They studied the drink menu in silence, heads bowed as for grace. The cheapest thing listed was a glass of Spanish red that even Alba had never heard of. Eventually, the lumberjack came out from behind the bar and down the gangway, carrying some green concoction in a tall glass.

"Someone ordered a Civil War?" she asked, giving them each a chance to accept, but they shook their heads.

"Though I'm tempted to order one," Lil said, "just to watch you work that mortar and pestle again."

Taking their order, the bartender insisted on noting both their names on her pad, not to lose them in the crowd. Once she was gone, Lil made a big show of toasting her hands over their candle. The chairs were red leatherette and even through their jeans and jackets they felt the cold.

At their feet, against the pontoon's dam, was an amoeboid pool of chocolate-colored sludge and seawrack, abob with tennis balls, beer cans, pine needles, and dozens of what looked like shoe polish tins, marked SKRUF. In the middle of the mess was a fat-assed wine bottle identical to the tables' candleholders. Lil pulled off a glove and reached into the sludge for the fugitive bottle. On the back of their drink menu, shielding her script like a schoolgirl, Lil began to write a message to ship out into the world. Alba grabbed at the thing, to kill the joke, but Lil slapped her hand away. She rolled the paper up tight and stuffed it down the long neck, then lit the bottle's candle from their own and replugged it. Shielding the flame, she carried it out onto the long walkway jutting from the pontoon. At first, her boots crunched nicely on the planks, but the farther out she went, the more the walkway flexed under her weight, until every step made the entire structure crackle and snap as the ice bridging the individual boards flexed and broke. At the far end, she knelt again, set the bottle in the water, and pushed it out.

By the time she got back, their drinks had arrived, and Alba had dragged one of the terrace's patio heaters right up against their table. Seeing that concession to the cold, Lil went to get two sheepskins from the central pile. They tucked them under their thighs, then finally lifted and touched glasses, looked each other in the eye, took a first sip, and both winced.

There was a line of old clinker-built warehouses all along

the far bank. Once used for whiskey blending, flour grading, lumber curing, the tourist map said. Somewhere in the world those trades were still carried on, Lil supposed, but here they were only postcards, faded logos varnished over to preserve their pretty state of decay.

Each took another sip of wine to resume. Tonight Lil's glass was perfectly clean.

"Make it last," she said. "At this price we're not having another one."

"At this price I wouldn't want it," Alba said.

"My sheep keeps trying to escape."

"Whatever this is, it's not sheep. Just feel how rough it is."

Lil leaned forward to peer at Alba's lap, to check if there wasn't some knack to tucking in the skin so it wouldn't wander. When Alba leaned forward too, it was only to pick the scabs of wax from their candleholder.

"*Made from Garnacha vines, some of which reach the grand old age of a hundred years,*" she read from the label, "*this wine nonetheless retains its sense of vigor, vitality, and all the good things in life!* They bang a big drum, but you'd get three or four bottles of it in any Figueres supermarket for what a single glass costs here."

"But not the snow," Lil said.

"Not the snow, no."

"And not the Vegas vibe."

"No."

"And not the lights dancing on the dark water, or Harry Connick, Jr., or the Rudolph rugs."

"No."

"Nor the charming company."

"No."

"And not," Lil went on, her voice beginning to break with long-fermented emotion and restraint, "—and not that warm solid knot in the pit of your stomach, which feels so good it almost makes you sick, because your son is awake and he can think and he can talk and he's going to live."

"No," Alba said, her eyes welling too. "No."

They sat for some time in a well-earned silence until an orange and blue snowplow came rumbling along the quay-side, scraping away the snow and sludge, spraying grit and salt from its tail like a tractor spreading fertilizer. The closer the low tectonic scour and rumble, the more visceral the threat, and both women kept quiet, readying themselves to meet it, because that is what their bodies were still primed to do. But then came the puny pitter-patter of the grit skipping off the quay and into the water. And then the threat was past and almost a disappointment.

"Do you think our bottle is still out there?" Lil asked. A genuine fear was alive inside her now, not only as to its safety but its future fate, and it was both galling and soothing that her anxieties could transfer so easily to an object so trite.

"I do," Alba said.

"Still afloat?"

"Probably."

"Still alight?"

"Possibly."

"Do you think it's going to survive?"

Alba didn't answer, afraid to jinx its chances with unreasonable hope. But she too was warmed by the thought of that bottle out on the water, merrily riding the waves, heading with its little flame for the open sea.

Lil took off her beanie because of the overhead heater,

lifted her chin, offering her face to the glow, and closed her eyes. The wine inside her was doing as good work as it ever had.

"Sit here too long, we'll get home with a tan and no one will believe our sob story," she said.

In Alba, however, the orange panels cued a memory of the two-bar heater her mother used in winter, and the glossy scars on the old woman's shins, from all the times she'd dozed off too close to the fire.

AFTER THEIR DRINK, ALBA SAID SHE WANTED to go back via the cathedral. Lil suspected she wanted to say a prayer of thanks or make some kind of payment, and didn't object, but when they got to the cathedral forecourt they found a huge crowd gathered around a stage set up in front of the portal.

Shoving their way through the bodies, they met a bearded man in a Viking helmet coming in the opposite direction, pushing a landau-type pram full of long metal batons topped with rags. The basket underneath held a zinc bucket of clear liquid—lamp oil? turps?—into which he dipped the batons, one by one, as he handed them out. Lil and Alba bullied their way past him, trying to get beyond the stage and around to the side door, where the cathedral entrance was, but beyond the landau the crowd was impassable. Even as they tried to retreat, more and more bodies kept piling from the side streets into the forecourt, crushing them so close that Alba could feel Lil's breath on her neck.

Jammed shoulder-to-shoulder, the crowd heaved and ebbed, lunglike, until a wide banner lifted into the air, and those holding its poles started to shuffle forward. It was a first hint of direction, and Lil made no effort to resist, let herself be carried along, and the next big heave—surge, squash, recoil—pulled them apart. It didn't matter to her what these people wanted, only that they wanted it so cleanly. *Torchlight procession.* The words alone had such appeal. The kerosene smell, the flames' fluster, the faces' dirty orange glow. The sense of a greater cause, and the threat it was entitled to. At any moment now she expected someone to start banging a drum, or a chant to start up—some reckless verdict she could enjoy much more openly than her own, shouted in unison with the rest of the crowd. But this was a very different kind of protest, apparently: even as they started, the marchers inched along in a silence that was absolute, and far more unsettling than any noise they might have made.

She spotted Alba outside the crowd, heading past the cathedral's Visitor Center, in the direction of the side door. So she turned and worked back against the grain, shouldering aside the silent bodies, trying to push her way free. From the Visitor Center's café tables, tucked under their sheepskins, a few tourists watched the show. A woman in the crowd waved her arm wildly, inviting them all to join in, and one of the men watching waved back, inviting her to join him for a drink. Already he had his phone out, and as she emerged Lil gave him what he seemed to want—her torch raised high above her head, steely-eyed pioneer of a better future.

She fully expected Alba to be waiting inside the cathedral door to take her hand and lead her up the aisle, to give thanks. Gratitude had always been such a big thing with her.

But Alba wasn't waiting. She had already walked alone to the altar, knelt under the crucifix, joined her hands, and bowed her head.

Refusing to play the spectator, Lil went to inspect the strange art hanging on the cathedral walls north and south. An explanatory panel said they were pieces on loan from the Berlin Bode Museum's medieval collections, most of which had been badly damaged in the Second World War. Nearest the north transept was *Christ Placed in the Tomb*, which (its card explained) had originally showed two angels carrying the dead Jesus. Now two gold-flecked wings hung mid-air above a headless female figure in copious robes. The woman's hands, too, were missing from the end of her outstretched arms, as though chopped clean off, Old Testament thief. On the wall alongside hung a shadow portrait of the original, to help the viewer imagine where the surviving fragments fit.

Back at the altar, unobserved, a dim blue display light fell on the pocked statue hanging over Alba, and the same light fell on her own slack skin, giving them both an air of absolute neglect. In that mineral light, in that musk cathedral, she began to cry silver tears. She had expected Pierre's salvation to be remedy, redress, or spur, but now understood it would be none of those things. As the first thrill failed, the disappointment it revealed had no obvious name or target, and at the altar, under the cross, her prayer was the opposite of appreciation.

"So be it," she said, nodding in concession to a contract of her own devising. Danger had dug a hole that deliverance had not filled, and now she needed to learn how to live in it. She nodded again, confirming the bid on her lot. She had what looked from just a little distance like a home, a family, a relationship. Maybe the shapes were enough. She thought of her father's solitary life. In the worst of her troubles with Lil, his independence from other people had often seemed enviable, even ideal. But she knew the withered ways he filled his days. In a very different way, she had also seen how loneness had rowdied her mother's mind. After years of being single, the woman was like an abandoned dog, loosed from the sanities of domestication. Without some anchor, of whatever form, Alba had small hope for herself.

Lil walked along the wall to the next sculpture, a tortured head and torso. The sad face dripped with blood from a missing crown, and the neck was a road map of bulging veins. *Crucifix (fragment). Siena. c1460. Limewood. 117 cm,* the card said. The shadow poster showed thin arms spread wide, but on the statue itself the left arm was ripped off at the shoulder, the right at the elbow, both legs were gone below the knees, and to Lil its pitiful state shouted suffering and mortal threat louder than the intact original ever could. Since her teenage years, she had insisted she was an animal, no more, no less—a primate with a superiority complex, at best—and the sight of anyone supplicant and beholden invariably angered her.

By the time she got back to the altar, Alba was no longer there. Probably she had gone to light a candle or make a donation, so Lil did another round, checking the niches and side altars, but couldn't find her anywhere. Only the altar in the north transept had candles: marshaled on an iron rack, four rows of white plastic tubes bearing flame-shaped filament bulbs. Just one was alight, its blue thread flickering left and right as though in the wind. The statue there was just two cracked heads suspended midair on stainless steel bars. *Prague, c1400, limestone, Heads from a Pietà, badly damaged post–WWII by fire in Friedrichshain bunker.* The Virgin's face looked more jaded than serene, and only the bottom half of the other head had survived, from the tip of the nose to His loosely permed beard. Whatever had once connected the two—the body holding and the body held—was completely gone. Curious effect: Lil couldn't look at the fragments without seeing the whole suggested by the shadow outline, and couldn't look at the outline without seeing the thing as it now was.

Outside, the silent protest had made a short token march through the city streets and returned to its starting point. On the stage on the cathedral forecourt stood a woman in a white chapka, a white bubble coat, tight white jeans, and black boots buttoned to mid-thigh. With clownish gestures, she was gathering everyone toward her to form a more compact crowd. Behind her, two Vikings held the banner that had led the march, a bedsheet spray-painted with one red word: *HØRE.* Beside her, two young girls in pink jumpsuits waited by a music stand. One was holding a megaphone, and when she began to speak into it, the woman in white began to sign. Her facial expressions and movements were very broad. Perhaps that was her personal signing style, or she felt she had to amplify for the crowd, or mimic the impact of the megaphone for those who could not hear.

As the monologue dragged on, Lil scanned the crowd. The watching faces were all lifted toward the stage and the light it cast, but none was the one she was looking for. By now the torches were all down to their last blue flickers or already burned out.

To end, the speaker held her megaphone away from her

face, her twin leaned in, and at the chapka's nod they both chanted some kind of motto in unison. Once they'd waved their approval, the crowd started to thin out and several children climbed onstage to join the girls. Their play was a mute opera of leaps, slumps, and hugs. As the crowd frayed, Lil kept searching, and in the end she too climbed onstage and stood at the edge looking out, but an overhead spotlight shone straight into her eyes, turning everyone in the audience into a blank silhouette. She put two fingers in her mouth and blew hard. Plenty of heads turned but no one waved. So she wolf-whistled again, louder, and this time almost no one looked. Taking their silence as permission, she lifted her chin and roared Alba's name. When she shouted a second time, there came a brash bark at her back. It was one of the girls, imitating Lil's *"Al-ba!"* through the megaphone. Lil ignored the mimic and shouted again, but again the megaphone echoed her, and with it, right in front of the stage, two older women threw back their heads and did likewise: *"Al-ba!"* At Lil's next shout, the chorus was almost universal. *"AL-BA! AL-BA!"* they chanted, their fists raised, punching the air at every syllable. The moment Lil climbed down, the megaphone girl took her place at the edge of the stage and made a grandiose bow, to much applause.

At the side of the stage, the big banner had been unpinned and rolled up, and a bunch of teenage boys were now playing with the poles. Lil lingered to watch the jousting, still hoping to see Alba emerge from the thinning crowd. From beyond the boys, a woman waved grandly, as though to catch Lil's attention, but at that distance, in the dark, amid the other silhouettes, hard to say who she might have been. The group she was with began to move off, but after a few steps the woman swiveled around and—walking backward—waved in Lil's direction again, as though beckoning her to follow.

Watching that stranger, Lil could feel the stiff smile pasted to her own face. The woman was still walking backward, waiting for an answer. Her smile, unlike Lil's, was tailor-made. A flurry of wind smeared her hair over her face and made her laugh and lift her hands in a token effort to hold it in place. She could laugh so happily because she had no idea what was waiting for her: a few steps farther on, right in her path, one of the teenage boys had gone down on all fours. The second the back of her knees touched him, her arms shot out and she toppled backward with a wicked shriek—but the others were waiting to catch her. Afterward, she sat on the cobbles crippled with glee. Lil caught herself staring and turned away and set off in the general direction of the hospital as calmly as she could. She didn't want to look like she was rushing, but wanted to get out of range of that laughter as quickly as she could. She had been ambushed, by envy and admiration. Falling, then sprawled, the woman hadn't looked in the least bit annoyed or angry. It all looked like good wholesome family fun.

Friday Morning.

O N FRIDAY MORNING THE THERAPIST brought a walker. One at each elbow, Lil and Alba stood him up like a drunk and parked him in the slot. They had to pry open his fingers, then curl them around the frame. His legs too were lazy and stupid, and even with the two women hovering at his side and the therapist kneeling behind, shoving his feet forward, left, right, to remind them of the mechanics, it took him ten minutes to reach the door.

As soon as he was back in bed, the new trainee nurse arrived with a shaving tray. For his electrodes, she said, presuming they knew what that meant.

"You can't do just half," Alba said afterward, as the nurse started to wipe him off.

When his whole chest was done, Alba ran her fingers over the hairless skin. "Feel it," she ordered the other two.

"Help yourselves," Pierre said.

As the trainee was leaving, Dr. Mya arrived with the neurologist. She asked Alba and Lil if they could be left alone for a few minutes with Pierre, and when they were gone, she sat on the edge of the bed and took his hand in her own. This was not out of affection.

She asked if he knew why he was in the hospital, and he said it was because he had the flu.

"Pierre, do you think your parents would come all the way from France just because you had the flu?"

"Maman would come if I had a nosebleed. Lil, I don't know." He was being diplomatic. His own private Lil was incapable of staging such obvious concern. Only once ever had she let him stay home sick from school.

"How long have you been here?" the doctor asked next.

Pierre thought about his answer. "Two or three days?"

She showed him the date on her home screen. The information had no obvious effect.

"Do you remember what you did last Friday?"

He tried to match the day with a memory, but could not.

"What's the last thing you remember before waking up in here?"

Again he tried to send himself back in time, but the effect was confusion, and in the end Dr. Mya explained everything as bluntly as she could, going through the past week day by day, up to and including the successful *réveil,* and he listened sullenly to this new version of his life, as if to a reproach. To end, she asked whether he had any questions. The neurologist so far had not said a word.

"Who saved me?" he asked as they got up to go.

"I believe it was the bus driver," Dr. Mya said.

"Can I call her?"

"Well?" Alba asked when the two doctors emerged. She and Lil had been listening just outside the door.

"We need to reactivate as many circuits as possible as quickly as we can," the neurologist said.

"Memory games, math problems?" Alba offered.

"If we could get him doing something complex with his hands."

"Knitting?" Lil joked.

"Knitting, jigsaws, arts and crafts . . . The therapist will show you the rehab material we have. It's mostly for older people, unfortunately."

"I meant to ask her, why is my throat so sore?" Pierre said when Lil and Alba came back.

"I'll explain when you're older," Lil smiled, but that produced only an adolescent scowl. "You kind of had to be there," she explained.

"I *was* there."

Still Lil hesitated. It was unknown territory, like a first joke on a first date.

"We should have filmed it for posterity," she said.

"The part where I died or the part where I came back?"

"The part where they pulled that enormous dildo up out of your throat."

"Sometimes I can still feel it," he said.

"Phantom dick syndrome," Lil said. "Welcome to the club."

At lunch, he struggled to lift a spoon of soup to his mouth. The arm seemed reluctant, even disobedient, as of someone catatonically drunk. When Alba leaned forward to help, he grunted her away. But it was too soon, his fingers were still too soft, and when he tried again the spoon drooped and dropped onto the front of his gown. Alba picked it up, licked it clean, dipped and held it to his lips.

"He has to learn to do it himself," said Lil, who had refused to intervene.

"He'll have plenty of time to learn later. Right now he needs to eat."

Once they felt it was safe, their friends back home started to call. Lil let Alba answer every time, partly because of the

obvious pleasure she took in telling the story, and partly for
the pleasure Lil herself felt at hearing that story evolve, to the
point where the happy ending soon sounded inevitable.

"He looks like I feel," Alba admitted to her father,
though, and it was one of the few things she said that Lil
thought absolutely true: disheveled, drained, adrift within
his own mind, Pierre looked a portrait of the distress they'd
both lived through, and the perfect companion to their
oddly unsatisfactory relief.

Within a day—sometimes hours—those same friends
were calling back. They were like children who wanted
to hear the same story over and over again. Likewise, all
through the day a steady stream of nurses stopped to look in.
Most made sure to catch Lil's or Alba's eye, to acknowledge
the remarkable outcome. Some didn't dare cross the threshold, but some walked right up to Pierre's bedside, reached
out to touch his arm or even his face, as though by right.
There are no private miracles in an ICU.

That evening, leaving to go down to the canteen for dinner,
they spotted Elsa ahead of them, waddling along the hall.
Heavier and older than they remembered. Without a word,
both women slowed and softened their steps until she turned
into the waiting room, where together they had waded the
hours, shared hard wisdom and sympathy, and stirred their
puny wooden spoons. Their luck suddenly felt like a sin or a
burden, and as by agreement both moved quietly and quickly
past the open door. She would have been obliged to offer
congratulations, they would have been obliged to accept,
and in return ask for news of her father, though they already
knew how bad that news was. He had lost consciousness two

days ago and never come back. Alba would have to promise to pray for him, they would have to tell her to stay strong and so on, and repeat almost word for word the nice lies she herself had offered them just a few days before.

The next afternoon, Lil handed Pierre a postcard bought on her latest trip into town: a stern official portrait of Their Majesties King Harald and Queen Sonja of Norway. He looked like the Kaiser in uniform: white gloves, cocked hat, epaulets and braid, brass buttons, big sash, and an outlandish array of decorations across his chest. She wore a floor-length evening gown of pistachio silk, with an emerald tiara and matching drop earrings, but also had a single medal pinned over her heart.

"For bravery above and beyond the call of duty," Lil explained.

With a pair of surgical scissors, she carefully cut off the queen's head.

"What the hell is this?" Alba said when she came into the room. Pierre's bed was covered with scraps of sheet music, timetables, menus, medical posters, tourist guides.

"Doctor's orders," Lil said without looking up. Now she was trimming a pair of boxing mitts from the Student Fair flyer she'd found in Pierre's jacket a week ago. Beside her, he was banging his fist lightly on the overbed table, again and again. There was a glue stick inside. His hand was still too stupid to hold it properly and this was his technique.

They'd already glued a photo of the ICU building to a big white card. In the sky above it, in buzzard formation, eight Friesian cows were circling, each with its own strange rider. The biggest was a wet-eyed old woman with angel's wings, and a vampire grin pasted to her face.

"Flight of the *Vache-Qui-Rits!*" Lil explained.

Pierre gave a scoff like a sick cat, but Alba refused to react. Afterward, she watched Lil carve a pumpkin carriage from a Halloween party poster, slide it under Pierre's fingers, then set her hand behind his elbow to support or steady it. Whether it was that hand or his own moving the carriage, Alba could not tell.

Lil sat alone by his bed that night, watching his chest rise and fall. She had watched strangers sleeping her whole life. It was always a return to the truth of the distance between her and everyone else. The sleeping body close by, vulnerable but unavailable, honest in its indifference, folded back into itself. And not just with other women. Like many parents, she had always felt slightly out of sync with her children too, by her well-meant lies about herself and the wider world.

Just when she was sure he was settled, his phone began to vibrate. She thought it might be Julie, then saw the French number and recognized it.

The good news was Valerie's excuse to call. It was also the only reason Lil had answered: Pierre spared could be the perfect payoff.

"You weren't answering your phone," Valerie said. "It kept going to voice mail, so I called your apartment and they said you'd lost—"

"You called my *home*? Are you *nuts*?"

"It's all right," Valerie said calmly, "I told them I was a friend and was just asking about Pierre." They had told her the news. "It must feel good," she said.

"It does," Lil said. "Thanks."

She gave her own version of the last few days.

"You're probably surprised I called," Valerie offered after a while. "But when I kept texting and calling and got no answer, I got so worried I was frantic. So then when they told me the news, I can't tell you the relief."

In the bed, Pierre began to moan. Lil shifted her chair closer.

"All the way through," Valerie said, "I kept telling myself, If he wakes up I'll leave her alone. I'll never contact her again. That's enough. That's the slate wiped clean."

Still Lil didn't soften.

"You know I'm not a believer," Valerie offered next, "but after our last call, when the news actually sunk in, I started to pray. To who or what I couldn't tell you, but I *prayed*."

"I'll tell Alba to send you the membership form."

"Maybe not a great idea."

"Maybe not. Anyway, I appreciate you calling." It was an exit line, if Val would hear it.

"So how does it feel?" Valerie asked. "Come on, I'm the one doing all the talking but you're the one with all the news."

In the bed beside her, Pierre gave a louder moan, and Lil set her hand on his chest.

"At first," she said, "you say to yourself, As long as his brain works. Then he's awake, and he's not a vegetable, and he can talk, and he can walk, and I'm not saying it's disappointing because it's not, you're ecstatic at first, of course you are . . ."

"Here comes the small print," Valerie said.

Now Pierre shifted slightly and gave another groan. Something wanted to surface, and Lil gave her hand more weight to calm him.

"That first day I got out of bed," Lil said, "I'd like to have stood on a scale to see what I actually weighed. Then it's the second day and you're still light-headed but not as much, and that's not a bad thing because it feels more real. You don't know it yet but you're coming down. And by the third day you can actually say to yourself, Jesus Christ, that was close." Too soon, she meant, it became another historical fact. So your son could move the fingers of both hands. So he could walk. Already, to revive the joy, you started looking backward, at where he'd been just twenty-four hours before. But every so often, for a masochistic thrill, you reminded yourself how far he still had to go.

Under her hand she felt him starting to struggle, and pressed harder, because they say you cannot feel two pains at once. By that pressure, she wanted to steer his dream.

"I'm sure he's going to be fine," Valerie offered. Like all happy people, her thoughts were highly contagious: *he* meant *everything*. It meant that this had all been just a scare, a false alarm, no reason things couldn't go back to what they were before.

How easily such fantasies came to Lil too, especially in a setting so unfamiliar as to feel inconsequential, almost imaginary. It made the real world—hard fact—France. It said this had all been a holiday, where nothing mattered, no meter was turning, everything would be exactly as they'd left it when they got back home.

"The body is tough," Valerie said with some authority,

because she'd had her own scares. "It can take more punishment than we think."

"Christ, you sound just like Alba," Lil countered. She needed to spoil not only Valerie's lenient mood but her own.

Valerie needed a moment to recalibrate. Then said, "I doubt that very much. I think you just like saying her name to me on the phone."

"Everyone keeps talking about luck," Lil went on, in an open-armed accusation. "A meteorite fell out of the sky and missed us by a hair's breadth. Is that good luck or bad?"

"*Le vent du boulet*," Alba had said just that morning. The cannonball whipping past. But for Alba it did not mean luck, or relief, or amnesty, as it did for everyone else. It meant the more vicious world in which they all now lived.

"Maybe this can be a fresh start for all of us," Lil offered when Val took none of her cues.

"I don't want a fresh start," Valerie said. "I like having a secret. I like walking around feeling that your real life is somewhere else, disguised by the drudge. That's what makes the drudge bearable, if you ask me."

"If you can stand the deception," Lil specified, not as a challenge but as a familiar fact.

"That's what people never get about affairs. It's not the deception you're drawn to, it's the truth. The relief of being with someone you don't have to keep convincing you're better than you really are."

Eventually Lil cut in: "Val, it was only sex." It was her favorite closing line. She had never yet heard an answer that didn't acknowledge—even inadvertently—some part of its truth.

"I should have known better," Valerie said. "I shouldn't have called."

Lil chose not to contradict her. It had taken her years to learn, but she knew now that the best exit was always to let the other person have the last word.

After she hung up, Lil kicked off her slippers and lay up on the bed as if on a ledge, reached her arm across his body, and snuggled up to him. Her little boy was alone in there, frightened, and she wanted to smuggle herself into his bad dream, to right it, or just to keep him company. So she pushed back his gel-stiff hair and stroked his face and rubbed his chest through his gown as though to warm him up, moving her hand in a circle, but still his cringing sounds kept up. Stroking his body, she felt the same anxiety she did whenever she succumbed to her need for contact and put herself in Alba's arms, and began that same circling motion that Alba felt so soothing, she knew. But then the circles would begin to widen, each orbit expanding, the hand with a mind of its own, the center refusing to hold, wider and lower, down onto Alba's belly, until something within her tightened, which of course Lil's hand could feel, and wanted—tried—desperately to relax, by doing more of what it was doing before, but which—twenty years had taught her—it would take far more than anything the hand could do to calm or cure or pry loose.

WHEN THEY CAME DOWN ON SUNDAY MORNING, they found him trying to get out of bed, because he wanted to shit in something other than the diaper they'd strapped to him. Alba rushed to help, but he waved her off. He also wanted to shower and shave, because he'd seen the madman in the photos they insisted on sending to family and friends.

"His girlfriend is coming to visit this afternoon," Lil said.

"She's not my girlfriend."

"Now's your chance, then. Ham it up. Some girls love to play the savior."

"That's how you got lucky?" he shot back.

Lil clutched at her heart, her legs went soft, and she slumped to the floor. She lay there groaning, then gasping, then dead.

Alba called for the care nurse, said they'd get a wheelchair and take him to their own bathroom upstairs. She too wanted to see him washed and groomed.

"I'm not getting into any wheelchair," he said.

"They brought you in here on a stretcher plugged to a pair of jump leads," Lil said from the floor. "The time for acting proud is long gone."

Later, with a trembling hand, he scrawled an X that marked his student residence on their tourist map. On a blank park he drew a map of his room, showing the hiding places for his money, passport, and laptop.

"His friends are coming to visit," Lil said. "He wants us gone."

"You're sure you'll be all right?" Alba said. His lopsided posture in the dentist chair troubled her. All that morning, even as she'd been chatting with him, she'd been ready to leap, he seemed so close to tipping point.

"Don't go anywhere now," Lil said as they left.

THOSE IN PIERRE'S ROOM DID NOT KNOW IT, but the partition door was open a crack, and in that crack was a woman's bloodshot eye. She had heard the ruckus out in the corridor, then heard them go next door. All the boys were in thigh-high nurses' uniforms, caps, and fishnets, and by the time Elsa got her bearings, they were well into a panto porn scene: "Oh Doctor, I think my tubes are blocked." "Oh Nurse Ratched, I need help with my suppository." They were talking so fast, one over the other, that she couldn't catch half of what they said, but the crass fun was welcome relief, they were so much the opposite of all her own visitors' curated concern.

"Minus five kilos," the friend with the stethoscope read from Pierre's chart.

"Wow, so you must be really ripped?" said the one with the elbow-length blue rubber gloves, pulling up Pierre's gown for a look.

Most of their jokes should have made her wince, but they made her smile. Now they were searching for his penile implant, holding down his arms, and the nurse shouted at them to be careful of the lines, but otherwise refused to interfere.

Elsa had heard a girl's voice as they arrived, but couldn't see her in the crowd. There was a strong smell of flowers, though, from somewhere close by. Perhaps she was standing unseen on the other side of the partition door.

Now the one with the stethoscope had picked up Pierre's clipboard and as casually as he could asked what was actually wrong with him. All the jokers, of course, had a ready answer. AIDS. Avoidant insecure attachment. Penis envy. As they ran through their jokes, and ran down their honest concern, Elsa shifted her eye up and down the crack, to keep track of him through the crowd. She had watched him jousting with his mothers and bantering with the nurses. His tone was always offhand, unflappable, but late at night, when he should have been asleep and thought no one was watching, he sometimes unbuttoned his pajama top and circled the edges of his electrodes with his fingers, around and around, harder and harder, desperate to get underneath and have a good dig.

On the whole, he and the girl were probably too similar to last, Elsa had decided. When she was alone with him, her face was clever, almost open, but with anyone else in the room, it was shrewd. She thought her absence of expression hid everything. An easy mistake at that age.

Now they were asking Pierre if it was true that he'd actually died. The ringleader was the one with the stainless steel Cyclops eye. Their gallows humor was loud but had no real threat. They were still too young—still had decades to go before they realized the body's one bald truth. She did not mean Pierre. In his unguarded moments, he looked like that truth had hit him with an iron punch.

They asked him had he seen the white light, did he feel special, grateful, and so on. A little genuine curiosity was finally creeping in.

"The doctor called it a miracle," the nurse told them, but

that too had to be cheapened: they fell to their knees, waddled to the bed, stretched their hands to touch the hem of his
garment.

When they left, it was with loud sobbing, fluttered hand-
kerchiefs, last good-byes to the condemned man. Only when
they were all gone did the girl move out to where Elsa could
see her. She sat at the bedside without a word and took Pierre's
hand. She liked to turn one of the rings on her finger, pretended most things were beneath her interest, but Elsa was
not fooled. The girl was another silent watcher. Sometimes
they played cards, dropping their cards one onto the other's
noiselessly, and she always refused to react when he flung his
winning card down.

He hadn't bothered to correct any of his friends' jibes with
sincerity, just as he didn't dare task his mothers with any
brutal truth. Perhaps these were baby steps toward true independence, which is letting error enjoy itself. These past few
days, however, whenever Elsa was tired of herself, she stood
and looked through the crack and soon felt better. Every day
she felt closer to him. They were like adults who've already
seen a film watching it again with children who have not. In
every feelgood movie she'd ever seen, such trauma as theirs
aged your innocence and ultimately made you wiser, made
you grow. Maybe that was how his friends imagined it—as
gifted insight—and were wary of the authority they thought
it conferred. Pierre had not contradicted them and Elsa
thought she understood his choice. All she'd gained through
these years chaperoning a terminal illness was a sense of her
own limitations, she sometimes thought—a sense of how narrow a range of feeling she had, even in absolute crisis.

NOW, WHENEVER HE WASN'T SLEEPING, he was messaging his brother or Julie.

"I see Monsieur's masseuse has arrived," Noah said.

"The speakerphone is on and she understands English, moron. Say hi to my baby brother," he told Ingerid, the care nurse.

She blew a kiss at the screen. A few minutes before, she had unplugged all his lines except one, and now was sticking four new electrodes to his freshly shaved chest. "Nice," Noah said in Catalan. "She's the one wipes your ass and everything?"

"Sure. Prostate massage, happy ending, the works. Normal life's going to be a big comedown after this."

Today she had a yellow barrette over her left ear that lifted her hair like a drape.

"The mothership has landed," Pierre warned.

They were coming to see him off: over his neck, Ingerid now hung what Noah immediately labeled his man bag. It was a mobile heart monitor. The nurse explained that they could track him from anywhere—not just his vitals but also his actual location, in real time. She sent them a link that opened what looked like a maze, black lines on white, with a flashing red dot all alone in a dead end.

"Go," Lil ordered, waving him toward the door.

"Where?"

The nurse hooked his drip bag to his walker's IV pole.

"*Out*," Lil ordered. "Anywhere but here. Go play with your new toy."

With both hands gripping the walker, he shuffled past the

end of his bed, turned by increments, then headed out into the hall. First the walker shunted six inches forward. Then the right foot followed. Then the left. His movements were deliberate but imprecise, like a conscientious drunk. Ingerid and an orderly went with him, one on each side.

"I never thought I'd see him doing that again," Alba said. They were standing at the threshold, leaning out as from the doorway of a departing train.

"Walking?"

"Learning to walk."

As he approached the nurse's station, someone gave a low whistle. He lifted his gown a few inches to show more of his pale, skinny legs, and they whistled louder, started catcalling in Norwegian and English.

"They keep that up, he'll never want to go home," Alba said.

"Why would he? Nothing waiting for him there that's as good as this."

Summoned by the whistle, Dr. Mya stood unseen in the doorway of Elsa's father's room, watching the little group advance. She was impressed to the point of suspicion. When they were out of earshot, she shook her head and said under her breath, "*Et mirakel.*"

Soon there would be sessions between the parallel bars in the basement, then on the treadmill, then the trampoline. But for the moment his slippers scraped along the floor, step by stupid step, all the way to the ICU double doors, where Lil and Alba had waited to be admitted on that first night. On the far side of the wired glass, normal patients and visitors strolled the corridors freely, and there Pierre looked back, unsure if he dared joined them, but Lil waved him on, flippantly, then grandly, bye-bye, bye-bye.

Every time they came back from a trip into town, they found his bed covered with shredded sheet music, menus, flyers, posters, magazines. Alba watched him slide the scraps across the card with what looked like no particular design, yet his collage was obviously the product of a singular mind. On the deck of a cruise ship wrapped in sausage tentacles stood a grand piano by a Christmas tree. At the keyboard sat a chicken hatching a clock. From the tree, in place of baubles, hung dozens of men's heads. The chicken's audience was a crowd of doctors and nurses whose arms and legs had all been put on backward, as by a mischievous child re-engineering its dolls.

As with something dubious or distasteful, Alba refused to get involved, but Lil was always eager to join in. Her goal was not to guide but to encourage him, she insisted—keep him working as long as possible, to stop him from dozing off, because if he slept at all during the day, that night he would lie awake, fiercely scratching his chest, sometimes even ripping off his electrodes, often pressing the alarm button, and when the nurse came she would find him on the verge of panic but never quite able to say what was wrong.

Alba had tried to talk to him, saying he should just think of this as the slate wiped clean, but the second she tried selling

Trondheim as a hidden blessing, or at least an opportunity, the shutters came down.

By Wednesday he was showing signs of exhaustion, and Dr. Mya had to prescribe sedatives.

"What more do you want?" Alba snapped at him one afternoon, maddened by his adolescent lethargy and his nameless angst. She meant that instead of being on life support, he could now breathe, eat, walk. Instead of being brain-dead, he could remember, think, talk.

She also meant that he was young, loved, and unbound, as she would have liked to be but was not. To those failings she could now add jealousy, of her own child.

Pierre heard but didn't understand the huge urgency in her voice, given how often she'd told him the danger was past. The story she and everyone else kept telling him had mortal threat, freak luck, and a storybook ending. He had been clinically dead. For how long exactly, no one knew. Then, magically, he opened his eyes and spoke. For everyone else, that's where his happily ever after began. His own version was very different: in it, he was walking along the street on his way to meet his girlfriend when he stepped into a wormhole, at the other end of which an older version of himself was lying in a hospital bed, tethered by a dozen lines to a dozen different machines, being told his heart was so damaged it had actually stopped and might give out again at any moment. He was twenty years old, had to have a pacemaker installed, needed lifelong medication, with who knew what other complications to come.

What more do you want? she heard herself snap. Just one of all kinds of phrases and facts she wanted to throw at him, not to throw them at herself. *Isn't this enough?* was another, to stop herself pairing off the present against a better version of itself. So she tried a softer tone: "Pierre, *amor*," she said, "it may not feel like it right now, but you were lucky." He hadn't collapsed in some backstreet but in a bright, accessible public space, and been found almost immediately, by a woman who knew exactly what to do. The ambulance had arrived in record time. The hospital they'd brought him to had a great cardiology unit, where one of Norway's best heart specialists happened to work. She meant that, apart from the actual catastrophe, everything had gone as well as it possibly could.

On Wednesday evening Lil went to the ward nurse's desk to get Pierre's file. She stole a pink Post-it and with her left hand wrote *BUSSJÅFØR* on it, and the phone number she'd gotten a week before. She had since texted the girl again, to give her an update on Pierre, to check if she was still willing to take his call, and to ask how she herself was getting on.

She asked the ward nurse to take the file to Pierre, to make the thing look more official. At his bedside, the nurse laid it on his lap, then curtsied, bowed her head, and held out her hand as though presenting a gift. There was a paper cut on her thumb. Pierre touched it with his left hand, and with his right—index and middle fingers erect—made the sign of the cross. "Be Well," he ordered. He was gaunt and sad and thinly bearded, like an Orthodox Christ.

"What was *that*?" Alba said when the nurse was gone.

"The King's Touch," Pierre said.

His file looked fatter than before. When they opened it, the bus driver's number was right there, on a pink Post-it stuck to the Admissions sheet. The police must have taken it at the scene, they supposed.

Pierre stood up to make the call. The new pajamas Alba had bought him were too big and he had to use one hand to keep the bottoms up. Pierre's friends, Lil noticed, had painted his toenails glitter gold.

"Hello, my name is Pierre Casals," he said in English. "I'm calling from the ICU in St. Olav's Hospital. I'm the guy whose life you saved. Yes. At the bus stop. Yes. Pierre. Pierre Casals. You too. From the hospital. Yes. Good, very good. The doctors, the nurses, all of it. I can't really say, so far I've only been eating soup and toast and things like that. Wednesday. Wednesday afternoon. They seem to think so. They're still doing tests but so far. Well they said it was lucky, that if I'd been out for another minute even. So I have you to thank for that. So thank you. Well, whatever you did, it worked. Well, that's what they said. They're both here. Since last week. They're pretty happy about it, as you can imagine. They say thanks too. I think they're going to spoil me now for a while. I know, I'll have to milk it."

The conversation went on far longer than even Lil had hoped. Alba too had expected to hear little more than a stiff thanks. The thought of his selfishness brought her such relief. It confirmed her own choice as not only right but brave, despite—because of?—the fact that she knew full well it would never get the open thanks that other woman was getting now, direct from the mouth of her son.

She watched him nod and smile, standing dreamily at the window. He had finally tied the drawstring on his pajama pants and was now picking Get Well cards off the sill, giving each one a single glance before putting it down again, difficult customer.

"What did she say?" Alba asked as soon as he hung up.

"She said gratitude is a very complicated thing, especially when it feels like an obligation."

"She actually said that to you?" Alba said, frowning. "Those were her actual words?"

"Yes."

"Interesting. What else?"

"She said she was very happy to hear I was recovering, and was very glad that I'd called."

"Come on, she said a lot more than that," Lil prompted. "You were more than ten minutes on the phone."

"She said I should exploit what happened to me. I should try to imagine that she never came along, that I was never resuscitated. Any worries or doubts I have from now on, she said I should just think of them as an aftertaste, as something belonging to the Pierre who died. Then she said, You've been given a second chance, so enjoy your second life, which is starting now."

Lil and Alba both smiled uneasily, for different reasons: Lil, because this was the very best version of what she'd asked the girl to say, and Alba, because it was so different from the imperative she'd recently given herself.

"Are they going to go in the front or the back?" Noah asked.

"Don't you know anything?" Already Pierre was unbuttoning his pajama top, with unusual care. "My fingers have this pins and needles thing," he said, frowning. "I don't know if that means they're dying or coming back to life."

The cartoon scar Dr. Mya had drawn was about two inches long, on the upper half of the left pectoral, just above one of the electrodes.

"That's *it*?" Noah said. Now that his brother had survived, his favorite drama was disappointment again.

"What were you expecting? Frankenstein?"

"I thought the heart was lower down."

"They can't put it where your heart is, dumbo. You know why?"

"Why?"

"Because your heart is already there."

"I thought it would be bigger," Noah said, trying to regain ground.

"It's actually a pretty minor operation. They don't even need to do a general anesthetic. They do you in the morning and you're back in your room that evening, watching the match."

"You want to be awake for something like that?"

"I think I'm pretty much at saturation point, as far as drugs go."

"I'd have them hit me over the head with a hammer if that's what it took."

"Easily arranged," Pierre shot back.

He was terrified of being chemically unconscious again. Every evening he flooded with fear as the moment approached when his mother would announce bedtime and give him his pills, which he would then have to pretend to swallow.

"The doctor says I'll be able to do everything I did before," he told Noah as brightly as he could.

"Skydiving, group sex, all that?"

"Normal service will shortly resume," Pierre said. He was beginning to store up private ambitions, the way some suicides do.

At about nine that night, Alba drew the big collage card away from him and began gathering up all the scraps—her way of telling him it was time for bed. She handed him his pills and a cup of water to wash them down. He mimed a giant swallow, then defiantly opened his mouth and stuck out his tongue.

They sat late by his bed, watching his chest rise and fall. After he closed his eyes, long minutes passed before Alba dared to relax. As babies, they seemed so fragile, then one day you began to suspect they were made to survive. There was no bright moment of epiphany. Their hearts just kept pumping. They kept breathing in and out. The proof wore you down.

"—*There*," Pierre cut in, opening his eyes.

They both gave him a blank look.

"You honestly can't hear it?" he said, baffled to the point of indignation. "It's every night now."

Lil went and stood in the doorway. When she came back, she stood up to the partition door, put her ear and two hands flat against it—exactly the pose a mime artist uses to show her audience a solid vertical plane.

"Upstairs, by the elevators," Alba said. "There's one on every floor."

To stop Lil marching up there in anger and causing a

scene, she herself went to find the source of the music. In her stockinged feet, she walked down the hall and started up the stairs, half expecting a young woman in Lycra with a rifle on her back to pass her in a sprint. Up on 6, it was just as she'd remembered: a stumpy upright piano with a black cellophane shine. She stood in its alcove and looked at the train station across the river, the sugared conifers framing it, the lone windows pinholed into the woods where the deer and wolves did their dance. There was an unattended piano up on 7 too, but the rumor was stronger there. 8 was a concert hall foyer. On 9, she found a woman in a dressing gown, plum-faced and bald, playing a fussy Chopin waltz with a champion typist's touch.

Alba waited while she played out the final phrase. Beside them, the stairs went up one more level, to what felt like her next logical destination: the helipad on the roof.

"Does it bother you?" the woman asked. She had lifted her fingers from the keys but still held the sustain.

"I love it," Alba said. "You play so beautifully. But right now it bothers my wife. She says it's keeping our son awake. You must have played professionally?"

"And what does your son say?"

"I think he's terrified of falling asleep and likes having something concrete to blame," Alba said. "And so does my wife." She was trying her best to make these things sound like simple statements of fact. "Personally, I could stand here listening to you all night."

"If you want me to stop, just say so. Is that what you want?"

A silver wig sat on top of the piano. The woman set it on her head, screwed it slightly left and right, then swiveled to face Alba. The transformation was astounding. She was at once the plum-faced virtuoso producing music as genial as the trickle of a mountain stream, and she was again the old woman in the 7-Eleven spilling her slop all over the counter, who had so disgusted Alba with her pathetic efforts at mopping it up.

When she was younger, Alba had quietly worshipped the possibility of change, much the way she worshipped God. Perhaps *potential* was part of what *God* meant to her. Few prayers ask for things to stay the same. Just as some say the silence between the notes is where the music really is, perhaps what Alba had never dared pray for was the fullest confession she'd ever made. Perhaps the mere idea of change had let her go on with things the way they'd always been. But this pianist was a radical rebuttal to such resignation. Here was a new formula: from that, *this*.

Friday.

"HELLO PIERRE," ELSA SAID, standing in the doorway. "Hello," he said suspiciously. He could see from the woman's face that he was meant to know her.

Sitting on the edge of his bed, she explained who she was.

"I thought that room was empty," he said, and said he was sorry for making so much noise. He meant his friends' visits, and all the loud conversations with Noah and Julie on the phone. Had this woman been listening in? He offered to go and apologize to her father the next time he was up.

"They're calling you The Miracle Boy," Elsa said.

"Who is?"

"The nurses. The doctors. Everyone."

He refused even to acknowledge the tag, which was less an embarrassment than a threat: it said he had been selected, was no longer the anonymous passenger he'd always felt himself to be in his old life. Instead he smiled at his visitor, discounting her claim as a harmless quip, but she didn't smile back. She said she'd seen him out walking the corridors and said it was incredible that he could be so mobile again, so soon.

They talked for a while, the woman mostly. Pierre sounded less than enthusiastic about leaving the hospital. He had caught Alba's lack of welcome for the next step: within a few days of having his pacemaker implanted (if the procedure went as planned), he would be transferred to a room on the far side of the double doors. *He* meant *they, her.* The ICU was a cocoon, a family, where you felt cared for—important, even—for a while, in so much more than a professional way.

Elsa said she understood. She said this wasn't the first ICU her father had been in, or the first coma, so she knew what she was talking about. "They always expect you to be so *grateful* when they announce you're going home."

Pierre nodded at the word. "That's what everyone keeps saying. You're so lucky! You got a second chance! But would they like to swap? They want my luck but not my pacemaker."

"We have a saying in Norway: the true thanks charity wants is silence," Elsa said. It was her way of agreeing with him, because of the favor she'd come to ask.

Pierre felt a more personal resentment toward the near future. The move down the hall to Cardiology was being sold as progress and felt like demotion. It felt like a public figure's quiet disgrace. It felt like his entire past, too, had been spoiled. Every plan he'd ever made had been a fantasy. Every premise false. The last twenty years had been a long walk across thin ice, thinking it solid ground.

"You walk out that door and the world is full of all the same splinters as before," Elsa said, pursuing a slightly different conversation from the one Pierre wanted to have. "You just feel a little less involved at first. And when things go wrong you think, However bad this is, and you tell yourself the hospital story again." First as a remedy, she meant, then as distraction, then reproach. "That works for a while, and then it becomes just words, and you just feel a bit worse than you used to for fretting about all the everyday shit."

He didn't want to be given back into his mothers' care. He preferred the way the nurses dealt with him. He liked the physical access and intimacy without the insinuation of rights. That had been the great relief of leaving home: gaining authority over his own body at last. In the hospital, as soon as he woke, they'd started treating him like a domesticated animal again.

Elsa said she would be delighted to take him up on his offer, if he really didn't mind coming next door to see her father. She didn't mean right now. The next time he was on his feet, whenever that might be. She said she knew it was a big favor, and wouldn't ask except that she felt she'd grown close to his parents, and in some ways to Pierre himself, over the past week. "No secrets in a foxhole," she smiled. She said she didn't mean to make him feel ill at ease, and maybe he thought that what she was asking him to try was silly, but what would it cost him, and what harm could it do?

Pierre didn't really understand what she was referring to, just kept nodding and giving her the occasional cue, letting her talk herself out, much as he did whenever Lil or Alba got heavy with him. The poor woman was on the edge of panic, he could see.

"I THOUGHT I THREW THAT AWAY," Lil said.

"You did," Alba said without looking up. She was repairing Pierre's oxblood sweater, the one the ambulance crew had sliced open right down the front.

"You fished it out? For what? A souvenir?"

Pierre was lying on the bed and Alba was leaning over him. She'd gotten him to put the sweater on, to hold its original shape and stand up the weave. At the neck, she found the top stitch to repair, found that stitch's twin opposite, and lined them up. Anchoring herself where the weave was still sound, she worked out to the damage, hopped across the slit, then worked herself into the damage on the far side.

Lil asked where she'd gotten the darning needle, which is not what her tool was, and which after twenty years together Lil should have known. Its top had an almost imperceptible kink, as though it had been twisted then straightened out. "Elsa?" Lil asked, and the name tightened Pierre's chest as though he'd been pricked. Her visit earlier that day had disturbed him more than he could admit. At first he hadn't properly understood why she wanted him to go into her father's room. His realization, later, of what she was actually hoping for—what gift she thought Pierre had—troubled him. The idea of special powers was too threatening and too tempting. The man would die and it would be Pierre's fault, or he would live and Pierre would be branded forever as a healer, which was even worse. It was the kind of presumption that would be punished, he knew.

While the repair work went on, Lil used Alba's phone to access her own photos folder online. The first picture she came across was of their wine bottle drifting down the dark river, a white-hot tip to its candle stub. Next was one of herself in the Little Big Horn restaurant. The smiling face looked alien, it was such a rare moment of undiluted joy. She flicked again, to a man in a hard hat on the scaffolding opposite, seen through one of the windows of the printed net, as though sitting inside the actual building, snug and safe and quietly eating his lunch. One by one, she reeled herself back through the days. A long line of footprints across a snow-covered park. Leg- and foot-shaped blocks of plaster on a lab shelf, like the body parts of an outsized doll.

"*Aie*," Alba said, as though she'd pricked herself.

Lil refused to look up. Browsing the photos, she was afraid of wiping a single one, as though they were some kind of guarantee. Alba, she suspected, would have liked to wipe everything.

A line of taxis outside the hospital entrance. The bronze wolfskin. Young women in winter sports gear in a dark play-ground, doing pull-ups from its climbing bars. In a slush-filled gutter, something that looked like a pair of old pants or roadkill. Alba asleep in the dentist chair. Pierre unconscious in the bed, with all his tubes still attached. The helipad, seen from the street below, as a chopper—in what looked like a nosedive—prepared to land.

Meanwhile, Alba hopped from one split stitch to its twin on the far side, worked out to where the weave was whole again, made a U-turn, dropped a rung, and started back.

"This is how they repair old tapestries," she told Pierre.

Using her left hand to flatten the wool against his chest, each time she threaded her needle under a stitch and up again, she gave a little tug, to pull the tail flush with the rest.

"That's Kristen," Lil said, switching the phone from landscape to portrait.

"Who's Kristen?"

"She was your nanny in the early days."

"Was she nice?"

Lil gave a low whistle. "The diaper change used to be your favorite part of the day."

Pierre lifted himself the better to see, but Alba pushed him down again. "*Mon cœur*, it's easier if you don't move. Then it just lies flat."

As a concession to Alba, Lil swiped the young woman's face away, to a close-up of one of those Nordic omelette things. Leaning over him, Alba too was coaching herself away from danger, in the polite but firm voice that parents use. "*No*, don't go *there*," she warned, pinching a loop of yarn to retract it. "Let's go back and try that again."

Lil showed him the view from the porthole over Oslo, the amber necklace of streetlights below. The plane on the tarmac in Barcelona. The green parrot in his grandfather's tree. She was walking backward through the gallery, rewinding herself shot by shot into an ever-improving past.

"You're just going to leave all those loose ends?" she asked.

"Five minutes ago you wanted to throw it away, now you want it good as new?"

"All I'm saying is, if someone starts pulling on those, won't it all just unravel again?"

"Someone," Pierre said. "Now who can she possibly mean?"

"I can't wave a magic wand and undo the damage," Alba explained. "What I can do—what I *am* doing—is put an exact replica on top of the original, to lock in all the broken yarn."

"I just don't see the point of so much work if it's going to look like that."

"Right now he's wearing it inside out, obviously. But outside out, who's going to know?" In fact, the color of the wool she'd found was not quite a perfect match. She would not have admitted it, but she hadn't searched too hard. She didn't want the scar to be invisible.

Back and forth, in tiny increments, she kept working down Pierre's torso. From Lil's low angle, it looked like she was stitching up the torso itself.

"Looks tricky," Lil admitted, to make peace. The only time she herself ever dipped a needle into anything was to dig a splinter out of her own skin.

"Actually, a nice clean cut like this is relatively easy. There's no threadbare," Alba said, rejecting the gift. "Normal wear and tear is much worse."

To finish, she wove the tail of her thread in and out of several adjacent rows to keep it tight, then lowered her head to his waist and bit down hard to cut the last loose bit of yarn.

ELSA CAUGHT PIERRE IN THE CORRIDOR the very next morning and steered him toward her father's room. Alba moved to go with him but Lil put a hand on her arm, holding her back. Just as they went in the door, Julie appeared at the far end of the hall with a bunch of blue flowers so big that she had to carry it with both arms. Alba would have liked to keep her out of it, and suggested that Julie come back later, saying it was not the best time, but Lil sent her after them. She was jealous too, but differently. In the vaguest way, with her own fantasy of revival, she wanted to be the body those young hands came to touch.

Lil and Alba went back into Pierre's room, where Alba lay on Pierre's empty bed to wait. She had made her plans, and this scene was not part of them. Lil stood with her ear against the partition and closed her eyes, the better to hear and imagine what was being done in the adjoining room.

"You know my father has always been crazy about fishing," Alba said now.

"The more I hear about that man, the more of a stranger he seems," Lil said.

"I used to think he just did it to get out of the house, but looking back, I think that's genuinely all he ever really wanted to do," Alba went on. "Trout mostly. Brown and rainbow. The Ter and the Freser and sometimes he'd drive up the mountains close to Andorra if he got word there was a feed on." The real purpose of her spiel was to drown out anything being said on the far side of the partition. She was far from indifferent to the cruelty of Elsa's vigil, yet felt deeply embarrassed at the quack cure—perhaps too close to her own bargain—that woman now wanted to attempt. What embarrassed her was not how pathetic her request to Pierre was, but how understandable. Who knew what she herself might be willing to try if one day her own father resembled the man next door?

"At a certain time of the month, every month, he'd get my mother to touch his fishing flies," she said. "Just rub her fingers on them, that was enough. We must have been the only family in Spain with the mother's schedule all marked out on the kitchen calendar. Because the biggest catches are always by women, apparently. All the specimens. You can look up the records, see the names. Something to do with the pheromones, which attract the biggest fish, which of course are always males. When my mother finally walked out the door, the only thing of hers he didn't throw out straightaway were her panties, and whenever he'd be fishing in a competition, before he left the house he'd rub his fingers on them, then rub his flies. Then when my periods started, it was my turn."

"I feel like you're trying to tell me something very important," Lil said, "but I have no idea what it is. I'm not saying I want to know. I don't." She had learned a long time ago that Alba's riddles—like her beliefs—were rarely worth the curiosity they provoked.

"There was nothing perverted about it," Alba insisted, talking more loudly now. "You know him. That's not the way he is. He'd just take my panties out of the washbasket. He was completely up front about the whole thing." Some conversations are the opposite of eavesdropping: they aim to drown out all rival thought.

"Why didn't you just tell him to stop?"

"Because some part of me liked it."

"You liked being bait?"

"I liked feeling there was something in me that was fundamentally *attractive*."

While Alba was making this confession—this veiled plea to Lil—next door Elsa was unbuttoning her father's pajama top and folding back the flaps. The pacemaker scar was about the same size as the one Dr. Mya had drawn on Pierre. When Elsa stepped back, Pierre shifted his body slightly to keep it between Julie and the old man, worried that from unthinking kindness she might reach out and lay her hand on him. The skin around the scar was puckered yet slack, like an old balloon. Pierre didn't want to touch it, knew with absolute certainty that he had no special power, contrary to Elsa's hope. He also knew he would make himself do whatever this desperate woman asked of him. This was partly to spare Julie from having to touch it, and part compassion, and part compulsion, born of the strangely familiar mix of pity, fear, and revulsion that sight provoked in him—a distilled version of what he felt for his own body now.

Sunday.

O N SUNDAY EVENING ALBA RETURNED from the canteen to find Pierre listing heavily in the dentist's chair, and the fear rushed her that he'd had another attack. But he was leaning, not falling, the better to see something in the next room. His physical therapist had mentioned that there was a TV in there, so he got her to open the partition door and give him the remote, then flipped around until he found a match to watch.

"Who's winning?" asked a voice from behind them. It was Dr. Mya, holding a bottle of whiskey and three *I ♥ Trondheim* paper cups.

Why didn't he just move in next door? she suggested.

"Everything?" Pierre asked, nodding at his own bed, where a body was lying under a white sheet. A large card lay on the chest, markered with big block capitals: DØ NØT RESUSCITÅTE. "We did everything we could," he said, "but she was too far gone."

"Lock, stock, and barrel," the doctor said.

They started to gather up his things.

"How's your arm?" Pierre asked.

She held up her de-cast arm and showed it off, good as new. She was another one who'd played the Miracle Touch game with him.

To speed up the move, Pierre told them to dump the magazines, stuffed toys, Get Well cards—everything but the absolute essentials. "Possessions possess," he declared, giving the thumbs-down to Julie's tired bouquet.

"From Deep Throat to Dalai Lama in three days," she said. "We're so proud."

Soon all that was left in his old room was the bed.

"Should I pull the plug?" Dr. Mya asked, kicking the wheelbrakes free.

"*Yes*," Pierre and Alba answered in unison.

"Put us all out of her misery," Alba said.

They steered the bed through the doorway and into the empty slot. Alba had expected the view from next door to be slightly different, but it was not. For days now she'd been watching workers in hard hats on the scaffolding opposite, behind the printed netting, tapping their tiny hammers at the facade.

"What's the name of that artist couple who completely cloak famous landmarks in brightly colored cloth?" she asked the window. *Couple* was not quite the right word. They did everything together but in a bizarrely blunt and detached way. She knew the legend that they'd been born at the exact same time on the exact same day, which in her mind made them more like bickering twins than lovers. "They used to wrap up dams, bridges, skyscrapers, entire islands—they did everything in these crazy screaming colors, always on a dramatic scale."

No one in the room could remember their names.

"On the Reichstag they used this silky silvery fabric you really wanted to stroke," Alba said. She had turned her back on the mirror building opposite and was waving her hands weirdly. "Which made it into this strange, almost sexual object. Just the fact that it was there made you want to go touch it. Which you could, for free, as much as you liked. Which was kind of the point." She stood behind Pierre and slid her fingers into his hair as a comb, but he shook her away. "It was there for two weeks," she said, "then one night they took it down and that was it."

"Sounds like a lot of work for nothing," Dr. Mya said. She had set her three cups and whiskey bottle on a locker.

"Look at the bed and take a mental photo of it," Alba ordered, and gave them a moment to obey. Then, magician's revelation, she whipped the sheet away.

"I thought it was a joke," Dr. Mya said, "but she's sound asleep."

Alba let the sheet dangle loosely, then snapped it hard. It ballooned, drifted down, took a few seconds to fully expire and marry the shape on the bed. "Now look again," she said, "and admit that you don't see exactly the same thing as before."

Dr. Mya uncorked the whiskey bottle and held it very close to the nose.

"That better be Irish," said a voice from under the sheet, "because I'm not coming back for anything but the best."

Dr. Mya poured the whiskey, they kissed rims, but Lil did not immediately have a taste. Instead she sat up in the bed and took the bottle and showed herself the label front and back.

"At least it's blended," she said. "If I have to listen to one more ignoramus raving about single malt."

It had the musical name of Bailie Nicol Jarvie, like three sons in a Scottish fairy tale. *Judiciously married, then mellowed with age,* Lil read.

"Something tells me you know your whiskey," Dr. Mya said. "Do you know this one?"

Lil shook her head. "But the label says it's out of the

Glenmorangie distillery, which means Islay, and Islay means peat, and peat I could put up with until maybe ten years ago, but those days are gone and nevermore." She looked and sounded deadly serious, but was only playacting at being her old curmudgeonly self, and putting off the moment of celebration the better to savor it. Finally, she drank, made a curious face, then drank again.

"Better than I expected," she admitted.

In the chair nearby, Pierre gave a chalky cough.

"Does the celebration mean you were less optimistic than you let on?" Alba asked.

"Most of my patients leave here on a gurney or in a wheelchair," Dr. Mya said flatly. "If I didn't celebrate things like this"—she pointed at Pierre—"I'd never celebrate at all."

"None for me, thanks," said his paper voice.

"Legend has it they used to wet the lips of the newborn heirs to the French throne with the finest Bordeaux," Dr. Mya said. She dipped her thumb into her cup, knelt before him, then—in a strangely formal but affectionate gesture—rubbed it across his lips, bottom and top.

"Stick or twist?" Lil cut in, cocking the bottle.

"Stick," Alba said, lidding her cup with her hand.

"I'm training tonight," Dr. Mya said.

"You'll sweat it out on the stairs," Lil said, pouring. "And won't it steady your aim?"

They all clunked cups again and took another taste.

"I'm tingling," Pierre said. His lips felt spiced and swollen, in a not unpleasant way.

Alba rolled his chair away from the doctor to the dark window. "*Trondheim*," she announced. "The Venice of the

North. The rooms across the hall have a view of the river, but at short notice this was the best we could get."

On the scaffolding opposite, a loose flap of netting lifted in the wind, showing where the facade's cracks had been chipped away to prep the repairs. The workers seemed to have attacked every trace of weakness, found fault lines everywhere, and trenched them out until it looked like a building after a small earthquake.

"Sometimes we get deer on the grounds," Dr. Mya said.

"Reindeer?"

"They come to eat in winter. Because of all the bushes. Especially when the wolves come down into the woods across the river. That drives them over the bridge."

In Pierre's bedlam hair, at the window, was a cheap blue halo he himself knew nothing about. It was an ambulance helicopter up on the roof.

"You can go up on the roof with a rifle and pick them off," Lil said, deadpan. "That's what Dr. Mya does to let off steam."

Dr. Mya took a sip and told Pierre, "She's kidding, but someone actually saw a man on the grounds last winter with a hunting rifle, in full camouflage. And six weeks ago I hit a stag with my car. They're like children. Look cute, but can be a real nuisance sometimes." She raised her de-cast arm as proof.

After a few more drinks, they all went to take the elevator up to the helipad, with Pierre in a wheelchair, swaddled in blankets and with the doctor's gun case across his knees. The elevator that came held two empty gurneys, so Lil said she and Alba would take the scenic route.

By the third flight of stairs, Alba's chest was heaving.

"When we get him home, how are we going to get him up to the apartment?" she asked, to slow Lil down.

"If he drops a few more kilos, I'll carry him fireman. Otherwise, an evacuation chair."

"Seriously," Alba said, dismayed to find Lil thinking of the future only in concrete terms.

"Seriously. Until his own two legs will hold him, you and me are going to schlep him up and down those stairs."

At the top, the elevator stood open, two empty gurneys still inside.

"It's physically impossible," Alba said. She was breathing noisily through her mouth.

"You mean it's going to be difficult and complicated. Not quite the same thing."

Out on the roof, Pierre and Dr. Mya already had the gun case open. Lil would have expected to see a disassembled rifle—stock, action, and barrel each in its own foam nest—but it was all of a piece: a queer but beautiful object carved from a block of richly veined walnut, with every extraneous part jigged out. Pierre tucked the stock to his shoulder and turned to his audience.

"Who wants to be first?" he asked pertly. "And who wants to see the others go?"

Alba's face soured instantly. "Boys and guns. How original."

"Actually, you'd be amazed at how calming it is," Dr. Mya explained. "Really cleans out your mind." She meant lining up the sights, budgeting her breath, divorcing the right index finger from the rest of her, over and over again. Each squeeze of the trigger brought a twinge—sometimes a surge—of physical relief, and each target dropped was its confirmation, as though she were killing off her own fears, failures, or unwanted futures one by one.

With the doctor pushing Pierre, they began a round of the helipad. It jutted beyond the roof edge, and Alba kept well back.

The rifle had only a peep sight: a pinhole in a round of metal above the bolt, to be lined up with the sight on the barrel's tip. Pierre scanned the park across the sludge green river for deer, but it was too dark. On the street side he tracked a car parking at the foot of the building opposite. A young woman got out and opened the back door, leaned in, and half pulled, half lifted out an eight- or ten-year-old boy. He was too big to be carried, and slack as rubber, but the woman somehow hefted him up so the head plopped over her shoulder, then arranged the child's limp arms around her neck and used her backside to slam the car door. She waddled across the icy road toward the entrance of the ICU, stopping every few yards to huff up the dead weight and grip him better under the thighs.

"You just let him point that thing wherever he wants?" Alba asked.

"Obviously it's not loaded," the doctor said.

"I thought you said it was laser?"

"I say laser because otherwise everyone thinks I'm up here shooting off live rounds."

"So you are?" Alba asked. A thrill of fear was niggling at the generous poise she'd planned for herself.

"*Live rounds* is a bit of an overstatement." As proof, the doctor showed one of the little bullets in her palm, and afterward showed them her setup, which was as safe as it was simple, she said: a heavy rubber sheet nailed to the side wall of the bulkhead, behind a metal cube about eight inches square, with a replaceable paper target as its outer face. Still Alba looked worried, so the doctor went to her case, clicked a magazine in place, and turned back toward the target. She cocked her hip strangely, tucked her left elbow to it, and raised the gun, and as she did this a subtle change came over her—a draining away of everything likable.

The round passed through the paper and clinked neatly inside the steel box. Left and right and above the target was eight feet of wall, and no chance whatsoever of a shot going astray, she said.

"You *never* miss?" Alba said. "Your hand *never* trembles? That's hard to believe."

"Do you see any dents in the sheet?"

"The target's too small," Alba explained.

"Too small or too far?"

"What's the difference?"

"I believe you," Lil said.

"I believe," said Pierre.

"What would it take to convince you?" Dr. Mya asked the skeptic.

"I'm not asking to be convinced."

"Although at the regulation distance . . ." said Pierre.

The jibe struck home. From her firing mat to the target was well short of competition distance. So she asked Lil to take the metal box to the corner diagonally opposite. Beyond was the river and the distant woods, which would swallow whole any stray. Instead of setting the box on the ground and stepping aside, however, Lil held it on her head. They all laughed, but Dr. Mya did not lower her rifle. In the distance, Lil was laughing too.

The fantasy's easy appeal allowed Alba not to protest

immediately. Neither did Pierre. But their silence was taken as sanction: the gun clacked. On the far side of the roof Lil wobbled, fell to her knees.

The surge of disbelief—almost joy—cleared rather than clogged Alba's mind, revealed too plainly what she was willing to believe.

"Don't worry, it's just the fright," Dr. Mya commented. "That was center clean."

Still Alba looked on as though at a dream—one endorsed by the doctor's continued calm: she now slid the bolt back and forward to reload. In the distance, the body on the ground gave out a loud moan, and a new doubt fouled Alba's face as she watched Lil come alive again, get her feet flat on the ground, and struggle awkwardly to stand. When she was stable, she reached into the target box, then held her hand aloft, forefinger and thumb pinching something too tiny to see at that distance in that light.

"Who's next?" the doctor asked, looking from Alba to Pierre.

Pierre began to wheel himself forward.

"*Pierre,*" Alba barked, "don't you *dare.*"

He showed no sign he'd heard. His trust was gratitude.

"Get *back* here," she roared, but did not chase after him. That would have been a failure of the very authority she was determined to impose.

By the time he set the box on his head, she was refusing to look at him, had turned instead to face the doctor full square. "You've proved your point," she said.

"So you trust me to open up your son's chest and tinker around inside his heart, but—"

"That was life-or-death!" I don't care how good you are, at

this or anything else, Alba wanted to shout, but stopped short of physically attacking the woman who'd saved her son. She was also shamefully aware of how little protest she'd made on Lil's behalf. Besides, some alien authority had entered the doctor again. Aiming, she was now the accessory: as in a relic, all power and purpose was concentrated in the gun. Even Alba felt its spell: it was not resistance but a kind of reverence that stopped her from grabbing the thing. In any case, it was too late, the index finger had already begun to squeeze and any sudden move now might spark precisely the disaster she had to avoid.

The gun gave a small jerk—noiseless, it seemed to Alba, in her trance—and Pierre slumped in his chair. All her thoughts were collapsing, falling away like robes. Then—a little too soon, a little too easily—he revived. Like Lil before him, he reached into the box, then held his hand aloft with its prize.

The others were all laughing grandly. No bullet had gone anywhere near Lil's or Pierre's head or anyplace else. The whole thing had been just a big practical joke.

Alba grabbed the rifle from Dr. Mya's hands. She squinted and scanned, found the rubber sheet, and pulled the trigger, to no effect. "Now's your chance!" Lil was shouting, arms flung wide marching toward her wife. Through the pinhole, Alba's world narrowed to that other woman's face. She blocked her breath and shot. Advancing, unstoppable, Lil jerked and grunted at the punch of each imaginary round, but each time righted herself and resumed her robotic stride.

In the distance, in his wheelchair, Pierre was shaking. But what about the shells, the clinks? How had that been done? There had been shells, hadn't there? Hadn't she seen them spat from the gun? She scanned the ground near her feet, and near the doctor's feet, but saw none. So had she imagined all that too, not just the danger but all its concrete details—everything but her own distress?

"You see what I mean about the release?" the doctor said with a grin.

A distant rumbling—a snowplow?—turned the others' heads, drew them toward the edge, though the wind there was sharp. An orange light was flashing beyond the junction, and Lil wanted to see the plow crawl past, pissing salt and grit. But the flashing light receded even as the rumbling grew, and as soon as they saw the actual source, they felt stupid to have ever imagined anything else: it wasn't a snowplow but a helicopter coming in, driving an immense wave of noise ahead of itself.

Had this all just been a test, then—of Alba's credulity? Just a heartless game, got up to show how near and far her fears went? She should have been ready to insult or slap or even spit on them, all three, but the absolute rage she needed to do so was slow to come. The rush of relief she still felt at Pierre's revival was no weaker for the threat being fake. Every joy takes time to age. Until it did, she was still echoing with a thrill she'd not felt since the old days—all those dumb stunts Lil used to get up to, sober and drunk, and that had cast their spell on her for a time.

Within seconds the rooftop was like the set of a war film: medics appeared at the bulkhead door with their gurney, scuttled into the bullying air blast as the chopper hovered overhead, leaning strangely forward and sucking twirls of white dust off the landing pad. It did not lower itself smoothly, but in capricious jerks, hanging tipsy in the air after each one—then pitched forward and hit the pad with a godly thump.

The rotor blades didn't slow. Bent almost double beneath the blast, hair maddened and ablaze, the medics slid the loaded gurney out into the storm of snow and noise and swapped their empty one in. There were big hand signals, not unlike the signing onstage a few nights before. The engine's whine did not wane. As though driven downward—not lifted—by the thudding whup, the chopper seemed flattened against the pad, the engine strained harder, near tantrum, and with a lunge—as on coiled springs—lifted off.

Waiting for her anger to come, Alba inched her way to the edge. The best solutions are the irreversible ones. They are also the least forgiving, when left undone. She should have climbed into the chopper just as it took off. She should have turned the gun on herself. She should have jumped. But the helicopter was gone, and the gun was a toy, and there were safety nets rigged all the way round the helipad, as on bridges and scaffolded buildings. Her wildest thoughts had been anticipated and ruled out. Now her only way out was the door she'd come through, back down those same stairs, into those same rooms, to more of those games where she was punchline or prop.

The protective netting of the building opposite was still rippling with downdraft. She wondered did they ever get it wrong—if netting with a picture of one building was ever put on another by mistake? And if it was, did anyone notice? And if they noticed, did anyone care? She wondered too what happened to the printed netting once the renovation was done. Would that life-size 2-D building be folded up and put in storage, as though at some point in the future it might be retrieved and given a solid frame again?

The night sucked the chopper down to the size of a spot,

then a speck. They were alone again on the roof. The remnant was not silence but resonance, cleaners in the concert hall.

Somewhere in the world, Alba supposed, in an anonymous warehouse, in optimal conditions, hundreds of those giant 2-D images were waiting for a second life—whole buildings folded up and stored away, like a dress too good to throw out but that in all likelihood would never again be worn or even see the light of day.

Author's Note

I want to express my deep gratitude to Blanca, Tof, Paul, Nil, and Carla for sharing their story with me, and for giving me the freedom to make it my own.

I thank Sunshine Erickson, Jeremy Page, Saskia Hampton, Brían Hanrahan, and Daniel Davis Wood for their careful reading and comments on the manuscript. Thanks to Laurianne Bixhain for her photography. Thanks to Isobel Dixon for her unfailing support and encouragement.

Bellevue Literary Press is devoted to publishing literary
fiction and nonfiction at the intersection of the arts
and sciences because we believe that science and the
humanities are natural companions for understanding the
human experience. We feature exceptional literature that
explores the nature of consciousness, embodiment, and
the underpinnings of the social contract. With each book
we publish, our goal is to foster a rich, interdisciplinary
dialogue that will forge new tools for thinking and
engaging with the world.

To support our press and its mission, and for our full
catalogue of published titles, please visit us at blpress.org.

Bellevue Literary Press
New York